Myth and Gospel
in the Fiction of John Updike

✳

JOHN McTAVISH

CASCADE *Books* • Eugene, Oregon

MYTH AND GOSPEL IN THE FICTION OF JOHN UPDIKE

Cascade Books
An Imprint of Wipf and Stock Publishers
199 W. 8th Ave., Suite 3
Eugene, OR 97401

www.wipfandstock.com

ISBN 13: 978-1-4982-2506-9

Cataloging-in-Publication data:

McTavish, John.

    Myth and gospel in the fiction of John Updike / John McTavish.

    xviii + 184 p.; 23 cm—Includes bibliographical references and index.

    ISBN 13: 978-1-4982-2506-9

    1. Updike, John Criticism and Interpretation. I. Title.

PS3571.P4 Z827 2016

Manufactured in the USA.

To Avalon

Every great literature has always been allegorical—allegorical of some view of the whole universe. The Iliad is only great because all life is a battle, the Odyssey because all life is a journey, the Book of Job because all life is a riddle.

    —G. K. CHESTERTON

A thing may happen and be a total lie; another thing may not happen and be truer than the truth.

    —LEAH WILSON

Irony is a disciplinarian feared only by those who do not know it, but cherished by those who do.

    —SØREN KIERKEGAARD

I think books should have secrets, like people do. I think they should be there as a bonus for the sensitive reader or there as a kind of subliminal quivering.

    —JOHN UPDIKE

I expect (the novelist) to show me man as he always is in the man of today, my contemporary—and vice-versa, to show me my contemporary in man as he always is. . . . [He] should have no plans for educating me, but should leave me to reflect (or not) on the basis of the portrait with which I am presented.

    —KARL BARTH

Contents

Foreword

"LET'S BEGIN BY MAKING one thing clear," the British novelist David Baddiel states in his review of Adam Begley's 2014 biography *Updike*: "John Updike was the greatest writer in English of the last century. Unquestionably, he was the best short story writer; I would argue the best novelist, certainly of the postwar years; one of the very best essayists and in the top 20 poets."[1] In fairness to the naysayers, however, Baddiel also puts the case that is often made against Updike, how he writes well but has little to say, that he is, in the oft-quoted words of Harold Bloom, "a minor novelist with a major style . . . but . . . the American Sublime will never touch his pages."[2]

I have no wish to participate in this argument. But I hope this book can clarify the *kind* of writer John Updike is. Admirers and detractors alike often speak as though he is a realist whose stories delineate character with psychological insight. While there is truth in this assessment, it misses the larger truth that myth plays a critical role in Updike's fiction, giving his stories much greater moral and theological *gravitas* than may first meet the eye.

In 1968, John Updike gave an extensive *Paris Review* interview to Charles Thomas Samuels in which he spoke about the mythic undertones in his work. Asked by Samuels why he had chosen to employ a mythic parallel in *The Centaur* (the one Updike novel where the myths break clearly into the open), Updike pointed out that the characters in *The Centaur* are guises, "concealing something mythic, perhaps prototypes or longings in our minds." Samuels then asked Updike why he had not done more work in this mode. "But I have worked elsewhere in a mythic mode," the author protested, citing some of the underlying mythic themes in *The Poorhouse Fair, Rabbit, Run,* and *Couples*. Still not satisfied, Samuels put one more question to John Updike: "Even if your other novels have underlying mythological

1. Baddiel, "Suburban Legend," New Statesman, May 2, 2014, 42.
2. Bloom, ed., *Modern Critical Views of John Updike*, 7.

or scriptural subjects, they don't obtrude as they do in *The Centaur*. So let me rephrase my question. Why didn't you make the parallels more obvious in other books?" At this point Updike stated the cornerstone of his literary strategy: "Oh—I don't think basically that such parallels should be obvious. I think books should have secrets, like people do. I think they should be there as a bonus for the sensitive reader or there as a kind of subliminal quivering."[3]

If John Updike "has nothing to say," it may be because the reader has been largely unaware of the allegorical way in which the questions that he raises and the issues that he explores are often presented. A writer can't help but appear shallow if the reader fails to notice the depths that are already there. I am by no means the first person to suggest that allegory is a key to understanding John Updike. In her 1973 study *Fighters and Lovers: Theme in the Novels of John Updike*, Joyce B. Markle makes much of Updike's "mythic underpinnings" in *Couples* and other early Updike novels.[4] George W. Hunt's 1980 study *John Updike and the Three Great Secret Things: Sex, Religion, and Art*, similarly shows Updike transcending the limits of realism and uniting "the keenly observed detail with the symbolic."[5] Even more penetratingly, Alice and Kenneth Hamilton explore the allegorical depths in Updike's novels and short stories in their 1970 pioneering work *The Elements of John Updike*.[6]

Since these early studies, however, critical interpretation has tended to overlook the allegorical nature of Updike's work, perhaps because Updike's allegories frequently nudge the reader in the direction of the Bible and the Christian gospel. Literary critics are not usually interested in the gospel. They may be interested in *religion* understood in a general or abstract kind of way. But Updike is no more abstract about religion than he is about sex. "Away with personhood!" his protagonist cries in *A Month of Sundays*. "Mop up spilt religion! Let us have it in its original stony jars or not at all!"[7]

---

3. Plath, ed. *Conversations with John Updike*, 35–36.

4. Markle, *Fighters and Lovers*. A large portion of Markle's discussion of *Couples* takes place under the chapter heading "The Mythic Underpinnings," 125–145.

5. Hunt, *John Updike and the Three Great Secret Things*. Hunt notes: "It is true that Updike's novels will, in the main, be 'realistic,' in that they refrain from distorting the world and our common-sense perception of it, and yet their metaphoric structure and the metaphoric probing within them allows these novels to transcend the limits of realism, and unite the keenly observed detail with the symbolic" (6).

6. Hamilton and Hamilton, *The Elements of John Updike*.

7. Updike, *A Month of Sundays*, 25.

The allegorical signals in John Updike's fiction direct us to faith convictions of a quite specific sort: religion "in its original stony jars."

The Hamiltons are especially skilled at uncovering the multiple layers of meaning that Updike repeatedly packs into these stony jars. Typical is their detailed discussion of "You'll Never Know, Dear, How Much I Love You" which runs almost twice the length of the story itself![8] Kenneth Hamilton once told me that he and Alice were planning to write a sequel to *The Elements* tentatively titled *The Myths of John Updike*. But then Alice took ill and they had to abandon the project. Their sequel, I believe, would have strengthened their allegorical argument significantly. Now that Alice and Kenneth have both died, it behooves us to follow their lead. This I am attempting to do with help from the Hamiltons themselves (cf. their myth-illuminating articles on *A Month of Sundays* and *Rabbit Redux* reprinted in this book).

I have also been helped greatly by family and friends. Thank you Bruce McLeod, Bryan Buchan, Biljana Dojcinovic, Harold Wells, Jim Taylor, Jack de Bellis, Robert Attfield, Philip Marchand, Muriel Duncan, Caley Moore, James Kay, and Donald Greiner for critical comments and stylistic advice. Thank you David Updike for the lovely introductory tribute to your father. Thank you Jan Nunley for your illuminating interview of Updike. Thank you J. D. McClatchy for your moving tribute in the wake of John Updike's death. Above all, thank you Sandra, Todd, Ian, and especially Marion for your never-ending love and support.

This book is published under my name and I stand by its contents. But more than most books it is a group effort which includes of course the friendly and capable people of Wipf and Stock, Brian Palmer in particular on the administrative side, and Rodney Clapp and Heather Carraher on the editorial side. It has been a joy working with you all.

I began this chapter with raves about Updike by a British critic. Let me close with the well known but truly prophetic encomium by the great American critic, William Pritchard: "He is a religious writer; he is a comic realist; he knows what everything feels like, how everything works. He is

---

8. Hamilton and Hamilton, *The Elements of John Updike*, 14–25. The Hamiltons wrote copiously but rarely gratuitously about Updike. I once asked Kenneth Hamilton why he and Alice hadn't discussed Updike's brilliant short story "Tomorrow and Tomorrow and So Forth" in *The Elements*. Hamilton grimaced and said that they had indeed written about this story but could not in the end decipher the symbolic significance of the protagonist's locker combination (18-24-3). Alice finally suggested they write to Updike and ask for help, but no, said Kenneth, that would spoil the fun.

putting together a body of work which in substantial intelligent creation will eventually be seen as second to none in our time."[9]

9. The well-known prophetic words are taken from Pritchard's 1972 review of *Museums and Women* in *The Hudson Review*.

Introduction

David Updike's "Tribute to Dad"

This tribute was originally delivered at a public gathering that took place in the New York Library on March 19, 2009 in honor of John Updike, who had died two months earlier. Among the twelve speakers were Sonny Mehta, chairman and editor-in-chief of the Knopf Doubleday Publishing Group; David Remnick, editor of The New Yorker; *Judith Jones, Updike's longtime editor at Alfred A. Knopf; Lorrie Moore, short story writer and novelist; and Roger Angell, writer and one of Updike's editors at* The New Yorker. *David Updike was the final speaker in the program.*

The tribute was later published in The John Updike Review. *I am indebted to both David Updike and James Schiff, the editor of* The JUR, *for permission to reprint this speech.*

TRIBUTE TO DAD

David Updike

THANK YOU FOR ALL of those wonderful tributes to my father, and thank you to the organizers for giving me a chance to add my own. I am sure he would agree that his career was blessed with wonderful editors, and you have been fortunate to have heard from five of them. That said, I should tell you, however, that this past fall, when I mentioned to him that something I wrote was being rather lightly edited and I hoped they weren't taking it too easy on me, he said, "That's good—the best editors are the ones who don't want to change a thing."

I want to introduce you to my father's family—his wife, Martha, and her sons Jason, Teddy, and John. My father had four children, of which I am one. My wife, Wambui, is here, as well as my sister Elizabeth and her husband Tete; my brother, Michael; my sister Miranda and her husband, Donald; and of course, our mother, John's first wife, Mary, and her husband, Robert Weatherall. Five of my father's seven grandsons are also present— Sawyer and Trevor, Seneca and Kai, and my own son, Wesley. Missing are the two eldest, Anoff and Kwame.

Here in spirit, too, are my father's own parents, Wesley Russell Updike, a high school math teacher and coach, and his wife, Linda Grace Hoyer, a bookish farm girl who gave her only child his first inklings of a creative life beyond their small Pennsylvania town. Their son, *Jahnny*, as they pronounced it, was not famous in 1950—he was a skinny, brainy boy bursting with creative energy, an aspiring cartoonist who also suffered from asthma, psoriasis, and a stammer, and in the high school hierarchy felt himself a considerable step down from the jocks, the athletes and their glamorous girlfriends.

Despite being ranked high in his class, he was not accepted at Princeton—admissions office take note—and so went to Harvard instead, and flourished there, in class and on the Lampoon. But an unexpected obstacle remained to his graduation: all Harvard graduates must be able to swim, and he could not. Inhibited as a child by the state of his imperfect skin, and despite the fact that his own father was, for a time, a high school swimming coach, he had shied away from public swimming pools and never learned. And so he dutifully went to swimming classes in the Indoor Athletic Building, and eventually managed two lengths of the pool—an achievement he seemed as proud of later as graduating summa cum laude. And for the rest of his life he swam with what I would describe as a rather studied but confident dog paddle.

In an art history class in his sophomore year, he met a smart and beautiful woman two years his senior, wooed her with kindness and wit, and spent his senior year in an off-campus apartment as a married man. His writing career began, as you know, at *The New Yorker*, but although he was a prolific Talk of the Town reporter, he was not yet famous then, and it took a lot of confidence and courage to pack his wife and two very small children into a car and drive north to set up shop in the small Massachusetts town of Ipswich in 1957. He borrowed money from his not so wealthy parents to buy a house and occasionally drove back to New York to write another Talk piece to bolster his income but had begun to publish light verse, short stories, one novel, and then another.

Hints of recognition, then fame, began to appear in our small-town life: interviewers from New York, articles and photographs in magazines, visiting Russians in fur coats and funny hats. But for someone who was getting famous, my father didn't seem to work overly hard: he was still asleep when we went to school and was often already home when we got back. When we appeared unannounced at his office—on the second floor of a building he shared with a dentist, accountants, and the Dolphin Restaurant —he always seemed happy and amused to see us and stopped typing to talk and dole out some money for movies. But as soon as we were out the door, we could hear the typing resume, clattering with us down the stairs like a train gathering steam.

As it grew, he wore his fame lightly, as his due, like one of his well-worn sweaters, hanging limply on his frame, thin at the elbows. He loved public institutions: libraries, schools, the post office—letters arriving and departing, the simple act of completion, dropping it in the slot. I did this for him this past January when he couldn't make it downtown himself—a small typed letter, a final correction for an English publisher who was reprinting the Maple stories. He had reread them in proof, he told me, "not without some pleasure." He was eager that this small letter, a final, important word in their correspondence, get in the mail, the truck, the plane—on its way.

He played in the same poker group on Wednesday nights for more than fifty years, along with the local cobbler, a doctor, the owner of the auto supply store. He learned to play golf on a couple of scruffy courses and looked most at home there, most himself. Later he joined a fancy old country club. But he always seemed slightly ill at ease there, like someone who had wandered into the wrong cocktail party and was afraid of being found out. He would worry about slow play—about slowing down the stalwart regulars who were coming up behind us—and would sometimes annoy me at the first hint of delay by rushing over, asking them if we were holding them up, and then letting them play through.

In late October we played at the same marshy course where he had learned the game, my brother and father and I and a friend, but he looked a little frail and had a tough time on a long par four, and I watched from a distance as he topped a couple of fairway woods before he finally caught hold of one. "Come on, Dad," I muttered to myself, "hit the Goddamned ball!" But he had a way of feigning disinterest in a match until it really mattered, and by the last hole, the match tied, I noticed in him a gathering concentration, a newfound focus. Politely competitive and gracious in defeat, he far preferred to be gracious in victory. He hit a good drive and a "useful" second, twenty feet short of the green. Our opponents were up in the familiar, ball-grabbing apple trees and I, after a good drive, had muffed my second into a greenside bunker. I watched him as he bounced a low, workmanlike chip to twelve feet, and while the rest of us bungled our way to sixes, he calmly two-putted for a five. He walked off the course quickly and wanted to get home—no soft drink or potato chips today. He was already ill. When he got home, exhausted and discouraged, he told Martha that it had been no fun and put his clubs away for the season. But I don't think he would mind my telling you that he won the last hole and match he ever played.

Among the last books he was reading was *Dreams from My Father*, by Barack Obama. He read it in bed in a sunny room overlooking the ocean, and I believe for him it was especially poignant, trying to catch up on the history he was about to miss, that was about to leave port without him. He was well aware too, that Mr. Obama shares with his three eldest grandsons a parentage both of America and of Africa, of Kenya and Ghana, and so connected him in a personal, familial way to this transcendent moment in American history.

Through it all, his unkind illness, he remained, in his wife's words, dignified and noble—continued to be what his own father called a *gen'leman*. And he continued to shave—each day, my sisters noted, even when it was perilous to do so. And as he so often did, he left for us a glimmer, a gift of himself, of his own cherished life on this earth, heart and mind conjoined. This is from his last published story, "The Full Glass," in the *New Yorker*, May 26, 2008:

> As a child I would look at [my grandfather] and wonder how he could stay sane, being so close to his death. But actually, it turns out, Nature drips a little anesthetic into your veins each day that makes you think a day is as good as a year, and a year as long as a lifetime. The routines of living—the tooth-brushing and pill-taking, the flossing and the water glass, the matching of socks and the sorting of the laundry into the proper bureau drawers—wear you down.

TRIBUTE TO DAD

I wake each morning with hurting eyeballs and with dread gnawing at my stomach—that blank drop-off at the end of the chute, that scientifically verified emptiness of the atom and the spaces between the stars. Nevertheless, I shave. Athletes and movie actors leave a little bristle now, to intimidate rivals or attract cavewomen, but a man of my generation would sooner go into the street in his underpants than unshaven. The very hot washcloth, held against the lids for dry eye. The lather, the brush, the razor. The right cheek, then the left, feeling for missed spots along the jaw line, and next the upper lip, the sides and that middle dent called the philtrum, and finally the fussy section, where most cuts occur, between the lower lip and the knob of the chin. My hand is still steady, and the triple blades they make these days last forever. . . .

The shaving mirror hangs in front of a window overlooking the sea. The sea is always full, flat as a floor. Or almost: there is a delicate planetary bulge in it, supporting a few shadowy freighters and cruise ships making their motionless way out of Boston Harbor. At night, the horizon springs a rim of lights—more, it seems, every year. Winking airplanes from the corners of the earth descend on a slant, a curved groove in the air, toward the unseen airport in East Boston. My life-prolonging pills cupped in my left hand, I lift the glass, its water sweetened by its brief wait on the marble sink-top. If I can read this strange old guy's mind aright, he's drinking a toast to the visible world, his impending disappearance from it be damned.

xvii

*Myth and Gospel in
John Updike's Early Fiction*

CHAPTER 1

Myth and the Problem of Nothingness
in *The Witches of Eastwick*

THE WITCHES OF EASTWICK appeared in 1984. The date of publication might be expected to put an allegorist like John Updike in mind of George Orwell's classic dystopian novel *1984*. However that may be, *Witches* certainly illumines the great theme of cosmic evil through constant use of myth and imagery.

Updike had earlier expressed his thoughts on the problem of evil in a review of F. J. Sheed's book, *Soundings in Satanism.*[1] Maintaining the traditional religious conviction that evil is a personal dynamic force, he nevertheless recognizes the implausibility of such a claim in the minds of many today in our secular culture. The thought of most people, the writer acknowledges, is that "if we must have a supernatural, at the price of intellectual scandal, at least let it be a minimal supernatural, clean, monotonous, hygienic, featureless—just a little supernatural, as the unwed mother said of her baby."[2]

Still, these grand ghosts, Updike notes, did not arise from a vacuum. Employing the thought forms of the Swiss Reformed theologian Karl Barth,[3] he proceeds to distinguish the power of evil from both the illusionary "nothing" of Eastern pantheism and the ontological "something" of such dualistic religions as Manichaeism. Neither nothing nor something in

1. Updike, *Picked-Up Pieces*, 87–91.

2. Ibid., 87.

3. Barth discusses the problem of evil in his *Church Dogmatics*, volume III, part 3 under the heading "God and Nothingness," 289–368. An abridgement of this section, which Updike probably consulted, is found in Helmut Gollwitzer's *Karl Barth, Church Dogmatics: A Selection*, 134–47.

the strict theological sense of the terms, evil is thought of here as the power of nothingness, real and malevolent and based somehow on the power of God's non-willing. That is, a potent "nothingness" was unavoidably conjured up by God's creating *something*. The existence of something demands the existence of *something else*. The resultant strange but real power, corresponding to what God does not will, is colloquially known as Satan or the devil.

The Witches of Eastwick shows the power of nothingness initially darkening the life of the editor of the weekly newspaper that serves the Rhode Island town of Eastwick. Clyde Gabriel's paper is called the *Word*, and his surname, Gabriel, evokes the angelic news bearer who tells Mary that the child in her womb is "the Son of the Most High" (Luke 1:32) and as such "the *Word* made flesh" (John 1:14). Eastwick's Gabriel, however, is anything but angelic, and soon proves ripe for the malignant power of nothingness. Under Clyde's proprietorship, the local *Word* degenerates into columns of small town gossip while Clyde's private life finds him taking to both the bottle and the *Word's* gossip columnist, a sensual redhead by the name of Suki Rougemont.

As Clyde and Suki's romantic relationship deepens, Clyde's attachment to the bottle deepens as well. One night, alone in his study, he is leafing through old college textbooks (shades perhaps of the old college textbooks that originally ambushed David Kern in "Pigeon Feathers") and drinking heavily when his wife, Felicia (happiness), returns home from a municipal meeting. Felicia immediately starts in about the "stupid people running this town" (144) and their decision at the meeting to change the name of Landing Square to Kazmierczak Square in honour of a hometown boy who had recently been killed in Vietnam. Clyde, however, refuses to show any interest in, let alone sympathy with, his wife's complaints, goading her to recall that Suki was also present at the meeting, "her piggy little nose in the air." Suddenly Felicia voices her deepest suspicions: "Don't you think, *ooh*, don't you think I don't know about you and that minx, I can read you like a book and don't you forget it, how you'd like to fuck her if you had the guts but you don't, you don't" (146).

Clyde continues drinking while Felicia goes on to claim that even their grown-up children, whose departure from home remains such a loss for Clyde, have lately expressed the wish that their father would leave the marriage, but recognize that he doesn't have the guts to do so: "A drunken weakling wants the entire world to go down with him. Hitler, that's who you remind me of, Clyde. Another weak man the world didn't stand up to. Well, it's not going to happen this time . . . *We're standing up to evil*" (147, italics in the text).

Clyde implores his all too talkative wife to cool it which, of course, only goads her to talk all the more. Finally, to stop this torrent of words pouring from Felicia's mouth Clyde takes the fireplace poker and slashes it across her head (149). Grateful initially for the heavenly silence that follows, the inebriated husband gradually realizes that in truth "happiness" has fled forever. After several more drinks, Clyde finds a stepladder and rope and ends his life.

The deaths of Clyde and Felicia bring their adult children, Christopher and Jenny, back to Eastwick where they are befriended by, of all people, Clyde's former lover, Suki. She eventually introduces them to an eccentric scientist who has recently moved to town from New York. This is Darryl Van Horne, a fast-talking inventor and magnet for a multiple of musical, athletic, and erotic activities that have been taking place recently in the crumbling old mansion where he lives. Suki, the journalist, along with her friend Alexandra, a sculptress, and Jane, a cellist, are all specially attracted to this colorful character bursting with super-demonic energy.

The three women, all freshly divorced, are given to making Voodoo dolls, love charms and other forms of black magic. While certainly not uncritical of the male species—"Men," Alexandra snorts at one point, and one of her sisters in witchcraft responds, "aren't they though?" (300)—they have no hesitation in bedding any number of Eastwick males. The women now throw themselves upon Van Horne who happily entertains them on his tennis court, in his indoor swimming pool, and on "the black velour mattresses" that are magically provided towards the end of their evenings together. Jennifer and her brother Christopher become part of this roiling coven. Jenny, in fact, eventually becomes Van Horne's special lab assistant in his quixotic quest to find a "loophole" in the second law of thermodynamics. And then his wife! After Jenny marries Van Horne, Christopher joins the household as well, making it a threesome of sorts. The witches had long suspected that a relationship had been brewing between Christopher and Darryl (299). But Jenny and Van Horne's marriage catches them by surprise and provokes so much rage that they decide to apply their amateurish yet intensely felt witchcraft to the young woman, fixing upon her a malignant, cancerous, death-inducing hex.

Jenny for her part begins attending Eastwick's Unitarian Church in search of spiritual solace and strength. Darryl joins her there, lending his rich baritone voice to the choir. The happy couple would appear to have found acceptance and joy in the family of Christ. Yet none of this prevents cancer from invading Jenny's body, spreading its malignant wings and taking her to an early grave. The story concludes with Van Horne and Christopher going off together to New York while the three witches manage to find new husbands and head out in various directions of their own, leaving behind "a scandal, life like smoke rising twisted into legend" (307).

Such is the bare plot of the novel. The allegorical signals, however, are what link this story with other stories, including the story of the Christian gospel. The metaphorical key here would seem to be the *Word* which, as noted earlier, is, at the earthly level, Clyde Gabriel's newspaper. But at the heavenly level, the *Word* is the divine Word that became flesh in the child whose birth was announced by the angel Gabriel. The incarnate Word may not seem like much in a town like Eastwick where the Word-attesting community has been reduced to a small, ultra-liberal Unitarian church whose minister has run off with a teenager, leaving his wife in charge of the parish. Nevertheless, it is the minister's wife, Brenda Parsley, who hits the nail on the head one Sunday by identifying the problem beneath all the other problems in Eastwick: "There is evil in the world and there is evil in this town . . . . It must not be tolerated, it must not be explained, it must not be excused. Sociology, psychology, anthropology: in this one instance all these creations of the modern mind must be denied their mitigations" (271).

If the malignant power of evil running amok in Eastwick cannot be explained by the contemporary social sciences, perhaps it *can* be illumined by the traditional science of theology. In the light of God's self-disclosure in the incarnate Word, evil is not underestimated and treated as though it were nothing. But neither is it overestimated and considered too overpowering for God's love as disclosed in the atoning death and victorious resurrection of the incarnate Word.

These thoughts, however, would not seem to take into account the fact that the power of nothingness is malignantly at work not only in human lives but in creation in general. As Updike notes in his review of Sheed's *Soundings in Satanism*:

> Man as organism is beset not by nothingness but by predators and
> parasites themselves obeying the Creator's command to survive
> and propagate. Disease is a clash of competing vitalities, and what

of those shrugs, those earthquakes and floods and mudslides whereby the earth demonstrates her utter indifference to her little scum of life?[4]

How to account for such parasites and predators in a world supposedly created by a God of goodness and love? The question is one that Updike himself never claimed to be able to answer, and yet he continued professing his faith in the words of the Apostles' Creed, convinced that, as he says in his review of Sheed's book, "no other combination of words . . . gives such life . . . so seeks the *crux*."[5]

These unresolved questions about the origin and nature of evil in creation are given voice in *Witches* in a secular sermon that Darryl Van Horne preaches one Sunday morning in his Unitarian church in the wake of the onslaught of Jenny's terrible illness. Speaking about the botched-up job of creation, Van Horne cites as evidence for his dark thesis the existence of such poisonous parasites as centipedes and tapeworms and tarantulas, especially the Cestode worms that lodge in our intestines. Van Horne wants to know who created these little monsters. Somebody up there must have thought they were a wonderful idea:

> They come in so many sizes, for one thing, from viruses and bacteria like your friendly syphilis spirochete to tapeworms thirty feet long and round worms so big and fat they block up your big intestine. Intestines are where they're happiest by and large. To sit around in the slushy muck inside somebody else's guts—that's their catbird seat. You doing all the digesting for 'em, they don't even need stomachs, just mouths and assholes, pardon my French. But boy, the ingenuity that old Great Designer spent with His lavish hand on these humble little devils (290–91).

Evil, it would seem, is built right into the universe, leading Van Horne to conclude:

> You got to picture that Big Visage leaning down and smiling through Its beard while those fabulous Fingers with Their angelic manicure fiddled with the last fine-tuning of old Schistosoma's ventral sucker: that's Creation. Now I ask you, isn't that pretty terrible? Couldn't you have done better, given the resources? I sure as hell could have. So vote for me next time, O. K.? Amen" (293).

4. Updike, *Picked-Up Pieces*, 90.
5. Ibid., 91.

7

Couldn't you have done better, given the resources? Perhaps so—*given the resources*. But then the resources are everything in creation. Once one grants the goodness of there being something rather than nothing, the question of how good or bad that something is can be examined as a separate issue. Van Horne's claim, however, that the universe itself is evil and brought into being by an evil will contradicts itself by assuming the goodness—the life, the *crux*—of the resources themselves. Van Horne is further refuted by the mute objects that witness to the goodness of the created world. The title of his sermon, for example, "THIS Is A Terrible Creation," is proclaimed in a signboard outside the church in moveable white letters. Van Horne's black words are thus contradicted by positive evidence that one can't even denounce the universe without using the universe, with its infinite variety, to do so.

Not surprisingly, Van Horne's sermon notes are scrambled and his face begins "thawing into nothingness" (293). Everything in fact that this man touches seems to be thawing into nothingness. For all the gaudy grandeur of his house, it is "like a stage set, stunning from one angle but from others full of gaps and unresolved shabbiness. It was an imitation of a real house somewhere else" (181). His tennis court dome is collapsing, his gate is crumbling, his plan to reconcile solar paint and electrical energy is proving to be fruitless. Even Van Horne's conversation seems "distracted by a constant slipshod effort to keep himself together" (47). Studying Van Horne closely, as one of the witches does early in the story, is like looking down a deep hole: "His aura was gone, he had absolutely none, like a dead man or a wooden idol, above his head of greasy hair" (47). Even the man's name, lawyers conclude after Van Horne leaves town and a trail of debts behind, had probably been assumed (307). Darryl Van Horne may not be nothing. But clearly he is not something either. He is a reminder rather of the strange, inexplicable power of nothingness, a power that, for all its terror, is no match finally for the Creator of all that *is*.

The Witches of Eastwick thus concludes on a hopeful note. Despite the fall from grace amidst the onslaught of nothingness, hints of reconciliation and the promise of new life occur throughout the story and especially at the end. Van Horne, for example, as noted earlier, returns to New York *(New!)*, taking Jenny's brother Christopher with him. "He was one of those" (297), remarks one of the witches, no doubt thinking along purely sexual lines. But this overlooks the fact that Christopher means "Christ-bearer," and as such could well be offering something more to Van Horne than simply human companionship and sexual pleasure. There may in fact be redemption for Darryl Van Horne in the company of the Christ-bearing herald of the New Creation. For that matter, there may be redemption for the three witches. They at least get out of town and manage to acquire new husbands.

Admittedly, this still leaves Jenny and her parents out in the cold, or rather down in the ground. Where is the sign of hope or promise for them? For an answer, we might note that when Jenny's parents died, Brenda Parsley, at Jenny's request, said a prayer at the undertakers. Suki later recalled the moment for Alexandra: "The Gabriels weren't anything really, though Felicia was always going on about everybody else's Godlessness. But the daughter wanted I guess some kind of religious touch" (163).

Some kind of religious touch! Readers of John Updike can't read a line like this without recalling David Kern, the hero of Updike's classic redemption story, "Pigeon Feathers." Early in this story, young David is found holding up his hands in the dark and begging Christ to touch them. He feels nothing and yet wonders if he may have been touched all the same: "For would not Christ's touch *be* infinitely gentle?"[6] Then at the end of the story the infinitely gentle touch of the dead birds in the barn speaks to David, silently, the actual words of Jesus: "Fear not, therefore; you are of more value than many sparrows" (Matt 6:26).

Might this same infinitely gentle touch be signalled at the end of the novel when we are told that "Jenny Gabriel lies with her parents under polished granite flush with the clipped grass in the new section of Cocumscussoc Cemetery" (307)? Might the "new" section of this very old cemetery in fact be quietly proclaiming new life in the face of death for all who are the recipients of God's grace as Jenny, by her very name (Jennifer/Guinevere), is?

Rhode Island's Cocumscussoc Cemetery itself may offer a classic redemptive touch insofar as, historically, it is part of a vast package of land given to the state in the eighteenth century by one Lodowick Updike.[7] Granted, no genealogical connection has been established between the Rhode Island Updikes and the New Jersey Updikes from whom the author was descended. Even so, one can't help wondering if this isn't, after all, John Updike's puckish way of saying, "Welcome home, Jenny."

6. Updike, *Pigeon Feathers*, 128.

7. Updike, *Self-Consciousness*. Cf. 186–93 for Updike's discussion of Lodowick Updike and John Updike's Dutch ancestors.

In such symbolic ways the author would seem to be signalling his conviction that just as evil is more powerful than anything the social sciences can describe, so its conquest through the Word is more decisive than anything the social sciences might dare to hope for. Might this not in fact be the religious touch that Jenny Gabriel requested when her parents died, and that she herself needed so badly after she died? In all events, lying there in the *new* section of Cocumscussoc Cemetery, in company with the philandering editor of the *Word* and his murdered wife, Jenny and her family lie under the promise and in hope of the *new* heaven and the *new* earth in which God and sinners are reconciled (Rev 21:1) and the night of weeping yields to the morning of joy (Ps 30:5).

John Updike was not—thank God—a religious propagandist. He would much rather bury the imagery in his stories and have them missed than approach readers as a heavy-handed Sunday school teacher. Still, the hints, the allusions, the secrets are there, inviting us to join in the cultural and religious debate that Updike's stories invariably initiate. *The Witches of Eastwick* for its part concludes with an unspoken invitation to recall the Word that became flesh in the child of Gabriel's promise. The incarnate Word that upholds the earthly child of the modern-day Gabriel's loins and gives Jenny's submission to death the promise of resurrection is none other than the one who can be heard saying in the *New* Testament: "I beheld Satan as lightning fall from heaven" (Luke 10:18).

Chapter 2 Introduction

The Centaur is John Updike's most overtly myth-laden book and also the book, Updike more than once claimed, closest to his heart. Interestingly, the picture on the back cover of Updike's memoirs, Self-Consciousness, *shows the author autographing* The Centaur *on the same page that features the Barth quotation which could well stand as a text for Updike's theological as well as literary creed: "Heaven is the creation inconceivable to man, earth the creation conceivable to him. He himself is the creature on the boundary between heaven and earth."[1] The book signing, incidentally, would appear to have taken place on a book tour in Czechoslovakia. No matter how far the boy from Shillington travelled,* The Centaur, *and its vision of earth as set under heaven, was never far, it would seem, from his heart.*

CHAPTER 2

Myth, Gospel, and *The Centaur*

JOHN UPDIKE WAS ONCE asked by an interviewer why *The Centaur* remained his favorite novel. "Well," he replied, "it seems in memory my gayest and truest book; I pick it up, and read a few pages, in which Caldwell is insist-

---

1. The quotation from Karl Barth that loomed so large in both Updike's life and work is taken from *Dogmatics in Outline* (59), which consists of lectures on the Apostles' Creed that the theologian delivered in the summer of 1946 in the semi-ruins of the University of Bonn. The primitive conditions that the theologian encountered in post-war Germany made it necessary for him to dispense with a manuscript for the first time in his life. The book, Barth informs us in the foreword to the Harper Torchbook edition of *Dogmatics in Outline*, was "a slightly polished and improved shorthand transcript" (5).

ing on flattering a moth-eaten bum, who is really the god Dionysius, and I begin laughing."[2]

This enchanting tale about a self-effacing high school teacher and his artistically gifted son, the teacher modeled on Updike's real-life father and the son modeled on the author himself, has endeared itself to many of Updike's readers as well. Yet for all the affection that *The Centaur* enjoys within the circle of Updike aficionados, the general reader often has trouble with the book. The symbolism is not in the background, as usually is the case with Updike, but front and center. Just as there is no avoiding sex in a novel like *Couples*, so there is no avoiding mythology in a novel like *The Centaur*. But once the reader has accepted this interpretative challenge, the story is quite accessible and enjoyable to read. *The Centaur* in fact may well be Updike's most hopeful and explicitly religious or gospel-imbued novel. Still, some explanatory remarks on the use of myth and symbolism in this novel, and in Updike's work in general, may be helpful.

When we speak of "myth" in this literary context, we simply mean the great stories and events and insights that have shaped our minds and colored our imaginations over the centuries. These stories may be rooted in history, as in the myth of Abraham Lincoln. Or they may be grounded in the world of the imagination, as in the Greek and Roman myths of antiquity. Or they may represent a mix of historical recollection and spiritual discernment, as in many of the stories of the Bible. Updike loved these old stories and cherished them as an important part of the world that his fiction attempts to describe. He took special delight in meshing the stories of the past with his own stories, sometimes transforming the old stories in the process, sometimes letting the old stories transform his.

Time magazine once reported that when John Updike was eight years old, he sat down at his mother's typewriter and pecked out his first story, which began: "The tribe of Bum-Bums looked very solemn as they sat around their cosy cave fire."[3] For the rest of his life, Updike remained a member of that solemn tribe. As he once told Charles Samuels,

> The author's deepest pride, as I have experienced it, is not in his incidental wisdom but in his ability to keep an organized mass of images moving forward, to feel life engendering under his hands.[4]

2. Plath, ed. *Conversations*, 35.

3. "View from the Catacombs," 73.

4. Plath, ed., *Conversations*, 44.

Most of the time the conversation between Updike's images and the images of the past is muted, subtle, indirect, and likely to go unnoticed. Still, the allusions, the parallels, the *secrets* are there, reminding us that all our individual stories, however ground-breaking, are told within the larger human context, told as it were by the tribe of Bum-Bums sitting around their cosy cave fire, sharing tales that will always be variations, to some extent, on perennial themes.

Updike's much-celebrated Rabbit novels offer a ready illustration of his intertwining of myths. Rabbit is the nickname of Harry Angstrom, the fleet-footed hero of *Rabbit, Run* (1960), *Rabbit Redux* (1971), *Rabbit Is Rich* (1981), *Rabbit at Rest* (1990), and the ghostly hero of *Rabbit Remembered* (2000). The nickname fits Harry's rabbit-like tendency to live within his skin, darting at the slightest external pressure, enjoying, above all, the sensation of running free. But the nickname also links Updike's protagonist with the naughty yet endearing lagomorph of Beatrix Potter's creation: the legendary Peter Rabbit who hops into Mr. McGregor's cabbage patch, tastes forbidden produce, and runs for his life when Mr. McGregor appears, rake in hand. *Rabbit, Run* finds Updike's human rodent running from his dreary job and pregnant, alcoholic-leaning wife, hopping into the bed of a prostitute's warren, tasting the forbidden fruit of extramarital sex, and running off again when his mother-in-law's minister—Mr. McGregor in a collar—comes after him with biblical injunctions in hand. Updike's Rabbit continues his adventures and misadventures in *Rabbit Redux* and *Rabbit Is Rich*, wriggling free from the various midlife traumas that, like the gooseberry net and sieve in Beatrix Potter's classic tale, would trap playful bunnies and squeeze the life out of them.

Yet all this running takes its toll. Just as Peter Rabbit sits down to rest after the chase only to discover "he was out of breath and trembling with fright," so Updike's Rabbit discovers that "little squeezy pains tease his ribs, reaching into his upper left arm" and he has "spells of feeling short of breath and mysteriously full in the chest, full of some pressing essence."[5] Rabbit's condition is further exacerbated by the heart attack he suffers during a near-drowning incident in the ocean—the counterpart to Peter Rabbit's shivering experience in the watering can in Mr. McGregor's toolshed.

On and on the symbolism rolls, but as raisins in the bun and not the bun itself. Updike, for one thing, doesn't worry about getting all the details exact. Peter Rabbit has three siblings—Flopsy, Mopsy, and Cottontail—and

5. Updike, *Rabbit at Rest*, 7.

not, as Updike's Rabbit has, only one (and hardly one who could be described as a "good little bunny"). The symbolism, in other words, is not vital to the story. It is there rather as a "bonus for the sensitive reader."

However, the symbolism in *The Centaur* is much more than a bonus. It is the very core of a story that has to do with the mythical impression of life that especially strikes us in adolescence. Is it not so that boyfriends, girlfriends, parents, friends of parents, teachers, classmates, bullies—almost everyone who walks into our lives during those early, formative, teenage years—assumes mythical, larger-than-life proportions, and to a remarkable extent retains those proportions throughout our lives? This is the life-defining truth that Updike attempts to capture on paper in *The Centaur*. Clearly, he believes that it is not enough in this case simply to deck out his fictional characters with mythical overtones. No, these characters who walk into our lives during our high school days are virtual gods whose mythical personae assume human form in the story. Chiron, the noblest and wisest of the centaurs, turns up as a high school teacher; Prometheus makes his appearance as the teacher's son; Zeus, as the school's principal; and so on.

The mythical story that Updike is telling overall is the tale of how Chiron, wandering the world in perpetual pain, willingly yields his immortality as an atonement for Prometheus. Zeus is punishing him for stealing fire from the gods. And since *all* of the characters in the story are mythical figures in human guise, Updike provides, at the beginning of the book, a summary of the controlling Chiron myth. Also, at the end of the book, he provides a mythological index to assist the reader in making connections with the lesser-known gods. Some critics consider the index superfluous. But for most of us, especially given that, as the novel itself points out, "few living mortals today cast their eyes respectfully toward heaven and fewer still sit as students to the stars," the index is a literal godsend.[6] Certainly, a reader who knows who's who in the story will appreciate the humor and ingenuity all the more.

An even greater problem than readerly confusion, however, may be aesthetic suitability. Many a critic has taken Updike to task for finding in ordinary high school characters the *dramatis personae* for some of the great mythological personages of classical lore. There is simply not enough nobility, they say, in *The Centaur's* human counterparts to warrant comparison with their mythological originals. However, if the critics are right on *this*

---

6. Cf. Edith Hamilton's *Greek Mythology* for an especially lucid introduction to the gods and goddesses of Greek mythology.

score, Updike is wrong not only in *The Centaur* but in almost every story he wrote. For the underlying thesis of his work is that there is nothing truly ordinary about so-called ordinary people just as there is nothing particularly special about the rich and the powerful. When an interviewer once asked him why he writes about the middle class, he readily acknowledged that he really only knows people in the middle. The poor, Updike said, he really doesn't know, and as for the glamorous, the very rich, "Well, glamorous people seem kind of special to me, and the few I have known . . . they're ordinary but they have the disadvantage of not knowing they are ordinary. So any native numbness or obtuseness is intensified by not even being embarrassed about it."[7]

Rich or poor or in between, what matters for Updike is life in all its beautiful perishing mystery. The writer accordingly makes no apologies for the analogies in *The Centaur*. Measuring human life qualitatively and not quantitatively, John Updike finds it perfectly appropriate for Mount Olympus to appear on earth in the form of Olinger High School; for Chiron, the wise centaur, to be portrayed as the antic but kind-hearted teacher George Caldwell; for Prometheus, the daring young god who steals fire from heaven, to be cast as George's fifteen-year-old artistically gifted son; and so on.[8,9]

The opening chapter of *The Centaur* reveals the complexity of Updike's mythmaking. George Caldwell is teaching a science lesson to a class of unruly students at Olinger High School. Caldwell, remember, is the human personification of the wise centaur, Chiron. As the story begins, he is struck by a metal arrow and limps off to Al Hummel's garage where Hummel/Hephaestus removes the arrow from his ankle. Caldwell then returns to the school through the basement in the hope of escaping the all-seeing eye of the school's principal, Zimmerman/Zeus. Passing through the girl's locker room, Caldwell morphs into Chiron and encounters Vera Hummel,

7. The audio interview was conducted by Terry Gross and can be downloaded from the *New York Times* Updike website at http://partners.nytimes.com/books/00/11/19specials/updike.htm1#audio2.

8. Referring in particular to his early short stories, Updike once famously summed up his whole philosophy of writing by saying that he felt he "was packaging something as delicately pervasive as smoke, one box after another . . . where my only duty was to describe reality as it had come to me—to give the mundane its beautiful due." Updike, Foreword, *Collected Early Stories*, xv.

9. James Wood once criticized Updike for finding "the same degree of sensuality in everything whether it is a woman's breast or an avocado." Cf. Wood, *The Broken Estate*, 192. Over and against such essentially aristocratic aesthetic judgments, Updike clearly chooses to go on his own democratic, religiously grateful, artistically unapologetic way.

Al Hummel's attractive red-haired wife who embodies Venus, the goddess of love. She proceeds to give Chiron—and the attentive reader—the lowdown on the gods whose human personae we will meet in the story. Remorphing as Caldwell, the teacher returns to the classroom and finds an angry Zimmerman waiting for him. Zimmerman immediately reproaches Caldwell for tardiness and stays in the classroom to monitor the teacher's lesson, which concerns the evolution of the solar system and the emergence of, eventually, human life. Although the lesson is brilliantly presented, the students become increasingly boisterous and rude, pushing Caldwell, who is in agonizing pain from his ankle injury, to the limit and beyond. Zimmerman, for his part, begins stroking the arm of one of the girls in the class, Iris Osgood/Io, managing before the class is over to slip the student's blouse and bra off. What, the reader might well ask, is going on here, not just mythically, but morally? And how realistic is it for principals to disrobe and fondle a student during a class? The scene does seem far-fetched until we remember that this is the mythological counterpart to the human story. Zimmerman is the personification on earth of Zeus, who is not only the principal god on Mount Olympus but also the most lecherous god in the field. The actions of the school's principal, therefore, are quite in keeping with the mythical figure that he embodies.

But this insight in turn only throws the question back to the ancient Greeks. What were *they* doing crafting stories of lecherous gods of Zeus's high standing? If there is going to be lechery should it not at least be carried out in some dark lowly corner where only the minor gods hang out? In fact, the luncheonette in *The Centaur* serves as the dimly lit meeting place for the wised-up, sexually wired students of Olinger High. The hangout is presided over, appropriately, by Minor Kretz/Minos. Lechery in Minor's luncheonette, however, is one thing; it is quite another matter when such seedy behavior is displayed by the principal god with thunderbolts at his fingertips.

Again the question is raised, what were these old Greeks thinking about? *Real people in real life.* That's what they were thinking about. The story of Zeus shows penetrating insight into the overriding power of sex centuries before Freud confirmed the matter with his psychoanalytic studies, and people like Bill Clinton and Monica Lewinsky played out the thesis in the corridors of high power. Who says the principal gods with thunderbolts at their fingertips are somehow above lecherous behavior? The moral question here hardly needs spelling out—and Updike doesn't belabor the obvious. Nevertheless, the question remains, and the alert reader can't help wondering afresh at the wild, powerful impulses that afflict not only the humble and lowly, but also and especially, it would seem, half-godlike, half-beastly characters like Zeus, like Zimmerman, like Mr. Clinton, like so many of us.

John Updike once told an interviewer that all of his novels in some way raise the question of human goodness. He hopes readers will wrestle with the question, not because the author hits the reader over the head with it, but because the story itself quietly inclines us to think about such matters. In *Rabbit, Run,* for example, we see human goodness betrayed as a result of Rabbit's need to run and breathe and remain free. While such a basic human need is understandable, we have to wonder, especially in the wake of the ghastly ramifications of Rabbit's behavior, whether the good, after all, may not consist, sometimes at least, in refraining from running and breathing free.

Of course, there is a price tag if one chooses not to run, and we find George Caldwell paying this price. The man remains in the classroom. He experiences the daily constrictions of life and work (and constantly lets everybody *know* how painful the constrictions are). He remains an old workhorse in harness, ploughing the field to the bitter end. For all the complaints, however, the price may be worth it. Certainly, the narrator of *The Centaur* thinks so. "Only goodness lives," he comments at the end of the story with Caldwell clearly in mind. "But it does live."[10]

Myth, then, has to do with stories that run deep in the human heart. These stories may be historically rooted or imaginatively based. Or a mix of the historical and the imaginative. The Christian myth is a prime example of the latter. It is rooted in the real-life story of the people of Israel and a first-century Jew from Nazareth. Nevertheless, the eye of faith, the imagination of the spirit, is required to discern in Israel's little defeats and victories the formation of God's covenant with his people, and the fulfilment of that covenant in the personal defeats and victories of the Jew from Nazareth.

As a man of faith himself, Updike takes the Christian myth seriously and makes considerable use of it in his fiction. Olinger High thus becomes not only Olympus, but also Bethlehem, and Caldwell is not only Chiron, but Christ. Christlike as well as Chiron-like, George Caldwell relinquishes his immortality and dies to self. This is basically done by staying in the classroom and also with his wife and family, thus resisting the temptation

10. Updike, *The Centaur*, 297.

posed by Vera/Venus. In any number of small and not so small ways, George Caldwell becomes, as Dietrich Bonhoeffer said of Jesus, "the man for others." He freely gives his gloves (a *Christ*mas present from his son) to a tramp. He ungrudgingly gives an insulting drunk his last handful of change. He unhesitatingly gives guidance and encouragement to his students. He gives his very life, and the shelter it affords, for his son. There is humor in Caldwell's antic generosity and steep self-deprecation, but there is also a genuine reflection of the self-giving Christ of the Christian story.

Updike more than once indicated that he originally planned *The Centaur* as a companion novel to *Rabbit, Run*, contrasting Rabbit, the engaging but exasperating human animal who lives entirely within his skin, with Caldwell, the Christlike character who cares nothing for his own skin and the "I" that it shelters. Caldwell is almost always thinking of the skin of others: literally, in Peter's case, as he worries about the effects that the spreading psoriasis might have on his son's arms and torso. But then Caldwell is also constantly worrying about the lives of those around him: his students, his colleagues, his wife, his father-in-law, etc. This is not to say that George is less than human. Indeed, he is acutely human (even as the man from Nazareth is acutely human) and understandably melancholy about the threat that death poses. Caldwell indeed feels the threat constantly churning in his bowels. Yet even here he is concerned about his own death mainly on account of the effect it is likely to have on others, Peter especially. The man for others simply does not worry about himself: "Don't worry about your old man," Caldwell tells Peter at one point: "In God we trust."[11]

When Hester Appleton/Artemis, one of Caldwell's teaching colleagues, shares with him her own confession of faith: *"Dieu – est –tres – fin. . . .* It's the sentence I've lived by . . . God is very fine, very elegant, *very* slender, *very* exquisite. *Dieu est tres fin."* Caldwell immediately agrees. "That's right. He certainly is. He's a wonderful old gentleman. I don't know where the hell we'd be without him."[12] The joking, colloquial tone aside, Caldwell's words remind us of Jesus' own fondness for the diminutive "Abba" or "Daddy."

And like Christ's self-giving, Caldwell's selflessness rubs off on others. There is an especially revealing moment when Peter and his girlfriend are having an intimate conversation in the bleachers during a high school basketball game. Self-conscious as usual about the scabs that psoriasis has deposited on his skin (a mythological allusion to the punishment that Zeus

11. Ibid., 168.

12 Ibid., 194.

is inflicting on Prometheus by chaining him to a rock and arranging for an eagle to constantly peck his liver), Peter turns to his girlfriend and says, "Hey. You have such beautiful skin." She replies, "You always say that. Why? It's just skin."[13]

Later in the story Peter shows her the scabs on the underside of his arm and even on his chest. When she responds with kindness and acceptance, he is amazed:

"Then you don't mind?"
"Of course not. You can't help it. It's part of you."
"Is that really how you feel?"
"If you knew what love was, you wouldn't even ask."
"Aren't you good?"[14]

Goodness and love appear throughout this story, inspired chiefly by Caldwell, which is to say by Chiron, the son of Chronos, the god of time, which is to say again by Christ, the Son of God, the giver of shelter and warmth to the whole world through his self-sacrificing example.

Commentary on a novel like *The Centaur* would not be complete without mentioning the role that real life plays in stimulating our most cherished myths. Updike never apologized for finding source material in his own life, especially his early years:

I suppose there's no avoiding it—my adolescence seemed interesting to me. In a sense my mother and father, considerable actors both, were dramatizing my youth as I was having it so that I arrived as an adult with some burden of material already half formed. There is, true, a submerged thread connecting certain of the fictions, and I guess the submerged thread is the autobiography.[15]

While lived experience needs to be shaped for literary purposes, there is nothing like one's own story for providing the larger-than-life texture that myth thrives on. Updike never claimed that his story was unique; only that, like's everyone's story, it bears recounting. He simply claimed for himself what he granted others: the freedom to discover in one's own personal journey the makings of myth.

13. Ibid., 228.
14. Ibid., 246.
15. Plath, ed., *Conversations*, 27.

Olinger High (the name, Updike explains, is pronounced with a long O, a hard *g,* and the emphasis on the first syllable as if to say "Oh—*linger!*") represents not only Olympus and Bethlehem, but also Shillington, the real-life borough on the outskirts of Reading, Pennsylvania, where John Updike lived with his family during his childhood, and where his father, Wesley Updike, taught high school. And Firetown is more than the tiny hamlet set in Galilee from whence Peter and his Christlike father set out for their three-day adventure. It is also Plowville, the real-life hamlet ten miles west of Shillington, on the outskirts of which the Updike family moved in 1945 when John was thirteen. Caldwell, therefore, stands not only for Chiron and Christ but also for Wesley Updike:

> I don't mind admitting that George Caldwell was assembled from certain vivid gestures and plights characteristic of Wesley Updike: once, returning to Plowville after *The Centaur* came out I was up-braided by a Sunday-school pupil of my father's for my outrageous portrait, and my father with typical sanctity, interceded, saying, "No, it's the truth. The kid got me right."[16]

And Cassie Caldwell is not only Chariclo/Ceres but also Linda Updike, John Updike's real-life mother. While *Of the Farm* may be the novel that features Updike's mother as the main character, she is still a vital, sustaining presence in the background of *The Centaur.*

In the late seventies, I was taking summer classes at Princeton Theological Seminary in New Jersey, the same seminary, incidentally, that Wesley Updike's father attended for two years around 1880. Rather presumptuously, I contacted Linda Updike (Wesley had recently died) and invited her out for lunch. She agreed, and I drove over to Plowville and met her at the sandstone farmhouse that her son has immortalized in *Of the Farm* and the valedictorian short story, "A Sandstone Farmhouse." As we then drove from the farmhouse into Shillington to find a restaurant, Mrs. Updike offered a running commentary on any number of places and turns in the road that figure in *The Centaur.* The real-life resemblance was uncanny.

A few years later I returned to Plowville. Mrs. Updike had died, and without her detailed instructions I had trouble finding the farmhouse. I finally stopped at a local garage and asked for directions. It was as if I had stumbled upon Hummel/Hephaestus, the garageman in *The Centaur.* My informant turned out to be the mechanic who had serviced Wesley Updike's car for years and before that had been one of his students. The picture that

16. Ibid., 26.

the mechanic painted of John Updike's father could have been lifted almost verbatim from the pages of *The Centaur*. "You could tell that Mr. Updike was a clever man," the garage man allowed. "But for a clever man he did a lot of crazy things." Country deference then kicked in and the garageman stopped talking. But I naturally pressed for details. "Well," the mechanic said at last, "one day Mr. Updike appeared at the garage and asked for a can of gasoline since his car had run out of gas. We offered to drive him to the car but, no, he insisted on walking. And so we gave him a can. Off he went only to return some time later with the empty can, having walked all the way back from his car." The mechanic shook his head at the memory of such self-tormenting nonsense.

But to me it was anything but nonsensical. It all seemed quite in keeping with the man I had come to know and love through *The Centaur*. Most of us complain about others and make excuses for ourselves. Not Wesley Updike! With strong whiffs of Caldwell/Chiron/Christ, he was the kind of man who praises everybody and punishes only himself. Crazy, yes, but in the zany spirit of the one whose cross "is foolishness to those who are perishing, but to us who are being saved it is the power of God" (1 Cor 1:18)

"Fiction," John Updike once said, "is a tissue of literal lies that refreshes and informs our sense of actuality."[17] The myth is the tissue, the exaggeration, the lie that catches the reader's interest. The myth grows, however, out of the real and constantly brings us back to the real, informing and refreshing us with its imaginative report of the things that lie deep.

17. Updike, *Picked-Up Pieces*, 17.

CHAPTER 3

Barthian Myths in Three Early Novels

BARTHIAN MYTHS? ISN'T THIS an oxymoron? Wasn't the father of neo-orthodoxy the great enemy of myth? To be sure, Karl Barth opposed a mythical interpretation of the gospel in the reductionist sense of the word. But this doesn't mean that he rejected myth in and of itself. And Updike for his part, while clearly loving myth, doesn't play it off against historical reality. Authentic religion connects us with reality, regardless of whether that reality is attested poetically or prosaically. Certainly, it was Barth's grasp of divine reality that Updike found so appealing in the theologian's approach to matters of faith. Asked by an interviewer once what elements of Barth's position attracted him to the theologian, Updike replied:

> I think it was the frank supernaturalism and the particularity of his position, so unlike that of Tillich and the entire group of liberal theologians—and you scratch most ministers, at least in the East, and you find a liberal—whose view of these (biblical) events is not too different from that of an agnostic. But Barth was with resounding definiteness and learning saying what I needed to hear, which was that it really was so, that there was something within us that would not die, and that we live by faith alone—more or less; he doesn't just say that, but what he does say joined with my Lutheran heritage and enabled me to go on.[1]

It really was so. The fact that Karl Barth understood the biblical witness to God's self-revelation in the history of Israel and Jesus Christ realistically, and not as metaphor, spoke to Updike and enabled him to go on. And there was a time in the writer's life when he wondered if he *could* go on. The threat of death began suffocating Updike's spirits to the point where Barth's

---

1. Plath, ed., *Conversations*, 102.

theology, and his theology alone, convinced him of the truth of the gospel and allowed him to breathe.[2]

However, it doesn't follow, as indicated earlier, that Barth's realistic understanding of revelation means that the theologian ignored or denigrated the poetry that is clearly part of the biblical witness to revelation. Karl Barth gladly recognized that the creation stories in Genesis, for example, are poetic in linguistic character, and certainly not empirically factual. Actually, Barth preferred to speak of "saga" rather than myth by way of indicating the kind of language the Bible uses when attesting the miracle of God's creation.[3] The important thing is not to conflate the poetry into the prose, or vice versa. We simply need to recognize that "it really *was* so." God truly did draw near in Christ, truly did endure nail prints in torn flesh, and truly did appear alive again. In the words of Updike's famous poem on the resurrection:

> Let us not mock God with metaphor,
> analogy, sidestepping, transcendence,
> making of the event a parable, a sign painted in the faded
> credulity of earlier ages:
> let us walk through the door.[4]

It is not a question of either demonizing or idealizing myth but of simply recognizing the role that it plays in the biblical witness to God's self-revealing presence and redeeming action in Jesus Christ. This is what Barth was so helpful in driving home for Updike. But we mustn't suggest that John Updike therefore spent the rest of his life reading Karl Barth! It is just that, as the writer once told Dick Cavett in a television interview,

> There was a time in my late twenties, early thirties when I was very frightened. Frightened of being alive, and somehow Barth eased

---

2. In his foreword to *Assorted Prose*, Updike writes, "The Barth article . . . was written in acknowledgment of a debt, for Barth's theology, at one point in my life, seemed alone to be supporting it [my life]" (ix).

3. In Barth's "Doctrine of Creation" (cf. *Church Dogmatics*, Volume III, part 1), the theologian distinguishes saga from history on the one hand and poetry on the other: "I am using saga in the sense of an intuitive and poetic picture of a pre-historical reality, of history which is enacted once and for all within the confines of time and space" (81). Barth recognized that the Bible "contains little pure 'history' and little pure saga, and little of both that can be unequivocally recognised as the one or the other. The two elements are usually mixed. In the Bible we usually have to reckon with history and saga" (81).

4. Updike, "Seven Stanzas at Easter," in *Collected Poems 1953–1993*, 20–21.

away the fear and enabled me to go on living. It's as simple and as complex as that. . . . the voice of the man aside from what he is saying . . . very comforting, kind of fatherly, gravelly, omniscient. Amused, even? He's a funny, a funny theologian. They're not all funny.[5]

John Updike's love for Karl Barth finds obvious expression in such full-blown Barthian characters as the Reverend Thomas Marshfield, the adulterous minister who serves as the protagonist and epistolarian of *A Month of Sundays*: "I became a Barthian, in reaction against my father's liberalism, a smiling fumbling shadow of German Pietism, of Hegel's and Schleiermacher's, and Ritschl's polywebbed attempt to have it all ways . . . ,"[6] and Professor Lambert, the cuckolded theologian who serves as the protagonist and narrator of *Roger's Version*:

> I took down my old copy (of Barth's *The Word of God and the Word of Man*), a paperbound Torchbook read almost to pieces, its binding glue dried out and its margins marked again and again by the pencil of a young man who thought that here, definitively and forever, he had found the path, the voice, the style, and the method to save within himself and to present to others the Christian faith . . . .[7]

While Barth's name looms large in such novels, his spirit looms even larger in three earlier novels composed while Updike's religious crisis was at its height. *Rabbit, Run* (1960) and *The Centaur* (1963) both explore Barth's covenant theology of grace in its vertical dimension while *Of the Farm* explores Barth's understanding of the covenant in its horizontal dimension. This chapter will attempt to draw out these Barthian motifs by way of illustrating the interplay between John Updike and Karl Barth.

---

5. "The Dick Cavett Show: A Conversation with John Updike," December 1978. Updike, incidentally, cites with appreciation Barth's expectation of the novelist: "I expect the contemporary novelist to show me man as he always is in the man of today, my contemporary—and vice versa, to show me my contemporary in man as he always is. . . . The novel should have no plans for educating me, but should leave me to reflect (or not) on the basis of the portrait with which I am presented" (Updike, *More Matter*, 834). Theologians are not all funny and neither are critics, it would seem, especially those who complain that Updike's novels don't sufficiently "educate us."

6. Updike, *A Month of Sundays*, 24.

7. Updike, *Roger's Version*, 40.

I

Rabbit, Run

> The motions of Grace, the hardness of heart;
> external circumstances.
> —PASCAL, PENSEE 507

UPDIKE'S EPIGRAPH FROM PASCAL is fleshed out in *Rabbit, Run* in the tale of an ex-high school basketball star whose days of glory have been tarnished by the slow yet relentless grinding of time. Harry "Rabbit" Angstrom is now in his mid-twenties and saddled with an unimaginative job and an even less imaginative wife who, pregnant for the second time, has taken to drink and TV. Feeling trapped by this inglorious net of external circumstances, Rabbit bolts for freedom, displaying at once the rodentine characteristics of his nickname and the Pascalian "hardness of heart" of Updike's epigram. While thoroughly animalistic in his ways, Rabbit is nevertheless pricked by spiritual urgencies. The motions of grace may have a difficult time penetrating his hard heart, but penetrate it they do even as the rays of the sun continue to strike the retina of the blind.

These invisible yet constantly pressing spiritual motions constitute the novel's deepest theme as announced by the epigraph. The theme is verbalized at one point during a spirited exchange between two clergymen: Fritz Kruppenbach, the Lutheran pastor representing Rabbit's side of the family, and the Reverend Jack Eccles, the Episcopal priest representing Rabbit's wife's side.

In both name and outlook, Kruppenbach recalls the early Karl Barth who stormed upon the theological scene in the 1920s with his thundering proclamation of the revelation of God that has broken into the world vertically from above in Jesus Christ. This utterly transcendent message gives rise to the enduring perplexity of the clergy person who is constantly dealing with something ultimately far more overpowering than the potentially solvable problems of daily life:

> Obviously the people have no real need of our observations upon morality and culture, or even of our disquisitions upon religion, worship, and the possible existence of other worlds. All these things belong, indeed, to their life and are bound up, whether they

know it or not, with their life's one need. But these things are not that need.[8]

The one great need that people have is God. This, Barth declares, is what, or rather who, we are ever hungering and thirsting for in and through all our material, emotional, and sexual yearnings: "When they come to us for help they do not really want to learn more about living: they want to learn more about what is on the farther edge of living—God."[9]

Yet it is precisely *God* that the clergy have so much trouble speaking about, either on account of embarrassed softness (Eccles) or clumsy hardness (Kruppenbach).[10] The *word* of course can easily be uttered. But the truth or divine reality indicated by this word can only be communicated by God himself in the transcendent act of breaking through to us in God's own self-revealing power.

The novel illustrates Barth's analysis of our situation vis-à-vis God's gracious being and redemptive action by showing a friendly hound of heaven pursuing Rabbit in the person of the Reverend Jack Eccles. The affable clergyman arranges for a game of golf with the mixed-up young Harry

---

8. Barth, *The Word of God and the Word of Man*, 188. The address was originally delivered in Germany in 1922.

9. Ibid., 189.

10. Something of the hardness and certainly the singleness of mind of Kruppenbach's own real life Barthian model may be glimpsed in an anecdote that James Luther Adams recounts in his preface to William Kimmel and Geoffrey Clive's *Dimensions of Faith*, 7. In 1936 Adams attended in Switzerland an international conference of students and faculties of Protestant theology, a conference in which Karl Barth was a participant. The first paper, presented by a theologian from the University of Geneva, dealt with the concept of religious experience, and it employed the language of psychology as well as of Christian theology. Before the speaker was well under way, however, Barth suddenly arose in the audience, interrupted the speaker, and addressed the chairman. "I shall not wait any longer. I want to ask the speaker a question now," he said, thereby of course throwing the meeting into an uproar of consent and dissent. The chairman replied that is customary for questions to be withheld until a paper is finished, but with questionable judgment the theologian reading the paper agreed to accept the question immediately. Barth thereby made a frontal attack: "Is the speaker reading to us a paper on Christian theology or on the psychology of religious experience? If the paper is on the psychology of religion, why should we here listen to it? This is a conference of Christian theologians; only the Word of God, not talk about psychology and religious experience, is appropriate here." Needless to say, heated debate followed. But the point is that Karl Barth (one of the few major German theologians of the day, incidentally, who unequivocally opposed the German Christians and their religiously rationalized embrace of fascism) was more of a soulmate for Kruppenbach than might first meet the eye.

Angstrom and, once on the green, tries to understand what makes Rabbit run:

> "Harry," he asks, sweetly, yet boldly, "why have you left her? You're obviously deeply involved with her."
>
> "I told ya. There is this thing that wasn't there."
>
> "What thing? Have you ever seen it? Are you sure it exists?"
>
> "Well if you're not sure it exists don't ask me. It's right up your alley. If you don't know nobody does."[11]

Eccles, his very name recalling the worldly wisdom of Ecclesiastes, doesn't know, he can't know this "thing" that Rabbit is talking about. Such knowledge requires wisdom from on high, and so Eccles seeks out Kruppenbach, who stands there on Mt. Judge armed with Karl Barth's searing, transcendent gospel (or at least a rough popularization of it). The meeting between the two clergymen begins with Eccles offering Kruppenbach a balanced and insightful but naturally all too this-worldly account of why Rabbit has fled his wife and forsaken adult responsibilities:

> "Do you think," Kruppenbach at last interrupts, "do you think this is your job, to meddle in these people's lives? I know what they teach you at seminary now: this psychology and that. But I don't agree with it. You think now your job is to be an unpaid doctor, to run around and plug up holes and make everything smooth. I don't think that. I don't think that's your job."[12]

Eccles naturally doesn't want to hear Kruppenbach tell him what his real job consists of any more than the worldly ecclesiastics of the roaring twenties wanted to hear Barth telling them what the real task of the ministry consists of. Nevertheless, Kruppenbach/Karl Barth tells anyway:

> "If Gott wants to end misery He'll declare the Kingdom now. . . . How big do you think your little friends look among the billions that God sees? In Bombay now they die in the streets every minute. You say role. I say you don't know what your role is or you'd be home locked in prayer. There is your role: to make yourself an exemplar of faith. There is where comfort comes from; faith, not what little finagling a body can do here and there; stirring the bucket. In running back and forth you run from the duty given you by God, to make your faith powerful. . . . When on Sunday

11. Updike, *Rabbit, Run*, 133.

12. Ibid., 169.

morning then, when we go before their faces, we must walk up not worn out with misery but full of Christ, hot"—he clenches his hairy fists—"with Christ, on fire: burn them with the force of our belief. This is why they come; why else would they pay us? Anything else we can do and say anyone can do and say. They have doctors and lawyers for that. It's all in the Book—a thief with faith is worth all the Pharisees. Make no mistake. Now I'm serious. Make no mistake. There is nothing but Christ for us. All the rest, all this decency and busyness, is nothing. It is Devil's work."[13]

Kruppenbach's words would seem to be a risible parody of Barth, and indeed there are parodic elements here, rich with humor. Still, Kruppenbach/ Karl Barth is "serious. Make no mistake." However outrageously insensitive and theologically one-sided Kruppenbach may be, he is pinpointing the secret need underlying all other human needs that makes Rabbit run. Here is Barth himself expressing the matter shorn of the entertaining parody:

> The people do not need us to help them with the appurtances of their daily life. They look after those things without advice from us and with more wisdom than we usually credit them with. But they are aware that their daily life and all the questions which are factors in it are affected by a great What? Why? Whence? Whither? which stands like a minus sign before the whole parenthesis and changes to a new question all the questions inside—even those which may have already been answered. They have no answer for this question of questions, but are naïve enough to assume that others may have. So they thrust us into our anomalous profession and put us into their pulpits and professorial chairs, that we may tell them about God and give them the answer to their ultimate question. . . . It is evident that [the people] do not need us to help them live, but seem to need us to help them die: for their whole life is lived in the shadow of death.[14]

Considered thematically as a whole, *Rabbit, Run* seeks to understand what makes Rabbit run from his wife and child, run into the arms of a prostitute, run back and forth between the two women, run until the poor bunny hardly knows where he is running any more, let alone why. What makes Rabbit run? Death, says Updike/Barth. This is the fundamental concern for thinking animals. And God and God alone can satisfy this grave concern. As another unsettled character conceded centuries ago: "Thou hast made

13. Ibid., 170.
14. Barth, *The Word of God and the Word of Man*, 187–88.

us for thyself, Lord: and our hearts are restless until they find their rest in thee."[15] What both the Eccleses of the church and the worldly wise beyond the church's walls don't understand is that, in the end, faced with the end, neither worldly wisdom nor worldly pleasure, nothing worldly at all in fact, can still our restless hearts. Only God's covenant of grace fulfilled in Christ and made real by the motions of the Spirit can still the storm that rages within. As long as that ultimate storm is not stilled, our hearts will remain restless, and, like Rabbit, we will go on running.

II

The Centaur

Heaven is the creation inconceivable to man, earth the creation conceivable to him. He himself is the creature on the boundary between heaven and earth.

Karl Barth

Barth's anthropological statement, taken from the theologian's exposition of the Apostles' Creed in *Dogmatics in Outline*, serves as the theme-announcing epigraph for *The Centaur*. We are creatures of the earth, dust through and through; and yet by virtue of the miracle of grace we are also citizens of heaven. *The Centaur's* protagonist, George Caldwell, dramatizes the centaur-like creature whose life straddles the boundary between heaven and earth. A high school science teacher by profession, and no spiritual athlete by temperament, Caldwell's utterly earthly heart remains open nevertheless to the motions of grace. One night, car trouble having stranded George and his son, Peter, in a flea-bitten, downtown hotel, George gets into bed:

> . . . after his body stopped rustling the sheets, there was a pause, and he said, "Don't worry about your old man, Peter. In God we trust."[16]

Caldwell's trust in God may not dissolve the problems of earthly existence; indeed, Caldwell remains almost as harried and anxiety-ridden as Rabbit

15. The unsettled character of course was Augustine (354–430), and the words come from his *Confessions*, 21.

16. Updike, *The Centaur*, 168.

ever was. Yet there is this difference: George Caldwell's earthly life is lived in the light of the watchful, caring eye of heaven. Through this vale of unending tears, Caldwell realizes that God is nevertheless his trustworthy partner. Earthly griefs and torments can and do break upon him, but they can't destroy this man who lives in the awareness of God's indestructible covenant of grace.

Throughout the novel George's faith is tested: everything from the threat of cancer to the peril of small-town gossip. The school secretary tries to slander Caldwell's name after he notices her popping out of the office of Olinger High's lecherous principal, the Zeus-like Zimmerman, looking, as Caldwell later described it to his son, "loved up." Responding to the secretary's concern about Caldwell's trustworthiness, Zimmerman attempts to reassure her:

> "The matter of trust has never come up between us."
> "But now?"
> "I trust him."[17]

In terms of the natural story line, the secretary is asking the principal of Olinger High to dismiss one of his most popular teachers. At the mythological level she is asking Zeus to kick the wise and gentle centaur off Mount Olympus. Theologically, she is asking the God of Israel and Father of Jesus Christ to tear up the covenant of grace. The request is bound to founder upon the rocks of reality:

> "You overestimate my omnipotence. The man has been teaching for fifteen years. He has friends. He has tenure."
>
> "But he really is incompetent, isn't he?"
>
> "Is he? Competence is not so easy to define. He stays in the room with them, which is the most important thing. Furthermore, he's faithful to me. He's faithful."
>
> "Why are you sticking up for him? He could destroy us both now."
>
> "Come, come, my little bird. Human beings are harder to destroy than that."[18]

Updike doesn't preach. He tells realistic stories with symbolic overtones that quietly invite us to enter the discussion. Here we are encouraged to consider the goodness of God whose partnership with us in the Christ-shaped

---

17. Ibid., 216.
18. Ibid.

covenant of grace may not solve our earthly problems. Yet within our blood-soaked world, it gives us a place to stand.

"Only goodness lives," the story concludes. "But it does live."[19]

Toward the end of the novel, Peter Caldwell

> remembered walking on some church errand with his father down a dangerous street in Passaic. It was a Saturday and the men from the sulphur works were getting drunk. From within the double doors of a saloon there welled a poisonous laughter that seemed to distill all the cruelty and blasphemy in the world, and he wondered how such a noise could have a place under the sky of his father's God . . .[20]

Then Peter recalled

> . . . his father turning and listening in his backwards collar to the laughter from the saloon and then smiling down to his son, "All joy belongs to the Lord."

The boy, we are told, takes the comment to heart, sensing that his father is voicing faith's deepest conviction concerning the creature's relationship with his Creator and the Creator's relationship with the creature:

> It was half a joke but the boy took it to heart. All joy belongs to the Lord. Wherever in the faith and confusion and misery, a soul felt joy, there the Lord came and claimed it as his own; into barrooms and brothels and classrooms and alleys slippery with spittle, no matter how dark and scabbed and remote, in China or Africa or Brazil, wherever a moment of joy was felt, there the Lord stole and added to His enduring domain . . . .[21]

III

Of the Farm

Consequently, when, in all honesty, I've recognized that man is a being in whom existence precedes essence, that he is a free being who, in various circumstances, can want only his freedom, I have at the same time recognized that I can want only the freedom of others.

19. Ibid., 297.
20. Ibid., 296.
21. Ibid.

—Sartre

The well-known words of the French existentialist Jean Paul Sartre supply the epigraph for *Of the Farm*. Updike thus signals his intention to turn the spotlight from our vertical relationship with God to the horizontal relationship with our neighbor. He develops the theme, however, not along Sartre's philosophical lines but in accord with Karl Barth's christologically grounded understanding of our humanity as created by God.[22] "In God we trust," George Caldwell said in *The Centaur*. *Of the Farm* now asks whether God can be trusted to know not only the liberating secret of our relationship with God, but the truth concerning our relationships with one another. Updike had earlier attempted to popularize Barth's theological understanding of the relationship between men and women in an essay only to have the essay rejected by *The New Yorker*. *Of the Farm* was subsequently written, he tells us, as a way of publicizing the essay's contents.[23]

Updike's original essay, suitably transmuted and condensed, appears in the novel in the form of a sermon that Joey Robinson hears on the morning of the third day of his weekend visit to the family farm. To this homecoming visit Joey has brought along his newly acquired second wife Peggy, his stepson Richard and, not least, his unresolved guilt and pain from shattered relationships in the past. Returning to his roots, Joey hopes to set these relationships right again.

The core of the problem involves Joey's relationship with his wife. The male-female relationship reaches its crowning intensification, for both Barth and Joey Robinson, in the husband-wife relationship. This is the great opportunity but also the great challenge posed by the horizontal dimension of the covenant. Updike's fictional minister trains his Barthian-inspired sermon on this challenge and opportunity.

The minister takes for his text the classic biblical passage that summons us to live together in community and not in isolation: "And the Lord God said, It is not good that the man should be alone; I will make an help

22. Cf. Gollwitzer, ed., *Karl Barth, Church Dogmatics*. Updike appears to have had especially in mind the section "Man and Woman" (194–229), which includes selected passages from Barth's discussion of the relationship between Man and Woman under the rubric "Freedom in Fellowship" in his *Church Dogmatics*, Volume III, Part 4, 116–240.

23. Thus claims the Catholic critic George Hunt, whose sleuthing work, reported in his book *John Updike and the Three Great Secret Things*, unearthed the origins of the novel (21). In a personal letter to Hunt, Updike is quoted as saying, "I wrote the sermon first as an essay no one would print, and then wrote the novel as a mounting for it" (83).

meet for him."[24] Exalted vision! Yet the moment steps are taken to realize the vision, the sexual challenge rears its awkward head: "And the Lord God caused a deep sleep to fall upon Adam, and he slept: and he took one of his ribs, and closed up the flesh instead; and the rib, which the Lord God had taken from man, made he a woman, and brought her unto the man."[25] Displaying his Barthian colors, the minister doesn't flinch from trying to understand whatever theological light the Bible might be attempting to throw on sexual politics here:

> [Eve] was taken out of Adam. She was made after Adam. And she was made while Adam slept. What do these assertions tell us about men and women today? First, is not Woman's problem that she was taken out of Man, and is therefore a subspecies, less than equal to Man, a part of the whole?
>
> Second, she was made after Adam. Think of God as a workman who learns as he goes. Man is the rougher and more ambitious artifact; Woman the finer and more efficient.[26]

The minister's observations trigger polite laughter from the pews—and that was years ago. Today his chauvinistic-sounding remarks would no doubt draw howls of outrage from people who are in no mood to joke about such matters. Indeed, the unguarded exegesis of the text displayed by the minister here is enough to make almost all of us wince (though Updike himself, in responding to my query about this sermon, didn't think "the minister's attempt to explicate Genesis had anything in it to apologize for, actually"). But clumsy or not, the sermon catches at something real. An abstract notion of equality today threatens to flatten out the sexual patterns of God's good creation, leaving us with a bleak and soulless vision of sexual ambiguity. Granted, the sexual differences here have traditionally been, and indeed continue to be, shamelessly exploited. Still, as the Catholics say, *Abusus non tollit usum.* Misuse does not negate right use. The differences between the sexes are intrinsically good and not bad; and the complementary needs and strengths that open up deepen and enrich our life together. Updike's fictional minister develops these themes, however clumsily, after the fashion of Barth's discussion in his ethics of creation:

24. Updike, *Of the Farm*, 149.

25. Ibid., 151.

26. Ibid., 151–52.

> "Karl Barth, the great theologian of our friendly rivals the Re-
> formed Church, says of Woman: 'Successfully or otherwise, she
> is in her whole existence an appeal to the kindness of Man.' An
> appeal to the kindness of Man. 'For kindness,' he goes on to say,
> 'belongs originally to his particular responsibility as a man.'"[27]

Kindness and appeal to kindness: these ethical concepts naturally need to
be distinguished from cultural categories. What is called for here is not a
patriarchal culture in which the initiative of kindhearted males becomes
confused with culturally conditioned expressions of male dominance while
the appeal of women to the kindness of men is confused with unhealthy expressions of female subservience. Granted, it's hard for most of us to avoid
confusing cultural patterns with ethical directives. Nevertheless, ethics and
not culture is what the novel—and the Bible—is speaking about here.

Male initiative in kindness! According to Barth, this is man's special
responsibility. When the man rebels against his calling by refusing to show
kindness to the woman, he becomes weak, however strong he may pretend
to be by way of compensatory psychological tactics:

> The tyrant need not be cruel or bad-tempered. There are quiet,
> gentle, amiable, easy-going tyrants who suit women only too well,
> and it is an open question in which form the male tyrant is worse
> and more dangerous. The distinctive characteristic of the tyranni-
> cal as opposed to the strong man is that he does not serve the order
> but makes the order serve himself.[28]

Female appeal to the kindness of man! This is the woman's special calling.
And when she rebels and refuses to let her whole existence be an appeal to
man's kindness, she becomes immature, however much she may compen-
sate for her immaturity by employing aggressive confrontational tactics. As
Barth notes, the woman is quite capable of playing on her side

> . . . the counterpart which the tyrant expects to see and which is
> necessary to the success of her own performance. She discovers in
> advance what is expected of her and fulfills it to the letter. She finds
> it convenient to make things as convenient as possible for him. She
> also finds it attractive—and the clever tyrant will certainly support
> this view—to be his pliable kitten, his flattering mirror. In pleasing

27. Ibid., 153.

28. Gollwitzer, ed., *Karl Barth, Church Dogmatics*, 224.

him she thus pleases herself. And she, too, will play her part all the more craftily because it is only a part.[29]

These ethical moves and countermoves, strategies and subterfuges, are dramatized in the encounters and conversations that fuel *Of the Farm*. Joey, to give but one example, recalls an incident with Peggy during an illicit weekend spent together before Joey left his first wife, Joan. He remembers Peggy saying:

> "Don't come again. I'm getting worse at saying goodbye. I'm sorry, I'm no good at this. I wanted to be a nice simple mistress for you but I'm not big enough. I'm too possessive. Go back and be nice to Joan, I've messed us all up by falling in love."[30]

Peggy here craftily plays up to Joey's weakness through her compliance. But there is no real appeal to Joey's kindness if only because there is no kindness to appeal to. Peggy's moral protestations instead simply give Joey a good conscience and help buck up his resolve to dispatch his wife and children. Joey remembers:

> And when I first—prematurely—offered to leave Joan for her, she cried. Oh no! Your children! I could never make it up to you![31]

How nice, we may think. A mistress with feelings! A home wrecker who actually cares! However, it is all a charade in which Peggy and Joey rationalize their moral failings. Joey is cruel to Joan and his children whom he readily sacrifices for Peggy, while Peggy feigns a guilty, conscience-struck spirit, thereby intensifying Joey's anguish but also making him proud of a woman who feels so morally anguished. All this in turn merely solidifies Joey's resolve to sacrifice Joan for Peggy. Joey in truth is a weak man, and Peggy is an immature woman, and all the psychological game-playing cannot alter the fact that the right relationship between men and women has been contradicted in their lives with—literally as well as figuratively—heartbreaking results.[32]

---

29. Ibid., 225.

30. Updike, *Of the Farm*, 87.

31. Ibid., 88.

32. The heart that actually breaks in this story is that of Joey's mother who suffers a heart attack on their way home from church. Cf. ibid., 157–62.

What remains unbreakable is the partnership between the sexes as willed by God and sealed in Christ's blood. As the minister in *Of the Farm* concludes in good Barthian fashion:

> Kindness differs from righteousness as the grasses from the stars. Both are infinite. Without conscious confession of God, there can be no righteousness. But kindness needs no belief. It is implicit in the nature of Creation, in the very curves and amplitude of God's fashioning.[33]

33. Ibid., 154.

CHAPTER 4

The Myth of Eros in *Marry Me*

MARRY ME RECEIVED A more sustained drubbing in John Updike's lifetime than almost any other novel that he published. Even when Michiko Kakutani was uncharacteristically gushing over Updike in a cover story for *Saturday Review*, claiming that he had defined "perhaps more persuasively than any other American author, the emotional territory of memory and desire,"[1] she still couldn't help bringing the novelist down a peg or two by suggesting that "his work has occasionally been uneven—his self-imposed quota of producing a book a year has resulted in such slight, imperfect works as *Marry Me* . . ."[2] I'm not suggesting Updike should never be brought down a peg or two. But *Marry Me*? Why pounce on this beautiful romantic novel to prove that the literary god of the cover story is still mortal? Yet this is the way it has so often gone with *Marry Me*: the critics are forever knocking the poor book. But *not* Adam Begley! Interestingly enough, Begley's recent biography of John Updike, while calling the novel "flawed,"[3] claims that *Marry Me* is "Updike's most underrated" novel.[4] Underrated it surely is, and I think I know why.

---

1. Kakutani, "Turning Sex and Guilt into an American Epic," 14.

2. Ibid., 20.

3. Flawed in Begley's curious judgment because of an insufficient connection with the great historical events of the day: "The white-knuckle trauma of the Cuban Missile Crisis doesn't figure in *Marry Me*, nor does the simmering violence of the civil rights movement—nor the assassination of the president" (Begley, *Updike*, 255). Forget the fact that the president's assassination took place well over a year after the events in *Marry Me*, why would the besotted lovers in this story ever be expected to have eyes or thoughts for anything other than their own love-enraptured selves?

4. Begley, *Updike*, 249.

The subtitle of the novel is "A Romance," and we all know how romances work, especially in fiction. Boy meets girl. Boy falls in love with girl. Obstacle materializes. Attempts to overcome obstacle fail and fail again until there's finally a breakthrough, sending the painfully thwarted lovers off into the sunset together and producing readerly smiles of vicarious pleasure. The obstacles may be real; indeed, they usually *are* real. It's the way they are overcome that normally begs the question of reality.

Consider, for example, how three popular twentieth-century romance novels undercut reality through a forced use of timing. In Erich Segal's *Love Story*, a brilliant, athletic Ivy Leaguer, the son of a wealthy New England lawyer, falls in love with a beautiful, brainy, talented girl, the daughter of a humble Italian baker. Blocking the romance is the boy's snobbish father (who hails, ironically, from the very town, Ipswich, Massachusetts, where Updike was living when he composed the original draft of *Marry Me*). The love obstacle is finally overcome when a mysterious blood disease takes the poor girl to an early grave. The old man's snobbery immediately dissolves and the young man is left with healing memories of love requited. The fanciful, unrealistic component in this instance is not, of course, the horror of the fatal blood disease but the calculated arrangement of its timing.

Timing also figures unrealistically in Robert James Waller's *The Bridges of Madison County*. In this romantic blockbuster, an itinerant photographer is passing through Iowa farm country on a *National Geographic* assignment and ends up enjoying a blazing four-day love affair with a middle-aged, Italian born, gorgeous farm wife. The obstacle—the farm wife's stolid but loyal husband and their unsuspecting children—is fancifully overcome by dispatching Dad and the kids to a four-day, out-of-state cattle fair while Mom and the stranger explore, unhampered, the joys of eros.

Still another example of a love story turning on forced timing is offered by Nicholas Spark in his romantic best seller, *The Notebook*. Here a summer love affair ignites between a poor, young Southern boy and a rich, young Southern belle only to run into class snobbery again, this time on the part of the girl's mother, who breaks up the relationship and effectively prevents the daughter from communicating with the boy anymore. An additional obstacle arises when the girl becomes engaged seven years later to a rich young lawyer. But that problem is easily taken care of. How many readers are going to feel sorry for a wealthy jilted lawyer who, as things turn out, is sexually impotent to boot? One can almost hear the cheers as the girl finally resists her mother's snobbish wishes, and ups and marries the poor but handsome Southern boy who has been implausibly waiting for her, it turns out, through all those seven long, libidinally charged years of non-communication.

Now compare these engaging but fanciful stories with the realistic romance that Updike recounts in *Marry Me*. In this story Jerry Conant is married to Ruth, and Sally Mathias is married to Richard. Jerry falls passionately in love with the lovely, tall, blonde-haired Sally even though, if not just because, she is not his wife. Has this sort of thing never happened before in the history of marital relationships? And when these romantic entanglements develop, is not the single most realistic obstacle preventing a satisfying consummation the stolid, unignorable fact of the marriages that are already in place?

Of course, marital obstacles can always be overcome by divorce. But it is much harder for writers of romance novels to make a convincing case for divorce when the lovers requesting it, and the spouses affected by it, do not include any comic-strip ogres or characters who conveniently pop off and die. No one dies in *Marry Me*, even though Ruth looks like she *might* die one day when her car skids off the road and hurtles through the woods. But the car ends up nuzzling "obliquely to a stop," and Ruth remains very much alive. Also, there are no ogres in *Marry Me*. The four protagonists all have their faults, but none of them is a monster.[5] There is no reason why these people can't, or shouldn't, continue to live within the marriages they have already entered upon. Jerry recognizes as much when he explains to Sally at the outset of the story, "I did a very bad thing in marrying Ruth. Much worse, really, than if I'd married for money. I married her because I knew

---

5. Nor is the author himself a monster, as more than one critic uncharitably suggested when *Marry Me* first appeared in print in 1976. Updike had recently filed for a "no-fault" divorce, and the following year he married Martha Bernhard. Yet the novel, for all its painful autobiographical overtones, is still a fictional work (composed mainly, as Begley points out, twelve years earlier), and there is no reason to believe that it was published against Mary Updike's wishes. In fact, a copy of the manuscript deposited in Harvard's Houghton Library shows annotations in Mary's hand. While her comments sometimes display signs of anger and hurt, it is clear that she is basically intent on making a good book even better. "I seem to be reading this as an editor rather than as an ex-wife defending her privacy," Mary says at one point in a summing-up statement. Her editorial suggestions concerning Richard in particular—"A little 'I-thou' between author and character would help. You must love your villains, too, or we won't love and believe you"—would appear to have led to a more empathetic portrayal of Jerry's arch-nemesis. Also, the concluding note to her ex-husband—"There is nothing you should change unless you find a comment of mine here or there compelling"—surely quashes all accusatory slurs against the author.

she'd make a good wife. And that's what she's done. God, I'm sorry. I'm so sorry, Sally" (12).

Jerry himself has understandably struck many readers of the novel as almost hopelessly romantic—a "twerp of twerps" in the words of the *Time* book reviewer. Nevertheless, he is not without redeeming qualities. And what is twerpiness, for that matter, when we are dealing with the innermost qualities of a man's life? Jerry's dread of death, in any event, is so fierce that he is driven to religion: "He read theology, Barth and Marcel and Berdyaev; he taught the children bedtime prayers. Each Sunday he deposited Joanna and Charlie in the Sunday school of the nearby Congregational church, sat through the sermon, and came home cocky, ready to fight" (78). The religiously pragmatic, Unitarian-raised Ruth hardly knows what to make of such behavior while the atheistic Richard sees it as a sign of psychiatric abnormality—"I'd never appreciated how neurotic this guy is . . . this death-wish sounds pretty psychotic"—and wondering if it has affected his work (88). Jerry, for his part, is convinced that he is surrounded by spiritual cripples who are not afraid of death because they lack imagination or soul.

Whatever outlook the reader favors, these are all real issues and understandable responses to them: the dread of death in the midst of life; religious faith as the answer to the heart's deepest concern; a quiet stoicism that would rather get on with the chores of life; and psychological illness as an expression of human emotion gone sadly wrong. These may be different issues for different people in different times of their lives, but there is nothing at all far-fetched or unreal about any of them.

Into this mix, Updike adds one more real-life concern: sex. Sex, however, is understood here as something more than a mere physical release of glandular fluid, more even than an expression of love freely offered and gratefully received. Updike understands sex as the expression of romantic love while romantic love is understood as a deeply surging force that seeks to heal a colossal metaphysical ache. As Updike once wrote in a lengthy review of de Rougemont's *Love Declared*:

> Our fundamental anxiety is that we do not exist—or will cease to exist. Only in being loved do we find external corroboration of the supremely high valuation each ego secretly assigns itself. This exalted arena, then, is above all others the one where men and women will insist upon their freedom to choose—to choose that other being in whose existence their own existence is confirmed and amplified.[6]

6. John Updike, *Assorted Prose*, 299. In the foreword to *Assorted Prose*, Updike

This free, loving, passionate choice of the other eventually leads to marriage. Yet once the lovers are married they are no longer able to love one another freely. Rather, they are *bound* in marriage.[7] Updike illustrates the predictable problem in *Assorted Prose* by citing a story from "The Well" by Vassilis Vassilikos:

> Once upon a time there was a little fish who was bird from the waist up and who was madly in love with a little bird who was fish from the waist up. So the fish-bird kept saying to the bird-fish: "Oh, why were we created so that we can never live together? You in the wind and I in the wave. What a pity for both of us!" And the bird-fish would answer: "No, what luck for both of us. This way we'll always be in love because we'll always be separated."[8]

Jerry patiently explains the conundrum to Sally, but Sally doesn't see why it needs to become a problem. If marriage is a problem, why not simply stay unmarried? Certainly Sally is happy to remain Jerry's mistress. However, Jerry counters:

> But I don't want you as a mistress; our lives just aren't built for it. Mistresses are for European novels. Here, there's no institution except marriage. Marriage and the Friday night basketball game. You can't take this indefinitely; you think you can, but I know you can't (53).

The point is that love inexorably drives the lovers to marriage and yet, once they are married, they are no longer free to choose "that other being in whose existence their own existence is confirmed and amplified." Thus the metaphysical ache opens up all over again, sparking ever fresh adulterous strategies to cope with it. The painful dilemma is one that Jerry has thought about for a long time. He truly wants to marry Sally. He honestly can't think of living without her. But he's not a cat or a frog or a snail. He is a human

retracts the earlier doubts that he had concerning de Rougemont's theories of Occidental love and declares that "his overriding thesis seems increasingly beautiful and pertinent; corroborating quotations leap to my eyes wherever I read" (ix). The medieval legend of Tristan and Iseult shows the lovers in love, not so much with each other, as with love itself: "Hence their passion secretly wills its own frustrations and irresistibly seeks the bodily death that forever removes it from the qualifications of life, the disappointments and diminishments of actual possession" (284).

7. The contemporary custom of living together without formal marital commitments doesn't essentially alter the nature of the relationship any more than the sexual orientation of the individuals involved alters the personal dynamics involved.

8. Updike, *Assorted Prose*, x.

being that foresees things. Jerry realizes that the moment Sally becomes his wife he will lose her as the healing balm to the metaphysical ache that is driving him to destroy his wife and wade through his children's blood in order to marry her in the first place. The only thing Jerry is going to get for his troubles is a load of guilt. "I've figured out the bind I'm in," he tells Sally. "It's between death and death. To live without you is death to me. On the other hand, to abandon my family is a sin; to do it I'd have to deny God, and by denying God I'd give up all claim on immortality" (55).

This is the fallen, imperfect world in which Jerry and Sally find themselves in love. When they first meet it is on a deserted beach where they share wine and lovemaking. Jerry cuts himself smashing the bottle open. It is only a nick, but enough to give the adulterous tryst the uneasy sense of a desecrated sacrament. The idyll concludes with Jerry looking up and cursing the heavens: "It won't stand still." He gestures upward and stares as if to blind himself. "The fucking sun won't stand still" (12). Sally accuses him of being melodramatic, but Jerry realizes that the sun—and the limiting conditions of life that it portends—will inevitably destroy their romance. It's not just that Sally will one day grow old and lose her beauty. Their romantic love for each other will dissipate because it can only lead to the actualities of marriage that in turn can only pull their dream relationship out of the ideal world and send it back to the impossible limitations of—reality:

> You're like a set of golden stairs I can never finish climbing. I look down and the earth is a little blue mist. I look up, and there's this radiance I can never reach. It gives you your incredible beauty, and if I marry you I'll destroy it (46).

Under the cursed sun, Sally can truly exist for Jerry only in his dreams. She is the ideal woman, after all, and not simply because she is more beautiful than anyone else on earth, more beautiful at least in Jerry's love-drenched eyes. No, Sally is ideal because she properly lives in the ideal world of Jerry's fantasizing mind. Only in our dreams can such love objects as Sally offer the healing balm to the metaphysical ache that stirs within the romantic hearts of people like Jerry. Real women and actual marriages invariably spell death to such dreams, even as the dreams themselves attack the actualities of real life. This is why Updike, in explaining de Rougemont's theory of romantic love, argues that eros is essentially docetic, life-denying, reality-renouncing:

> The love-myth, simply, is the daughter of a creed that holds Creation in contempt. She stands in the same relation to fruitful

THE MYTH OF EROS IN *MARRY ME*

marriage as does Dualism to the Christian Monism precariously
hinged on the dogma of the God-man. Her essence is passion
itself; her concern is not with the possession, through love, of another person but with the prolongation of the lover's state of mind.
Eros is allied with Thanatos rather than Agape; love becomes not a
way of accepting and entering the world but of defying and escaping it. Iseult is the mythical prototype of the Unattainable Lady to
whom the love-myth directs our adoration, diverting it from the
attainable lady (in legal terms, our "wife," in Christian terms, our
"neighbor") who is at our side.[9]

The actualities of existence ultimately pose as much of a threat to Sally as
they do to Jerry. And so we find her eventually squirming whenever Jerry
hints at the ephemeral nature of their love. She doesn't want to confront,
any more than he does, the truth that spells the end to a love that can survive only in an ideal, otherworldly context. There is a telling moment when
Sally and Jerry are trapped together in an airport in Washington, unable
to get back to their home in Connecticut. Jerry has yet again been reflecting on the tragic, transitory nature of their romance while Sally has been
attempting to avoid the issue by directing Jerry's thoughts toward the next
flight home. Still, Jerry keeps hammering away at the critical point in all
this:

> Don't shut me up quite yet. Please. Listen. I see it so clearly. What
> we have, sweet Sally, is an ideal love. It's ideal because it can't be
> realized. As far as the world goes, we don't exist. We've never made
> love, we haven't been in Washington together; we're nothing. And
> any attempt to start existing, to move out of this pain, will kill us.
> Oh, we could make a mess and get married and patch up a life
> together—it's done in the papers every day—but what we have
> now we'd lose. Of course, the sad thing is we're going to lose it
> anyway. This is just too much of a strain for you. You're going to
> start hating me (46).

The romantic thesis of *Marry Me* is played out in the novel with the inevitability of a Greek tragedy. The cruelty that emerges in Jerry's actual marriage and family life while he pursues the dream relationship with Sally is
shown in a number of small but telling ways. For example, early in the story
Jerry phones Sally. During the conversation, Sally attempts to discipline
her young son Peter, who is eating candy early in the morning. Jerry asks,
"Who's there?" Sally quickly replies, "Nobody. Just Peter" (15). In the wake

9. Updike, *Assorted Prose*, 285.

of the all-consuming romance, Sally's children have all but ceased to exist for her. They have become in effect little nobodies.

The cruelty of it all eventually disturbs Jerry to the extent that he confesses the affair to Ruth. She responds by paying Sally a visit and begging her to stay away from Jerry for at least the summer. The summer past, Sally then registers her own strain of living a dream life in the actual world by confessing the affair to Richard, who promptly reads the riot act to Jerry and Sally. The two accordingly go off with each other to look for a home where they can fulfill their romantic dream only to have Jerry realize, this time with piercing clarity, the difference between fantasy and reality, and he immediately calls the marriage with Sally off.

The story concludes with Jerry returning in his mind to two romantic visions. First, he fantasizes about marrying Sally and flying to Wyoming with her and her children. Then he imagines taking Ruth and their own children to France for a second honeymoon. Finally, and this would seem to be what actually happens, Jerry flies to the Caribbean by himself and then returns to marry Sally, or at least to ask her to marry him, in the one dimension where romantic love can truly thrive: the ideal world of our fantasies.

Marry Me is a delicious romantic novel—until that final sentence in the book which decisively undercuts the whole phenomenon of romantic love. Perhaps this is why the novel, for all its gorgeous prose and reams of reader-friendly dialogue, has been slow to attract a wide circle of readers. How many romantically hungry readers are going to enjoy a love story that is essentially telling us that romances are impossible? Yet does *Marry Me*, in truth, undercut romantic love? Updike, after all, has never fallen for an unqualified pessimistic creed any more than he has ever embraced an unrestricted Pollyannaish creed. His fictional goal has always been to reflect the subtle, ambiguous "yes-but" quality of reality. And so here, surely, John Updike is saying "yes" to romantic love, "but . . ."[10]

---

10. In an iconic 1968 interview published by *The Paris Review* (editor George A. Plimpton) and given to Charles Thomas Samuels, Updike explains what he means when he says his work says 'yes, but.': "Yes, in *Rabbit, Run* to our inner urgent whispers, but—the social fabric collapses murderously. Yes, in *The Centaur*, to self-sacrifice and duty, but—what of man's private agony and dwindling? No, in *The Poorhouse Fair*, to social homogenization and loss of faith—but listen to the voices, the joy of persistence. No, in *Couples*, to a religious community founded on physical and psychical interpenetration, but—what else shall we do as God destroys our churches?" Plath, ed., *Conversations*, 16, 33.

The depiction of Adam and Eve that graces the cover of the novel signals the story's paradoxical message.[11] The original biblical couple is seen in paradise with Adam offering Eve a kind of priestly blessing while Eve holds the apple of temptation in her hand, the two of them covering their sexual organs with fig leaves while the serpent curls around the tree and speaks to Eve the words recorded in the biblical saga, "Did God say, 'You shall not eat from any tree in the garden?'"

Updike would seem to be inviting us here to understand Jerry and Sally's romance in the light of the innocent setting and compromised nature of the relationship that originally obtained between the primal romantic couple. The novel indeed is filled with literary allusions linking Jerry and Sally with the myth of Adam and Eve. Both couples live in a lush, garden-like setting, a paradise of sorts. The garden of Eden is filled with trees that are "pleasant to the sight and good for food," while little committees meet in Sally's home "to render Greenwood even more of a Paradise" (125). Both couples begin their lives with God—and each other—in an original state of grace. The biblical saga makes a point of saying that Adam and Eve knew no shame when they first stood together in the naked glory of their humanity. Likewise, the Conants and Mathiases know no shame when they are first observed on (note the name) Grace Island enjoying an innocent evening of games and drinks, and later undressing and going swimming, "their naked shapes making chaste blurs in the whispering dark" (80).

Both couples also eventually fall from grace and are driven from the garden and its innocent glories. A cherubim with flaming sword prevents Adam from returning to eat from the tree of life and thus eternalizing his primal sin. Similarly, a "Negro" airline attendant, flashing an exhilarating grin, "a great smile dazzling in the depth of its pleasure, its vengeance, its comprehension, its angelic scorn," prevents Jerry and Sally from boarding the plane that would allow them to return them to their suburban paradise in Greenwood (48).[12]

---

11. The front-of-jacket photograph of the garden of Eden is from the sarcophagus of Valerius Adelphia (fourth century) in the archeological museum of Syracuse, Italy. Updike's cover designs are carefully chosen and almost always cleverly illumine the book's theme.

12. The airline attendant is referred to several times in the text as "the Negro." This may be the author's way of distinguishing the attendant from the white couple attempting to reenter the spoiled paradisical garden. But it may also be a way of identifying the attendant with the dark-skinned Middle Eastern cherubim guarding "the way to the tree of life."

Most important is the "yes-but" message found in both stories. "Yes, God says to Adam and Eve, 'You may freely eat of every tree of the garden. *But* . . . of the tree of the knowledge of good and evil you shall not eat, for in the day that you eat of it you shall die'" (Gen 2:16–17). The two nevertheless do eat from the forbidden tree; their eyes accordingly are opened, and they become "like God, knowing good and evil" (Gen 3:5). Realizing that they are naked, they cover their genitals with fig leaves.

In this way the biblical poet states the theological conviction that our good and beautiful humanity has somehow gone sadly wrong. The essence of sin, the Genesis myth seems to be saying, consists in the denial of our created nature. It is the proud attempt to become like God, "knowing good and evil." Adam and Eve may still live morally exemplary lives, but they do so now on guilt-inducing terms. For they now live, not according to the Creator's command and within the restrictions imposed upon creaturely existence, but on the basis of their own godlike powers to determine what is good and what is evil. This is the path that Jerry and Sally essentially take in their own romantic rebellion against the creaturely limitations placed upon them by their marriages. They would rather forsake their actual spouses for the sake of an ideal relationship not bounded by the restrictions laid upon their creaturely, God-appointed condition.

In the face of these rebellious actions, both *Marry Me* and the Genesis story are saying "Yes—but." Yes, they say, to naked flesh and erotic relationships, to love and sexuality. There is no need to cover one's genitals with ancient or modern fig leaves any more than there is any need to solve the problem of eros by eliminating it from marriage altogether and opting, as the Eastern world has traditionally done, for forced, arranged, potentially passionless marriages.

But . . . these romantic relationships take place within the limitations of creaturely existence. We are not God. We are not permitted the godlike freedom to transcend the particular. Our love is always a human and limited love, and must therefore resist the attempt to transcend the built-in limitations of the creaturely realm. We live *under* and not *as* God.

Jerry and Sally originally fell from grace on a deserted beach. Significantly, "the beach was unusually shaped: an arc of flat washed sand perhaps half a mile long was bounded at both ends by congregations of great streaked yellowish rocks . . ." (4). Towards the end of the story they return to the same beach. Again it is described as an "arc of sand between two congregations of great streaked rocks" (270).[13] The "congregations" of rocks suggests a religious context for the story. At the beginning of the affair, Jerry and Sally fall from grace. At the end of the affair, Jerry realizes that he won't be marrying Sally, that he *can't* marry her in the flesh-and-blood world of reality. For Jerry is not God. He is a limited, bounded creature, even as the rocks limit the beach on which he walks, the very beach on which their affair was originally given life.

Jerry is thus forced to return and focus again on the concrete relationship, the actual marriage to which he is bound as a creature living under God. But, and this would seem to be the underlying theological point here: creaturely existence is not ultimately a bad but a good thing, and even very good. "God," Jerry exclaims while walking on the bounded beach with Sally at the end of the affair. "This is the most beautiful place I've ever seen!" (270) Consciously, Jerry is recalling their first romantic tryst. Unconsciously, he is reveling in the sheer beauty of limited, bounded creaturely existence as lived under the providing hand of an ultimately good and gracious God.

A musical analogy comes to mind here. More than once Updike has drawn attention to Karl Barth's singular love for the music of Mozart. Unlike the relatively unrestrained composers who followed Mozart in the Romantic era, or the even more excessive composers of the modern and postmodern periods, Mozart played by the rules. As Barth once observed, Mozart "moved freely within the limits of the musical laws of his time, and then later ever more freely. But he did not revolt against those laws; he did not break them."[14] The Romantics, the modernists, the postmodernists: all in their own way sought to transcend the musical limitations of their time, and did so with varying degrees of success. Yet Mozart's music, bounded by the customs of eighteenth-century Classicism, nevertheless retains its incomparable life-giving beauty and charm. "With an ear open to your musical dialectic," Barth once wrote of Mozart, one can be young and become old, can work and rest, be content and sad; in short, one can live." To which Updike adds: "Those who have not felt the difficulty of living have no need of Barthian theology; but then perhaps they also have no ear for music."[15]

---

13. The picture of the author on the flyleaf shows John Updike standing on what appears to be the far edge of a sandy beach with a congregation of rocks in the background. The photographer is Updike's son, Michael.

14. Updike, *Odd Jobs,* 229.

15. Ibid., 230.

A similar "Yes" to life, spoken within the bounds of creaturely existence, is sounded throughout Updike's fiction and not least in *Marry Me*. The limitations of life are certainly there, and often enough rebelled against by Updike's characters. Nevertheless, the limitations ultimately make sense in a world that comes from God and goes to God. The beaches on which Updike's characters enjoy their idyllic adventures are bounded by *congregations* of rocks. But this is ultimately a good and even very good thing, beautiful, as Jerry might say.

"Yes, but . . ." writes Updike in his essay on de Rougemont: "But what of that thunderous congestion in the chest, that suffusion of emotion as harsh as a blow, which Tristan endures at the sight of the Unattainable Lady, or even at the mention of her name?"[16] What, in other words, of that stab of desire produced afresh by the mere sight or even thought of the ideal woman (or man) of our romantic dreams? It is a good question and one that can never entirely be silenced in our incurably romantic hearts. This is why, surely, Updike's novel concludes with that threefold reverie in which Jerry first imagines the marital consummation of his romantic relationship with Sally, then imagines the marital consummation of his romantic reunion with Ruth, and finally imagines a suitably romantic entry into that *dimension* where Jerry can meet his ideal woman at an ideal party some day and stand, "timid and exultant, above the downcast eyes of her gracious, sorrowing face, and say to Sally, '*Marry me.*'"

Yet one has to wonder if this essentially unrealizable fantasy is not offering in the end a kinder and more hopeful understanding of life and love than the unrealistic promises of all those romantic novels that ultimately ignore the limitations of creaturely existence, and encourage us to believe that we *can* exchange the actual for the ideal and still live happily ever after.

16. Updike, *Assorted Prose*, 299.

Interlude with the Hamiltons

Chapter 5 Introduction

LIKE MANY YOUNG READERS in the 1960s, I first discovered John Updike by reading Rabbit, Run, *and then I pounced on* Couples *when it appeared in 1968. Two years later Alice and Kenneth Hamilton brought out the first full length critical study of Updike under the title* The Elements of John Updike. *The Hamiltons, it turned out, were fellow Canadians. Alice taught English at the University of Winnipeg, and Kenneth taught theology at the same university. Their book opened my eyes to the astonishing depths of Updike's allegorically driven fiction.*

Kenneth Hamilton was especially equipped to understand a writer like John Updike. One of Updike's theological heroes, after all, is Søren Kierkegaard, the complex theologian whose work Hamilton had recently elucidated in his 1969 study, The Promise of Kierkegaard. *Also, the Hamiltons, as a writing team, were unusually gifted in interpreting dense symbolic literature: witness their remarkably lucid treatment of Beckett's plays and novels in* Condemned to Life: The World of Samuel Beckett. *When* The Elements *appeared, I seized the opportunity to review the book for* The United Church Observer, *the denominational magazine of the church that both Kenneth Hamilton and I represented at the time as ministers. Here is my review.*

THE ELEMENTS OF JOHN UPDIKE

By Alice and Kenneth Hamilton (Eerdmans, 1970)
Reviewed by John McTavish in *The United Church Observer*

In *The Elements of John Updike*, Alice Hamilton, who teaches English at the University of Winnipeg, and Kenneth Hamilton, who teaches theology at the same university, refute the charges that John Updike is "a dealer in trifles . . . out of touch with our age of apocalyptic terror." He is, they say, one of the most serious authors of our age. That Updike refuses to be heavily pretentious merely serves to reveal the smugness of his critics.

Like his seventeenth-century literary mentor, Robert Herrick, Updike looks "light" but is not. For those who have eyes to see—and a knowledge of the Bible and Christian theology, the Hamiltons suggest, helps to develop such eyes—a vision of truth and reality, a searing commentary on our betrayal of that truth, and a glimmer of "the way out of the weeds" is elegantly given.

Still, as the Hamiltons candidly concede, for readers desiring dramatic events and the clash of "interesting" personalities, the plots in Updike's stories usually have little to offer. The way into his theme is almost always through the imagery, which provides the justification for the story line, and not vice versa. For an illustration of this literary device, we are directed to a passage in Updike's recent novel, *Couples.*

In this particular passage, Foxy, new to the community and at a dinner party with a plate of consommé set before her, blushes, bending her face "to the shallow amber depths where the lemon slice like an embryo swayed." Foxy blushes because she has inadvertently let slip the fact that she is pregnant. To escape the mockery of the couples she turns her eyes downward to her plate of soup. She sees the lemon slice in the soup as an embryo because of the nagging of physical discomfort caused by the fact that her first pregnancy at twenty-eight has proved unexpectedly burdensome. But her blushes are also prophetic of her next pregnancy, when the couples will again mock her, only more cruelly. The embryo in the soup she sees seems to be swaying. This time it will sway towards life, but the next time it will be pulled toward death. But Foxy is also aware of the lemon slice apart from its resemblance to an embryo. Lemon is also *leman*—lover. When she summons Piet, her soon-to-be paramour, to repair her house, she will welcome him in lemon-colored clothes and serve him lemonade.

On and on the symbolism rolls.

The best way to approach the allegorically charged Updike may be to read his second novel *Rabbit, Run,* which concerns the high school athlete who finds adult life an anticlimax after his achievements in adolescence. Then tackle Updike's short stories (the finest of which, I believe, are found in the collection titled *Pigeon Feathers*) and poems (*The Carpentered Hen and Other Tame Creatures* and *Telephone Poles and Other Poems*). Now read the Hamiltons' book and see what you missed on your first reading of these. I think you will be amazed at what escaped you the first time through.

Then (but probably only then) you should take up Updike's controversial *Couples. Couples* is a delicious but also savage account of how the choosing of pleasure rather than justice leads to slavery instead of freedom in the case of people who are—in Updike's judgment—God's creatures standing on the boundary between heaven and earth.

That we constantly deny that we stand on this boundary, deny therefore that earth is really only earth in its relationship to heaven and the moral-religious dimension that heaven proclaims, Updike's characters often attest. Such denials, however, don't alter the fact that God's grace keeps breaking in upon us: this is the glorious truth that shines through the books of this remarkable young American writer.

Shortly after this review appeared in The Observer, *I received the following letter from Kenneth Hamilton.*

The University of Winnipeg

Winnipeg, Canada

15 June, 1970

Dear Mr. McTavish,

Martin Rumscheidt, who was here at The Canadian Theol. Soc.'s meetings last week, drew our attention to your review of *The Elements of John Updike* in the Observer. I had just returned from a 2-months stint of teaching in the U.S., and Alice had put the Observers aside until my return, so we had not happened to see it as normally we might have.

You have obviously read the book quite thoroughly and with a great deal of sympathetic understanding. In fact, all that we might have asked is whether you did not find some deficiencies in our exposition and whether you thought that it would be fully intelligible to the general reader who might not come to it, as you yourself do, with a theological background.

At any rate, we know that in the limits set for a review you cannot say everything; and we are most appreciative of the fact that you paid us the compliment of suggesting that readers might take the book as a guide to seeing Updike's intention and the load of meaning which he packs into all his works. We are also personally grateful that the reviewer *was* some one who is theologically literate, and who did not think that we were simply reading into the Updike corpus something that could not possibly be there because literature can have nothing to do with dogma.

Thank you again. One of the things that constantly amazes us is that we can read Updike and always find there something that we have overlooked in previous readings. Sometimes concentration upon a writer leads to boredom, when one finds that familiarity means, if not contempt, at any rate lessened enthusiasm. This doesn't happen in this instance.

Sincerely,
Kenneth Hamilton

Thus began a long distance friendship that ended only when Kenneth died in 2009 at the age of ninety-one. I didn't get to know Alice nearly as well, but I do remember meeting her at a conference once and asking why so many women readers seemed to dislike Updike so intensely. Alice looked around to make sure no one was listening, and then in a throaty, conspiratorial voice whispered: "Because he knows us so well!"

The Hamiltons worked well together, in fact so well that when Alice died in 1991 Kenneth not only stopped writing about Updike but stopped even reading Updike for several years. Kenneth once told me that he and Alice always found that the way into J. U.'s stories was "through chewing away at little indications of what Updike called his 'little secrets' given by hints, persevering until a pattern became visible. Other indications, then, would show whether or not we were on the right lines."

They chewed together, and the results speak for themselves.

The two chapters by the Hamiltons that appear in this interlude were originally published in journals. "Can A Novel be Christian? John Updike and A Month of Sundays" appeared in the May–June 1979 issue of the evangelically oriented magazine Radix, *and "John Updike's Prescription for Survival" appeared in the July 5, 1972 issue of* The Christian Century. *The articles demonstrate, I suggest, the strengths of an allegorical approach to the myth-laden writings of John Updike.*

CHAPTER 5

Can a Novel Be Christian?
John Updike and *A Month Of Sundays*

By Alice & Kenneth Hamilton

WHAT HAS ATHENS TO do with Jerusalem? asked Tertullian, the second-century Church Father. In our day it might equally be asked, "What has fiction to do with faith? Can there be Christian novelists and Christian novels?"

The question has no easy answer in general, and we shall try to explore it in particular by looking at one contemporary novelist: John Updike. We shall concentrate upon just one of his novels: *A Month of Sundays*.

I

A Month of Sundays raises the issue of the "Christian novel" rather sharply. Updike's narrator in this book is a Christian minister who discusses on almost every page what it means to have faith or to lack it. On the other hand, the storyteller and his story seem to undermine rather than support what are generally called "Christian standards." The incidents he describes and the language he uses are certain to offend many Christians. (We know of one denomination, identified with progressive and "open" views, that put a notice in its official journal stating how *A Month of Sundays* had been taken off the shelves of its bookstores, since it was not the type of book a church should promote.)

The narrator, the Reverend Thomas Marshfield, is a minister in disgrace. Banished from his parish after the discovery of his multiple sexual adventures with women parishioners, he has been sent to a home for delinquent clergymen. There he undergoes a month's "therapy" of rest and exercise, with each morning spent in free writing—presumably for the purpose of self-discovery. Marshfield's confessions make up the book. He writes with gusto about the events leading to his downfall, showing little guilt or shame as he recalls in loving detail the various episodes of the past year. Any repentance he may feel is overshadowed by what looks like strenuous self-justification. His last piece of writing before returning to whatever future awaits him (he expects to be sent to a remote country parish) describes a sexual encounter with the woman supervising the program at the home, one Ms. Prynne—first name unknown.

A Month of Sundays is not an edifying novel, at least not in its plot. But then, the novelist's chief concern is not to edify. Their calling is to reflect the world as they see it and to dissect human existence as it is and not as it ought to be; to show us ourselves with a clarity we could never achieve on our own, and thus to shed new light upon the human condition. In this respect novelists are totally unlike the preacher, whose sermons *should* edify.

Marshfield's narrative contains four sermons, one for each Sunday morning of his confinement. These sermons explain the title of the novel, and they actually provide the central key to the novel. The sermons are there, not because they edify but because they show what is going on in Marshfield's mind and how his therapy is proceeding.

Updike says that he is a Christian, yet he says also that he thinks novels should not be sermons or moral directives to the reader. In this he divides himself from Christian writers who adopt the fictional form in order to present the Christian message—from C. S. Lewis, for example. Such writers are essentially preachers or teachers of theology who enclose their Christian teaching in an envelope of literature. The envelope may be of high artistic quality, yet the literary packaging is always separable from its didactic contents. This is "Truth embodied in a Tale" (as Tennyson put it), and what counts is that the truth be heard. The tale is simply a means to an end.

"Christian novelists" who are preachers and teachers are really fabulists rather than novelists. This is why their tales so often turn to the fantasy world. Imaginary worlds can be created where the ambiguities of existence are smoothed out and things and events *clearly* illustrate those spiritual laws that the writer-teachers wish their readers to learn.

Updike stands fully in the tradition of fictional realism. He begins always with the world just as it is. He refuses to edit the pictures that his observer's eye records in the interests of any preconceived theories about the nature of the universe. This is why he is especially punctilious about placing his characters in an actual place and an actual time, and nearly always in those places and times with which he himself is thoroughly familiar. He is concerned to be true to living experience, to capture in words the actual texture of our days upon earth and not to distort or simplify this texture at the behest of an ideology, however persuasive.

Of course, as a Christian, Updike has an "ideology." Viewing the world from the standpoint of faith, he is already ordering the data of experience and imposing a special kind of pattern upon the flow of events. Updike knows this, and he is vigilant not to let his religious convictions interfere with his novelist's calling. In this respect he does not want to be a "Christian novelist." At the same time, because Christian faith accepts the earth as God's creation, he sees no incompatibility between the novelist's calling to report on existence as he finds it and his Christian convictions that God's grace is the underlying reason for all that is.

A Month of Sundays is written to Updike's usual prescription. It is about the reactions of one contemporary American, living in one of the eastern states during the last months of Nixon's presidency, and (like many today) preoccupied with a sense of emptiness in his life that seeks relief in a quest for sexual fulfillment. Because Thomas Marshfield also happens to be a Christian minister, his social position is directly involved as well as his personal integrity. Torn by moral uncertainties, Marshfield still feels himself called to proclaim the Christian gospel in which he most surely believes. Though the novel is a record of events, its core is Marshfield's attempts to wrestle with the nature of relative and absolute standards of conduct, sin and sanctity, judgment and forgiveness. Though not a "Christian novel," *A Month of Sundays* shows that its author is convinced that a true report of what it means to live in America today has to reckon with this question: *If* Christian faith gives the truth about human existence, *how* does it demand that we, present-day Americans, are to think, feel, and make decisions in the concrete circumstances of our lives?

II

Because novels reflect how people are living their lives, Updike says his books are all invitations to the reader to join in a moral debate. He thinks novelists should not impose their views upon their readers. So he rejects both the novel which tries to be a sermon and the novel of "moral imperatives." (He faults, for example, Saul Bellow's tendency to nudge his readers into accepting the author's prescriptions for the betterment of life.) A moral debate, however, is possible where the author shows his characters making decisions, right or wrong, without passing judgment upon them. The readers can then join freely in the debate, because they are not being maneuvered into taking one side or the other.

Novelists can give their readers another freedom. They can suggest how the particular story they are telling is to some degree a continuation of other stories told in the past. As all literature examines the basic problems of human existence, every moral debate has been pursued down the centuries. Moral problems don't change—only the social context in which they are set.

Early in *A Month of Sundays* Marshfield mentions Ms. Prynne. Later, he tells us that his father-in-law is a Dr. Chillingworth, professor of ethics at the seminary he attended. The names are taken from characters in Nathaniel Hawthorne's *The Scarlet Letter*, the classic story of a clergyman's adultery in seventeenth-century New England. Roger Chillingworth was the husband of Hester Prynne, the woman in Hawthorne's novel who would not reveal the identity of the father of her child. Chillingworth, a scholar and a doctor, devoted himself frantically to hunting down his wife's lover, discovering him to be the Reverend Arthur Dimmesdale of saintly reputation. Updike is telling his readers that his story has definite connections with Hawthorne's, even though the sexual liberation proclaimed in the America of today is the opposite extreme to the rigid ethical code that ruled Puritan America.

Hester Prynne was forced to wear an embroidered capital "A" (for Adulteress); and when Arthur Dimmesdale died, this same letter was seen to be scored upon his breast. In Updike's story, Marshfield notices that the home in New Mexico to which he is sent for rehabilitation is shaped like an *omega*, the last letter of the Greek alphabet. His punishment is not public shame but a relaxed month's stay in what has every appearance of being a luxury motel. The opposite extreme indeed!

At the end of *The Scarlet Letter* Hester Prynne comforted women who came to her with sorrows akin to her own. "She assured them, too, of her firm belief, that, at some brighter period, when the world should have grown ripe for it, in Heaven's own time, a new truth would be revealed, in order to establish the whole relation between man and woman on a surer ground of mutual happiness." *A Month of Sundays* is set in this "brighter period." American society now assumes mutual happiness to be the sole basis for marriage, so that no "fault" in one of the marriage partners need be proven in order to terminate the relationship. Ceasing to call adultery a sin has undoubtedly made things much more pleasant for adulterers, since they are now viewed with sympathy rather than detestation. But is this a "surer ground" for establishing the relationship between men and women? People continue to be unhappy in marriage and out of it—and morally confused in the bargain.

These are the issues Updike raises in *A Month of Sundays*. He does not take sides, except indirectly. By setting over against Hawthorne's "A" an "Ω" instead of a "Z," though, he suggests that all our moral codes lie under the judgment of the One who is the Alpha and the Omega, the Almighty (Revelation 1:8). Christians in any age are not necessarily more morally enlightened than their unbelieving neighbors, but they know they are accountable not merely to society but to God.

III

Novelists convey much through names. The two sides of Hawthorne's tragic hero Arthur Dimmesdale appear in his two names. *Arthur* ("noble") gives the public image of this cleric-adulterer, the man who seemed to his contemporaries to be a courageous saint. The name recalls the legendary King Arthur, noble champion of Christendom. *Dimmesdale* identifies the inner self hidden from view, the soul that walks in that dim dale, the valley of the shadow. This private self walks fearful and uncomforted, having lost the presence of the good Shepherd. Knowing his deeds to have been evil, Dimmesdale hates the light (John 3: 20). Under cover of darkness he mounts to the pillory where Hester Prynne was punished, but he refuses her plea that he stand there with her openly in the daytime. He speaks to her freely only when she meets him in the forest where the trees dim the sunlight.

Updike's Thomas Marshfield is, as he himself remarks (4), a "doubting Thomas." Yet he never doubts the reality of God. His doubt is like that of Thomas the disciple: a refusal to believe the joyful news of Christ's resurrection (John 20: 24–29). He is slow to trust in the power that can raise him to a new life after sin has revived in him and he has died (Rom 7: 9). In the end, though, he believes, as Thomas did. His last name is explained by his remark, "For what is the body but a swamp in which the spirit drowns?"

(46). His transgressions come from letting his demanding body rule him, much as he desires to be spiritually alive. When the seed of the Word is sown in the field (Matt 13: 3, 24), it needs good ground to grow in. A marshy field is not ideal ground. Nevertheless, Marshfield never despairs of forgiveness as Dimmesdale did. He wishes to live in the light. His chief difficulty lies in deciding just where lies the division between light and darkness, life and death. Puritan America and its heavily ruled lines separating righteousness and sinfulness is gone forever. In a world of relativized values, how do we follow the path toward the light?

IV

So we are back with the moral debate. In *A Month of Sundays* Updike uses other writers besides Hawthorne to clarify the issues. He brings in one of his "heroes," Søren Kierkegaard. Kierkegaard wrote of three different "stages on life's way," that is, choices of paths to walk on. He called these: the aesthetic, the ethical, and the religious. These three choices are seen in Marshfield's choice of female partners.

His wife Jane represents the ethical path of life. The daughter of a professor of ethics and without religious convictions, Jane ("The Lord graciously gave") is a loving and understanding wife and the mother of Marshfield's two sons. For twenty years he had been completely faithful to her, and their marriage has been a true blessing. They seem a perfectly matched pair—they even have come to look alike. But habits that seem "good" can quickly be broken at the appearance of something which seems to be a "higher good." Marshfield falls in love with his church organist, Alicia Crick, a divorcee of thirty, pert, blonde, and nearsighted. Infatuated, he soon deserts the ethical path.

"Life, that's what we seek in another," he explains in describing how their affair began (28). Alicia ("noble cheer") Crick ("painful spasmodic affection of the muscles") lives up to her name. She cheers Marshfield with her vitality and wins his affection with her love-making. The attraction is almost completely physical.

Kierkegaard says that the aesthetic path, the path dominated by feeling, is the choice of both the sensualist and the artist. It is essentially pagan, knowing nothing of sin or guilt. Marshfield feels this, saying, "How the fallen world sparkled, now that my faith was decisively lost!" (39) But Kierkegaard also says that the aesthetic vision is shortsighted. Turned inward

CAN A NOVEL BE CHRISTIAN?

upon egotistical pleasure, it loses sight of the conditions of our actual existence. Aesthetic persons find that their joys quickly fade, leaving them to face emptiness and despair.

Even in his first infatuation, Marshfield realizes that Alicia does not really love him. She loves her own body. Just as she is expert at playing any kind of organ music, she would make love to any available man. But Alicia also desires a man who will support her. In order to force Marshfield to divorce Jane and marry her, she first tries to make him jealous by seducing his young assistant minister and then, as a last resort, tells Jane about their affair. That is shortsighted of her because it drives Marshfield not into her arms but into despair. He knows that he no longer wants her. The aesthetic choice was a mistake. Yet he cannot return to the ethical path with its restrictions now that he has tasted freedom. The fact that Jane is so *good* and ready to forgive him is a torment, since he cannot forgive himself. His marriage seems to him a prison and Jane a jailer.

Kierkegaard's third path is the religious. He says that the ethical stage of life makes us feel guilty because we cannot live up to it. Kierkegaard here is following the Apostle Paul's teaching: it is the Law that makes us conscious of sin, so that we know ourselves to be under God's judgment and are freed only by God's grace that comes with Jesus Christ (Rom 2–5). Kierkegaard explains that the religious choice is the choice of faith. We trust in God to perform the impossible: to forgive the sinner *because* he or she stands before a holy God. In faith we sinners discover that we can bring nothing to offer God except our own incapacity.

Believing his vocation to be that of directing his fellow human beings toward the religious path, Kierkegaard said that all his writings carry the warning, "Away from the aesthetic!" In Marshfield's church Frankie Harlow, wife of the chairman of the board of deacons, comes to him with a complaint. She is distressed about Mrs. Crick being encouraged to take over too much of the church services with her music. She thinks that the Word of God should be the chief concern of worship. In other words, she tells Marshfield, "Away from the aesthetic!" Marshfield notes that Mrs. Harlow (unlike both Jane and Alicia) is a believer, sincere in her faith. But she is also a woman, and she is unhappily married. He decides that here is the one woman who can make him happy. And he finds her willing.

The name *Harlow* suggests *harlot*. In the New Testament Rahab the harlot is cited as an example of faith (Hebrews 11:31). *Frankie* (Frances, "free") *Harlow* therefore represents the faith that is free, opposed to the works of the law. "For freedom Christ has set us free; stand fast, therefore, and do not submit again to a yoke of slavery" (Gal 5:1). Marshfield feels that he has been living the life of a slave, a slave to his passion for Alicia and a slave to the moral goodness of Jane. Frankie Harlow seems to offer his way out. He himself refers to his sermons as being "fashionably antinomian" (26). (Antinomianism is the heresy teaching that obedience to the moral law is not required of the person of faith and may even be a hindrance to the reception of grace.) If he practices what he preaches, his antinomianism offers him a new vista of hope through sexual union with Frankie, the "harlot" who embodies faith.

Alas, Marshfield has forgotten the words of Paul, "What then? Shall we sin, because we are not under the law, but under grace? God forbid" (Rom 6:15). Perhaps he does remember subconsciously, for when Frankie freely offers herself to him he finds he is impotent. Out of bewilderment and frustration, he turns to commit adultery with various women who come to him for counseling over marital troubles. But he still desires no one except Frankie, and at the same time sees his continued impotence with her as "the survivor in me of faith, a piece of purity amid all this relativistic concupiscence, this plastic modernity, this adulterate industry, this animated death" (139). Taking the religious path is a dangerous choice, because those who take it may be halted in their tracks and turned round in the other direction—which is what *conversion* means.

V

Marshfield's last act as parish minister is to dismiss Alicia from her position as church organist. Jane tells him it is morally wrong, but he does it all the same. Whether he does it out of revenge, to try to please Frankie, out of belief (as he imagines) that she is distracting the congregation from worship by playing too much music, or in order to precipitate a crisis, the outcome alone is clear. Alicia goes to Mr. Harlow and tells him all about Marshfield's adulteries known to her or guessed. In short order, the disgraced minister is flown to his rest-cure in the West.

In the omega-shaped building Marshfield writes a portion of his story each weekday morning. Sunday mornings he composes a sermon which fits into the mood of that portion of his narrative written the previous week. His first sermon is on the text "Neither do I condemn thee" (John 8:11), and his conclusion is "We *are* an adulterous generation; let us rejoice" (47).

Recalling in his record of events his first sense of joyous freedom with Alicia has made him turn to use this first sermon to justify his adultery. Thus he argues that Christ's forgiveness of the woman taken in adultery implies that fidelity in marriage is an impossible ideal. The coming of Christ (so he argues) banishes all legalism, and it is the scandal of Christianity that it frees us for earthly joys.

The sermon, of course, is fully antinomian. It is a justifiable protest against the kind of savage legalism that Hawthorne described in *The Scarlet Letter*, but otherwise it is clearly special pleading. The same holds, to a lesser degree, of Marshfield's second sermon. It is on the miracles of Jesus, taking the text, "Woman, what have I to do with thee? Mine hour is not yet come" (John 2:4).

Marshfield has written the day before of Alicia telling Jane of her husband's adultery and of his own subsequent feeling that Jane's forgiveness of him has trapped him into a relationship with her which is all duty and no joy. So the words, "Woman, what have I to do with thee?" are partly his angry words to Jane. Anger lies under the words of the sermon (which deal with Jesus censuring his followers for their little faith) and flares out in the final paragraph where he curses his imaginary congregation and himself for having no faith in miracles. It seems that Marshfield, reliving the time when he still loved Alicia, knows that only a miracle could give him both Alicia (sexual freedom) and Jane (family life and social acceptance). Yet his anger comes not only out of his frustration over wanting the impossible. It is also directed against himself for wanting a purely selfish miracle. He says, "The hard lesson is borne in upon us, alleviation is not the purpose of His miracles, but demonstration" (104). The lack of faith he curses is chiefly his own inability to subordinate his private desires to the will of God for him.

The third sermon has the text, "He found him in a desert place" (Deuteronomy 32:10). Marshfield's narrative of his fall has now reached the climax of his disgrace. His sermon is inspired by the unfamiliar desert country surrounding his place of forced retreat. He notes that Death Valley is called in Spanish, *La Palma de la Manos de Dios*. He draws the conclusion that we can always see our situation—and America is becoming more and more a desert, physically and spiritually—either as hopeless or as providentially guided (held in God's palm). In the desert, life barely sustains itself, yet life is perpetually renewed. His message is, "Live, brothers, though there be nought but shame and failure to furnish forth your living" (166).

Marshfield's last sermon is on the resurrection. Though he gives as his text only the words, "We are of all men most miserable" (1 Cor 15:19), it is to affirm that Christians do not think, as most people do, of hope in eternal life as one hope among others. If Christ is not raised, they have nothing to hope for at all. In this sermon Marshfield addresses himself and his fellow sinning clerics (thinking of them as he sits alone writing), saying that their calling is an essential one. They "stand as steeples stand, as emblems; it is our station to be visible and to provide men with the opportunity to profess the impossible that makes their lives possible" (210). He adds, "let us take comfort at least from the stiffness of our roles, that still stand though we crumple within them" (211).

It seems that, after all, the therapy prescribed for Marshfield within the omega-shaped building has been successful. He no longer tries to justify his past or use Scripture to voice his own inner turmoil. He ends with the question asked by Pascal, *Qui m'y mis*—Who has set me here? And he answers, "There is a *qui*, a Who, who has set; we have not accidentally fallen, we have been placed" (212). Now, knowing that fallen human beings (including fallen ministers) still have a place in God's gracious purposes, he is ready to be returned to his work as a minister of the gospel, no matter where he may be "placed."

There is a penciled note written at the end of his fourth sermon: "Yes —at last, a sermon that could be preached." He believes that the supervisor, Ms. Prynne, has put it there.

VI

Because Ms. Prynne is in charge of the program at the omega-shaped home, Marshfield thinks she reads his written confessions. He addresses her as "Ideal Reader."

The Ideal Reader, though, is also the reader Updike always has in mind when writing his novels. This reader is not necessarily a Christian (novelists write for everybody), but one who knows literature well, including the Bible.

For this Ideal Reader, Updike has prefixed two quotations to *A Month of Sundays:* "My tongue is the pen of a ready writer" (Ps 45:1); and, "This principle of soul, universally and individually, is the principle of ambiguity" (Paul Tillich).

The second quotation is to help Updike's reader join in the moral debate. Marshfield, the sinning man of faith, is (like Hawthorne's Dimmesdale) an ambiguous figure. Only a very simplistic moral outlook would judge him all good or all bad. The first quotation indicates why Marshfield is a divided, tormented man who can neither be a conventionally respectable minister nor leave the ministry and become one of the many faceless fornicators in today's scene. Marshfield *is* a ready writer; and many readers of *A Month of Sundays* find his obvious relish in writing about his sinning to be one of the most offensive things about him.

But the reason for the quotation is not to tell us that Marshfield enjoys writing and is a bit of an exhibitionist. Psalm 45 is a song celebrating a royal marriage. It has been interpreted as an allegory of Christ and the church. But Marshfield will not accept a faith that spiritualizes everything. He wishes to celebrate *both* human sexuality *and* divine grace. Neither the contemporary church nor contemporary society show him how this can be done; and so he is pulled first in one direction and then in another by his belief that sexuality is good in itself and by the call to serve God which seems to say it is sinful, though permitted when legalized.

Marshfield comes to a resolution of his problems by the time he writes his fourth sermon. At least, he knows that for him the one thing needful is to preach the gospel. Whatever we have done, we can be born again. But Marshfield's decision to put his spiritual vocation first cannot be all he has to tell us, or he has abandoned his belief that serving God can coexist with celebrating human sexuality. It is not and he has not. The last pages of the novel describe his seduction of Ms. Prynne.

This seduction seems an incomprehensible act in an adulterer newly reformed. It also seems very unlikely that a woman in the position of Ms. Prynne would jeopardize her job (to put the matter on the lowest level) in order to accommodate one patient out of many. In addition, though Marshfield has been irresponsible, he would hardly be so irresponsible now as to leave in his room a detailed account of his sexual encounter. He does not know for certain that it is Ms. Prynne who reads what the patients write. The reason Marshfield gives for hoping Ms. Prynne will give herself to him is that he needs one more sexual adventure to complete his "cure," and he thinks Ms. Prynne is kind!

The whole episode is unconvincing at the realistic level, unlike Marshfield's accounts of his other seductions. There are two indications on the other hand, suggesting that this final episode is not a literal record of events.

One is that Ms. Prynne is also Updike's Ideal Reader. The other is that her name suggests "misprint."

Marshfield tells us that, from Ms. Prynne's way of dealing with those needing her help, he has come to understand "that love is not an e-motion, an assertive way of putting out, but a *trans*-motion, a compliant moving *through*" (217). On one level, then, Updike is telling his Ideal Reader, through his account of his satisfying love-making with Ms. Prynne, how through sharing written words an author and his reader can really meet and understand each other. It is not just a matter of the author "putting out" his story. Without believing that there can be a *trans*-motion in which the reader responds to the story, the author's work would be barren and loveless.

The second level of Updike's closing narrative is the more central one in relation to the novel. All through the story Marshfield makes mistakes in typing. For example, he means to write "throats," thinks about "thoughts," and writes down "throughts." These conflated "portmanteau" words come in the printed book as *misprints*. Now Marshfield's theology, so he is always telling us, is taken from Karl Barth. Barth's theology is a "theology of the Word." It teaches how faith consists entirely of God's Word: the Word Revealed (Christ); the Word written (the Bible); the Word preached (the witnessing church). Marshfield believes in the Word, but he does not know how the World—the world of generation—can be related to the Word, though he is sure that it must be, somehow. Then he sees how easily we could mean to write *Word* and write *World* instead. *World* is a misprint of *Word*! Can it be that not just the word *World* but the actual, material World itself is akin to the Word though distinct from it? Doesn't Scripture teach that the World was made through the Word (John 1: 3)?

Marshfield's writer's eyes have seen Ms. Prynne as an Earth-Mother: large, solid, dressed in earth-colors, directing the physical conditions of those in her charge impartially, stern yet kindly in her ministrations. In sexual imagery he describes his reconciliation to the World through Ms. Prynne.

Updike's method of storytelling offends many people, particularly Christians by whom Updike might expect to be most readily understood. Yet is it perhaps life itself, which Updike insists upon describing completely and without reserve, that offends? At any rate, Updike has many readers. Some of them are led to join in the moral debate that he initiates in each of his novels. Some notice that he always raises the issue of Christian faith as giving the perspective needful for any genuine insight into the human condition. Somewhere there must exist the Ideal Reader for whom John Updike writes.

CHAPTER 6

John Updike's Prescription for Survival

By Alice & Kenneth Hamilton

IN 1969, DURING A radio interview in Britain, John Updike commented: "I seem to see all my books in terms of children's drawings. They are all meant to be moral debates with the reader, and if they seem pointless—I'm speaking hopefully—it's because the reader has not been engaged in the debate." Whatever moral debate Updike may have meant to stimulate in his latest novel, *Rabbit Redux* (Knopf, 1971), it has not to any significant extent engaged readers who have written reviews of the book.

The early reviews ranged from the laudatory to patronizing, from calling *Rabbit Redux* the best book of the decade (*New York Times Book Review*) to protesting that it is not up to the author's usual standard (*Newsweek*). Most reviewers praised the precision with which Updike has caught the apocalyptic mood of 1969, the year of his story's action. But they had some reservations over his apparently ambivalent attitude toward the events he records. Charles Thomas Samuels, writing in the *New Republic* (November 20, 1971), explicitly finds fault with what he considered a failure on Updike's part to express judgment, probe motives, and suggest a prescription. Contrasting *Rabbit Redux* with Saul Bellow's *Mr. Sammler's Planet*, Samuels says that Bellow is strong "in fathoming causes and asserting judgments" when he analyzes "the chaos of the present," but Updike "remains too mute about questions of motivation to keep *Rabbit Redux* from having the dispiriting effect of a sordid story that is told to no clear purpose."

Now, since Samuels interviewed Updike for the *Paris Review* in 1968, he should be the first to remember that Updike at that time mentioned his discomfort over the way in which Bellow's books are continually "inviting us to participate in moral decisions," and stated his belief that books should have secrets and that the author's methods should not be obvious. Thus it is false to conclude—simply because it is not as evident as it is in *Mr. Sammler's Planet*—that moral debate is absent from *Rabbit Redux*. As in all his previous books, so in this one Updike gives judgments and prescriptions in terms of the story and its telling, rather than in a commentary tacked on to the narrative. Any story must seem pointless and "told to no clear purpose" if the reader ignores what the author offers because he expects to hear what the author deliberately refrains from saying.

Updike told Samuels that his deepest pride as an author was in keeping "an organized mass of images moving forward." It is in the images of *Rabbit Redux* that Updike renders his judgment upon "the chaos of the present" and his prescription for surviving it.

I

The most obvious image is that of space travel. When Updike wrote *Rabbit, Run* (1960) the beatniks were engaged in finding themselves by traveling around America. Harry "Rabbit" Angstrom, the hero of *Run*, made his own effort to find freedom through leaving his home and family. The book ended with Harry running blindly, trying to escape the obligations which seemed to him a net spread to trap rabbits. In *Redux* we learn that Harry, in fact, looped back to his wife and three-year-old son. Now, ten years later, he has stopped running. In 1969 travel is for astronauts, not for rabbits. He has grown stout, and no one calls him Rabbit any more. He owns a shabby house on the outskirts of his hometown, Brewer, Pennsylvania.

Each of the four sections of *Redux* ("Pop/Mom/Moon," "Jill," "Skeeter," "Mim") is introduced by fragments of the recorded conversations of American or Russian astronauts. In the opening section the first Apollo moon flight is in progress. Soon Harry learns that Janice has left their "pad" and has flown to join a lover. Harry's own experiences during the course of the novel can be seen as a flight to the moon, a journey ending safely when he and Janice "dock" in a motel bedroom on the same street where, ten years before, he had been running blindly.

Before Janice leaves him, Rabbit is alone one evening with his son, Nelson. He is distracted by the television depiction of the Apollo flight. The news, the thinks, is "all about space, all about emptiness." "They keep mentioning Columbus but as far as Rabbit can see it's the exact opposite:

Columbus flew blind and hit something, these guys see exactly where they're aiming and it's a big round nothing." His thoughts move to the "nothingness" of the TV dinner he had put into the oven. He tries to open a beer can and the pull-tab comes off. Channel-hopping on the TV set provides nothing worth watching except a comedy sketch parodying the Lone Ranger radio series of his boyhood and making the once faithful Tonto the secret lover of the Lone Ranger's wife. The radio show used to open with the cheery call "Hi-ho, Silver!" But now silver bullets are trampled underfoot by TV actors to raise a cheap laugh.

In *The Centaur* (1963) Updike treated the theme of the passing of the Golden Age. In *Redux* the Silver Age has passed. Silver coinage, like the mass media, has become debased. The silver face of the moon has been proved to be nothing but gray dust. And while in classical mythology the Silver Age was followed by the ages of Bronze and Iron, we have arrived at the age of plastics and metal substitutes. Rabbit has learned his father's trade and has worked beside him for ten years as a linotyper. Sitting at his machine, a vat of molten metal at his side, Harry has known his happiest hours. But before the book ends he loses his job; the printing works in Brewer will be closing shortly. Offset processes, bypassing the use of metal entirely, are replacing type.

The printing firm employing Rabbit is called Verity Press. So the space age is the era when no verity can be trusted to endure, when "sterling" qualities are mocked and the cheap substitutes we live by go to pieces in our hands. The cities of America, raped by bulldozers, have become full of vacant lots resembling the landscape of the moon.

Rabbit's mother, so strong before, is now sick and partly paralyzed, kept alive by drugs that give her hideous nightmares and grotesque erotic urges. Just so the nation—the "Mom" of all Americans—has fallen into sickness. She too walks with difficulty, is unable to use her arms or to give advice and encouragement to her children. Nightmare riots shatter the national morale and sexuality gets out of hand.

II

Thus Updike suggests that ours is the confusion of a world deliberately traveling, like a spacecraft, toward nothingness. In such a world imagined impossibilities become actualities. Early in *Redux* Harry, wanting some excuse to cut off his conversation with his father at the printing shop, says that he should be getting home in case the house is burned down or a madman gets in. Also, having heard rumors of Janice taking a lover, he wonders whether she has left home; but he dismisses the idea—"Who'd have Janice?" The three unthinkable events happen, in reverse order.

In *Run*, Rabbit was a man motivated by feeling. In search of an erotic ideal unlike the dreary actuality of his marriage, he left Janice twice. After the second flight, the dispirited Janice accidentally drowned their baby daughter. Rabbit returned contrite, but soon after ran away for the third time—and kept on running. Updike described Rabbit's irresponsible behavior by the image of moon-worship. In seeking the abstract female principle, the "nothingness" of woman, Rabbit was courting death in the romantic tradition of love for the pale, dead moon.

In *Redux* Rabbit has turned realist. He accepts Janice's departure—to her surprised annoyance—without trying to fight back. By what seems a casual chain of events, however, he takes into his home Jill Pendleton, the runaway daughter of a wealthy Connecticut family. The silver-haired Jill is a moon-maiden, offering the same blend of sexuality and mysticism that Rabbit formerly tried to steer his life by. He sees her as made "out of air," a spirit to be given substance through erotic encounter, so that his violence upon her undeveloped body becomes "completing creation." He sees her as his dead daughter given back to him. Memory of the baby's death had killed him for all spontaneous delight in sexuality, but now, as Jill lies beside him, he can believe that the Silver Age has come again.

Those who travel to the moon, however, must be prepared to meet its dark, farther side as well as its silver face. Darkness comes suddenly in the shape of Skeeter Farnsworth, a black youth who proclaims himself the messiah of nihilism, and declares that "confusion is God's very face."

Skeeter is on the run from the police on a charge of drug-pushing. Rabbit's first impulse is to attack him physically, but he lets the self-styled messiah stay and listens to him as he expounds his philosophy. He does not interfere when Skeeter gets Jill back on drugs and fornicates with her in the lighted window of his house. Seeing this performance, the neighbors react by burning down the house, with the drugged Jill inside it. Then, knowing that Skeeter has let her die rather than risk recapture by the police, Rabbit helps him escape. He is thanked by Skeeter's spitting into the hand extended in friendship.

This is where Samuels professes himself most puzzled by Updike's failure to show sufficient motivation. Why is Rabbit so blind to what is going on, so passive when he discovers the tragic outcome of his refusal to see what is before his eyes?

There is no simple answer, because Updike does not traffic in simplistic moral judgments. He has put it on record that he does not wish his fiction to be less ambiguous than life itself is. But one part of the answer is that Updike evidently believes passivity on the part of the male to be a phenomenon of our day. In the 1969 radio interview, speaking of *Couples*, he observed: "The women in that book are less sensitive perhaps to the oppressive quality of cosmic blackness, and it is the women who do almost all of the acting . . . I don't want to say that being passive, being inactive, is wrong in an era when so much action is crass and murderous."

Couples was set in 1964—a time when John Kennedy's assassination seemed an isolated act of madness, though Updike judged it to be a symbol of the age. By 1969 multiplication of violence, fear, and frustrated anger throughout the nation has made the oppressive quality of cosmic blackness evident to all. In *Redux*, certainly, Janice—a very unimaginative woman— acts while her husband chiefly reacts. Also, Rabbit's very self-assured sister Mim is the one who finally intervenes to end Janice's love affair. It is undeniable that Rabbit's passivity is a link in the chain of circumstances leading to Jill's death. Yet it can also be argued that, given the situation he finds himself in, Rabbit's inaction is probably less destructive than almost any action open to him. Jill, in any case, is doomed to destruction by her own choice of life style. Updike's image for her is the white Porsche she drives, ignorant of the fact that it needs oil as well as gas, until its engine is ruined. In consenting to join Jill and Skeeter on their "trip" Rabbit makes his most fateful mistake. His spiritual moon-flight almost means being sucked into nothingness. Yet he finally returns to earth. *Redux* means "led back"; it also means "restored to health"—for space travel inspired by moon-worship is a sickness.

III

To understand how Updike distinguishes between sickness and health, we must look at the images connected with Rabbit's work at the Verity Press. The critics find the bread-winning Harry of *Redux* much less attractive than the moon-struck Harry of *Run*. Samuels sees the older Rabbit as "meanly conservative," a chauvinist no longer in revolt against his culture but "a perfect example of its repressiveness." It is doubtful, of course, that Updike wishes to present Rabbit as a perfect example of anything, and more than doubtful—given his declared opposition to doctrinaire liberalism—that he regards Rabbit's conservatism as mean. What Samuels dismisses as Rabbit's "mediocre job" Updike connects with "the golden age of machinery." At the printing works Rabbit is a master of a craft. This is the basis of his conservatism. A father himself, he honors his own father and his country, the *patria*.

His work at the press has made Rabbit value straight lines. The "chaos of the present" cannot shake his conviction that reality has its own shape apart from our desire and capacity to manipulate it. When Janice's friend Peggy Fosnacht tells him, "Living is a compromise, between doing what *you* want and doing what *other* people want"; he interjects, "What about what poor old God wants?"

In one important respect Harry's conservatism is decidedly not mean. He refuses to claim that he knows for certain what God wants. He has learned from his work that to be human is to make mistakes. The pages of *Redux* are peppered with paragraphs for the local weekly, the *Brewer Vat*, as these originally come from Rabbit's linotype machine—full of faulty lines that need to be done over again. There is only one person who arouses savage hatred in Rabbit: a doctor who once held his hand in a tight grip which said, *I know best*. Being ready to admit that he does not know everything, Rabbit is able to give others the same liberty.

Peggy Fosnacht cannot understand why Rabbit will not blame Janice for leaving him. When he comments that Janice too has a life to lead, she explains, "You're so forgiving, Harry." Also, Jill tells him that "pig laws" have put him into a "greasy job" and turned him into a "gutless creep." Evidently Peggy, Jill, and the critics all share the view that Rabbit, when not a repressive reactionary, is pitiably weak—and perhaps a reactionary because he is weak. Thus R. Z. Sheppard wrote in *Time* (November 15, 1971), "Like so many lifers with little hope of parole, he defends his prison because he must live in it." Perhaps Rabbit is weak in relation to Jill and Skeeter. At the same time he genuinely wishes to understand, without prejudging, these visitors from a world unlike his own. While his neighbors do not hesitate to act the part of God and consume the wicked by fire, he leaves vengeance to heaven. If he lacks wisdom, he does not lack compassion. Skeeter, as they part, tells him, "Never did figure your angle." "Probably isn't one," is the answer. Rabbit, literally, plays it straight.

In *Run* Updike says of the young Harry that he "lacks the mindful will to walk the straight line of a paradox." The mature Harry possesses this will, and he exerts it when he first learns that Janice has lied to him about having a lover. "It comes to him: growth is betrayal. There is no other route. There is no arriving somewhere without leaving somewhere." Fittingly, as he drives Skeeter out of Brewer, he gives him $30. The price of his own growth in understanding is the price once paid a betrayer.

IV

Many of the news items in the *Brewer Vat* concern the past history of the town. They show, for anyone who can make connections, how constant through the centuries are the problems of life in America. People today concentrate upon space and ignore time. Yet life is continuity in time. Rabbit himself realizes that what is wrong with the age is that nothing connects.

Connections with the past are waiting for us to recognize them. One of Updike's heroes is James Buchanan, the US president who, many believed, made the Civil War inevitable through his efforts to placate all parties. Yet Updike suggests that Buchanan's way of mediation is, in the end, the sole alternative to intensifying hatreds and bringing on permanent chaos. There is a Buchanan in *Redux*, a black employee at the Verity Press and a friend of Skeeter's father. Wishing to help Rabbit after Janice has left him, Buchanan takes him to Jimbo's Friendly Lounge and introduces him to Jill and Skeeter. To Harry's father, Buchanan is simply another unreliable nigger, and to Skeeter he is a contemptible Uncle Tom. His work of bringing together the worlds of conservatism and radicalism seems to end in tragic failure. Yet, because of him, connections have been made that did not exist before; and the pattern of breaking connections (symbolized in Jill's flight from *Connect*icut) has been reversed. In spite of all appearances, Buchanan may have achieved something. Rabbit chooses to regard Skeeter's farewell gift of spittle as a blessing. Perhaps it was.

One connection is definitely made in *Redux*. This is foreshadowed early in the novel when the Brewer Vat proudly reports that one tiny component for the Apollo vehicle has been manufactured in Brewer: a switching sequence for a navigation computer responsible for the spacecraft's safe return from the moon. At the end of the book Harry and Janice meet, like space module and space capsule making a connection, in a long and narrow motel bedroom. Rabbit has his burrow in Brewer, under the sign of the "Safe Haven Motel."

V

In the chaos of our age, however, few hope to find their safe haven. *Redux* offers Updike's prescription for survival, given through the mouth of a blues singer called Babe. Sitting in Jimbo's Friendly Lounge, Rabbit hears her sing "in a voice that is no woman's voice at all and no man's, is merely human, the words of Ecclesiastes. A time to be born, a time to die. A time to gather up stones, a time to cast stones away. Yes. The Lord's last word. There is no other word, not really."

The third chapter of Ecclesiastes begins, "To every thing there is a season, and a time to every purpose under the sun." The Preacher goes on to comment on the wickedness of men, how they fall under God's judgment and how God lets them see that they are beasts. The characters in *Rabbit Redux,* in fact, are shown to be beasts. Skeeter is a goat, Jill a spring chicken, Buchanan a buck, and so on. Jill's mother (herself a flamingo) tells Rabbit when they meet after Jill's death, "You are a beast." He replies, "O.K., sure." But the important theme of the book is that life has its seasons.

Time, rather than space, is the dimension with human meaning; and time is not a void, for it is marked by seasons connecting in definite sequence. Rabbit is aware that for him, as for most people today, there is no clear consciousness of the seasons. One day follows another with pallid sameness. Yet the seasons are there. The problem is that men neither observe the individual season nor take the action appropriate to it.

Updike carefully fashions each of his novels to a season. *Run* was a spring-to-summer book. *Redux* begins in high summer and ends in October, the season when nature is preparing for the sleep of winter. The prospect for America seems bleak, since nothing except death appears to lie ahead. Mim, Rabbit's sister, flies from California to see her mother. She tells Rabbit that the brown Californian desert is spreading eastward and soon there will be nothing green anywhere. (So much for the "greening of America!") She is also certain that Mom is dying. Yet Pop believes that Mom is doing much better than anyone could expect under the drugs that allow her to sleep—in spite of nightmares. If she can only hang on, he assures Rabbit, the doctors may yet discover a cure.

Pop's hopes may be wishful thinking and Mim's hard-headed realism may be the true diagnosis. Nevertheless, the chill winds of approaching winter are perhaps heralds of sleep rather than portents of death, and a springtime resurrection may lie ahead. Beside Rabbit's house there is a maple sapling. It seems not to be growing. Yet, as Rabbit sweeps up its fallen leaves, he marvels that there are so many. For Updike the maple is the American tree. America is sick; it is not yet dead.

Redux ends, after a season of moon madness and flaming terror, with a measure of cautious hopefulness. In the motel bedroom Rabbit and Janice strike a truce for the time being and meet in bed—not to copulate but to sleep. For as Ecclesiastes said, there is "a time to embrace, and a time to refrain from embracing." This is God's last word, and America may not have ears to hear it. Yet if America observes the signs of the times, it will know that this is the season for sleep and the restoration of wasted powers. Updike's last word in *Redux* is brief and direct: "He. She. Sleeps. O.K.?"

*Myth and Gospel in
John Updike's Later Fiction*

CHAPTER 7

John Updike's *Rabbit* Tetralogy and
Alan Ayckbourn's *Norman Conquests* Trilogy

WHO TODAY REMEMBERS IGNAZ Holzbauer, Johann Baptist Vanhal, Leopold Kozeluch, Antonio Salieri, or Wolfgang Amadeus Mozart? Actually we all remember Mozart. And many of us may also remember Salieri but only because he allegedly tried to poison Mozart. It's really only Mozart and his music that we remember from this list of major (at the time) eighteenth-century composers. The rest have pretty much been forgotten.

Which contemporary writers will people remember a hundred or two hundred years from today? Two speculations were offered recently: one by the American Pulitzer Prize-winning literary critic William McPherson, and the other by the well-known British director, Peter Hall. McPherson suggested that "John Updike may be America's finest novelist and . . . likely to be scrutinized a generation or two or three from now as runic clues to the times we live in." And Peter Hall predicted that "if, in a hundred years, anyone wants to know what it was like to live in the second half of the 20th century, I am quite sure they will turn to the plays of Alan Ayckbourn before they look at historians or sociologists."

It might seem odd at first to link Ayckbourn and Updike. Yet the similarities in their highly praised works are striking. Both men have inspired the highest critical as well as popular acclaim for their realistic portrayals of domestic life. Both combine traditional linear story lines in the telling of their stories with ingenious and yet accessible forms of experimentation in the telling. And both have been astonishingly prolific. Updike in his lifetime gave us over sixty books while Ayckbourn, at last count, has given us eighty plays, half of which have received productions in London's West End.

Both Ayckbourn and Updike, moreover, are only children of mothers who were themselves writers. Both married young, eventually divorced, and married, lastingly, again. Both, too, have largely eschewed the pleasures and distractions of urban life for the quieter, closer-to-ordinary life offered in small towns. Updike spent most of his adult life in small towns on the eastern seaboard in America while Ayckbourn currently resides in the British seaside town of Scarborough, where he has lived more or less since he was in his late teens.

Finally, and by no means least, both writers are best known artistically for a series of popular works that follow an ordinary Joe through his life. In Updike's case the protagonist is Harry Angstrom, a used-car salesman who hops like a sexed-up American bunny through a quartet of *Rabbit* novels in *Rabbit, Run* (1960), *Rabbit Redux* (1971), *Rabbit is Rich* (1981), and *Rabbit at Rest* (1990).[1] Meanwhile, the protagonist in Ayckbourn's 1974 *Norman Conquests* masterpiece is Norman Dewers, an assistant librarian who romps like an English sheepdog in heat through *Table Manners, Living Together,* and *Round and Round the Garden.*[2]

Harry Angstrom and Norman Dewers are certainly not clones. Each has his own highly distinctive psyche and personality. Still, in a number of ways they are soulmates, reflecting striking commonalities of religio-philosophical thought going on in the minds of their creators.[3] Consider, for example, some of the ways that Updike's Harry and Ayckbourn's Norman encounter love, affirm life, and face death.

1. An Everyman's Library edition of John Updike's quartet of *Rabbit* novels has been published as *Rabbit Angstrom: A Tetralogy.* Citations to this work are given in the text in parentheses.

2. Ayckbourn, *The Norman Conquests: A Trilogy of Plays.* Citations to this work are given in the text in parentheses.

3. Of course, to fully appreciate these soulmates we need to be sensitive. As Updike says somewhere, for a book to be good it is not enough for it to be good: the reader has to be ready. And in Ayckbourn's case the theatergoer not only needs to be ready but the actors need to play the material for the truth and not for laughs. For an excellent illustration of Ayckbourn's special brand of truth-telling in a production of *The Norman Conquests,* consult the BBC's YouTube broadcast of the 2015 adaptation of the 1974 *Norman Conquests* trilogy as prepared for BBC's Radio 4.

Encountering Love

We begin with the encounter of love, or more precisely the way in which love encounters Harry and Norman. The two protagonists are virtually infamous for reminding us that we are sexual beings in nearly every cell and filament of our humanity. This does not mean that they are simply copulating machines. Both men are still emotional, moral, even spiritual beings—besouled bodies, or embodied souls. We may be able to distinguish between the soul and the body, but we can never entirely separate the two primal components. Our humanity consists in the thoroughly integrated and yet dualistic nature that makes us all—and this is what Harry and Norman illustrate so well—perpetually restless and unsatisfied.

Harry initially attempts to dissolve the persistent body-soul tension by running away from his wife, Janice, and his job. He simply hops into his car after work one day and heads south:

> . . . down, down the map into orange groves and smoking rivers and barefoot women . . . drive all night through the dawn through the morning through the noon park on a beach take off your shoes and fall asleep by the Gulf of Mexico. Wake up with the stars above perfectly spaced in perfect health (25).

Heaven! Except that the earthbound, bodily side of Harry causes him to become increasingly drowsy. He ends up taking a wrong turn and loses precious time while driving through the night. Then, frustration piling on frustration, Harry lands in a dead-end petting grove. By dawn our thoroughly exhausted wannabe runaway is back in his dingy hometown, maybe not restored to his wife and family, but with the body-soul tension still firmly intact.

Norman also attempts to resolve the body-soul tension by fleeing to the sunny South, or at least what passes in Britain for the South: "Ah, the sun, the sun, the sun . . ." (165). Unlike his more idealistic American soulmate, however, Norman has a more feasible, if modest, game plan. The idea is to go off with his wife's younger sister, Annie, to a nearby industrial town where Norman and Annie can lie together in their room in a hotel. Norman and his sister-in-law plan to meet first in the village, at the back of the post office, and then steal away on the bus to the hotel. As Norman explains, "Forget everything, everybody, just lie anonymously in each other's arms. Just for a day" (98).

There are, naturally, complications. In addition to having a devoted if painfully indecisive boyfriend (Tom, the neighborhood vet), Annie is the main caregiver for her invalid mother with whom she lives in an old Victorian country house in Sussex. Annie has nevertheless arranged for older brother Reg and his wife Sarah to come down for the weekend to relieve her of her filial responsibilities. When they are late in arriving, however, Annie stays with her mother rather than force the hapless old woman to fend for herself. Norman eventually walks in from the village to find out why Annie is not coming and is told to go away for an hour until Annie's brother and his wife show up. "I don't want you here when Reg and Sarah arrive," Annie explains. "And I've got to see them in. I've got to show them where everything is for Mother, all her bottles and pills and God knows what. And which is their towel. I mean, there's masses. I can't just rush off. Anyway, Tom's here" (166). When Reg and Sarah finally arrive, Sarah wastes no time worming the truth out of Annie and convincing her to call off the tryst with Norman. A much annoyed Norman ends up staying at the family homestead for the weekend.

"Other people are hell," Sartre famously claimed. Whether this is always true or not, it is certainly the case that other people often form the chief obstacle thwarting whatever plans we might have for resolving the body-soul tension.

As Updike once explained to a British interviewer,

> Take Harry Angstrom in *Rabbit, Run*: there is a case to be made for running away from your wife. In the late fifties beatniks were preaching transcontinental travelling as the answer to man's disquiet. And I was just trying to say: "Yes, there is certainly that, but then there are all these other people who seem to get hurt." That distinction is meant to be a moral dilemma.[4]

From the soul's perspective, the most common obstacle preventing the body from dissolving the agonizing tension within is quite simply the injurious effect that our actions are likely to have upon the defenseless and often blameless people around us.

The itch to resolve the tension nevertheless persists, and Harry and Norman are at least honest in acknowledging as much. As Norman explains to his brother-in-law,

---

4. Plath, ed., *Conversations*, 50.

> It's not fair, Reg. Look, I'll tell you. A man with my type of temper-
> ament should really be ideally square-jawed, broad-shouldered,
> have blue twinkling eyes, a chuckle in his voice and a spring in
> his stride. He should get through three women a day without even
> ruffling his hair. That's what I'm like. That's my appetite. That's me.
> I'm a three a day man. There's enough of me in here to give. Not
> just sex, I'm talking about everything (45).

Not just sex! Norman Dewers desires to give his whole body and soul to
Annie—and doesn't see why everybody else doesn't feel the same way about
the Annies in their lives. The prissy, interfering Sarah, however, is one person who quite forcefully rejects Norman's thinking. Why, she demands to
know, would he ever consider doing anything so sordid as to run off with
his wife's sister? "I'm appalled at you, I really am. . . . Annie of all people.
How could you? What on earth made you do it?" (96). Norman explains
that it was going to be something different for Annie—exciting. Besides, he
says, "she's beautiful" (97). Sarah is naturally disgusted with this shallow,
self-centered thinking. Yet before the weekend is over her actions betray
the fact that she too has trouble coping with the psychic tension within.

Norman for his part remains convinced that what he is doing is not
only good but right. As he says to Annie,

> Believe me, it's right. We have right on our side. . . . Don't you see,
> we're not alone? We've got the whole tradition of history behind
> us. We're not the first lovers who've ever done this—stood up to
> the whole establishment and said to hell with the status quo, we
> don't care what's meant to be, we mean this to be. Us (102).

Those who would send Norman on a guilt-trip for trying to bed Annie
perhaps don't understand that Ruth's sexual indifference alone is enough to
drive a man like Norman to embrace adultery: "I tell you, if you gave Ruth a
rose she'd peel all the petals off to make sure there weren't any greenfly. And
when she'd done that, she'd turn around and say, do you call that a rose?
Look at it, it's all in bits. That's Ruth" (45). Romantically wired characters
like Norman Dewers not only crave but deserve, certainly in their minds,
romantic trysts.

Harry Angstrom also argues that his adulterous actions are morally le-
gitimate. Only Harry's argument, unlike Norman's, reflects the more Puritan culture of America, and thus takes on more of a religious or theological
coloration. An important confessional moment occurs shortly after Harry
has returned to his hometown and hooked up with an ex-high-school

acquaintance and part-time prostitute, a young woman by the name of Ruth Leonard. One day Harry decides to drive back to his apartment so that he can pick up some clothes and leave the car for his wife. (The "almost paralyzed" Janice, expecting their second child, has been living with her parents since Harry abandoned her.) While walking back to his paramour's apartment from his, Harry is overtaken by the hound of heaven in the form of the minister of Janice's family, the Rev. Jack Eccles.

Harry is surprised at first that Eccles doesn't bawl him out. The man "doesn't seem to know his job." But eventually Eccles gets around to the matter and puts the critical question to Harry: "What did she do that made you leave?" Harry replies,

> She asked me to buy her a pack of cigarettes . . . it's the truth. It just felt like the whole business was fetching and hauling, all the time trying to hold this mess together she was making all the time. I don't know, it seemed like I was glued in with a lot of busted toys and empty glasses and the television going and meals late or never and no way of getting out. Then all of a sudden it hit me how easy it was to get out, just walk out, and by damn it was easy (91).

Harry continues to parry the minister's questions with straightforward, sensible responses, forcing Eccles at last to play his theological trump card: "Do you believe in God?" "Yes," replies Harry unhesitatingly. "Do you think, then, that God wants you to make your wife suffer?" Harry is ready for this question with one of his own: "Let me ask you. Do you think God wants a waterfall to be a tree?" (92).

We are not told what Harry is thinking here, but we can guess. Ever since he was a fleet-footed high-school basketball star, people have called him Rabbit. And like his namesake, Harry was not only once quick on his feet, but he remains driven by an extremely powerful sexual urge. It is this urge that has driven him to leave his wife and seek out someone like the plump but voluptuous Ruth Leonard. The question is, who planted this powerful urge in Harry's groin? Who is driving him to realize the fullness of his humanity by running the way Rabbit likes to run? Who, one might ask, but God?

The question at least makes Eccles think. Finally, he counters Harry's suggestion that God might prefer a vibrant, voluptuous waterfall to a static, sexless tree with the remark, "No, but I think he wants a little tree to become a big tree." This moralistic jibe makes no impression on the fast-moving, testosterone-driven Rabbit: "If you're telling me I'm not mature, that's one thing I don't cry over since as far as I can make out it's the same thing as being dead" (93). What can Eccles do now but confess his own limitations: "I'm immature myself," Eccles offers, leaving Harry, certainly in Harry's mind, the clear winner of the debate (93).

The problem of innocent people getting hurt nevertheless persists. And the people especially hurt by Harry's actions include his wife and son and, most drastically, an infant daughter born to Harry's wife while Harry is still sharing Ruth's bed. Even Ruth ends up getting hurt in the end. The problem is not one that can easily be moralized away. It nags Harry through the day and even into the night, materializing in his subconscious while he lies sleeping alongside the ex-prostitute. Harry dreams of an old wooden icebox in his parents' house. The melting cake of ice is surely his wife Janice (January ice) whose psychic meltdown horrifies him in his subterranean if not waking life. Even when he's awake, the consequences of Janice's meltdown are such that Rabbit is soon running back to his wife and the fast-spreading watery mess he has left behind.

No sooner does Harry return to Janice, however, than an unexpectedly impregnated Ruth begins manifesting her own psychic meltdown. What can Rabbit do now but run back and forth between the two women, finally running off the last page of the novel altogether, demonstrating that there is really no place in the end for any of us to run. Like a trapped rabbit, Updike's erotically embroiled protagonist demonstrates that however much we might dart here or there, we can never entirely break free from the underlying tension of the body-soul condition. This may be discouraging news for the human species, yet it lifts us above the animal world and makes us something more than mere rabbits running around with clothes on.

Norman Dewers can also be found continually attempting to dissolve the psychic tension within—and just as continually failing to do so. Norman, as we have seen, is initially foiled in his attempt on Friday night to run off with his wife's younger sister, Annie. Then he is further stymied when sister-in-law Sarah summons Norman's wife Ruth to come down to the family homestead to keep an eye on her husband. Finally, on Saturday night, Sarah catches Norman giving Annie what appears to be an innocent good-night kiss. Her cries of righteous indignation bring Norman's wife running from her bedroom, and the long anticipated moment of recriminations materializes.

Ruth slaps Norman's face hard and says, "Well, I think this is it, don't you? I think this is where we say thank you very much, good-bye" (142). It appears that Norman has his freedom at last. But now that he has it, does he really want it? One has to wonder when Norman immediately tries to change the subject. He begins arguing with Ruth. He gives her that "awful doggie look." He even crawls over to her and starts licking her hand. Clearly, Norman is having trouble walking away from his marital prison cell, even and especially when the doors have been flung wide open.

Then on top of everything else, recalling Harry's drowsiness while attempting to drive through the night to Florida, Norman realizes that he is dead tired and desperate for a place to sleep. Ruth is kind enough to tell him that he can sleep in the living room. *Ruth*: "We'll talk about this in the morning. You can sleep down here." *Norman*: "Where?" *Ruth*: "I don't know. In a chair. You're certainly not coming up with me. I refuse to be number three in a night" (144). What can Norman do now but exactly what Rabbit did (as we learn in *Rabbit Redux*, the sequel to *Rabbit, Run*) but re-seduce his wife so that he can at least get a good night's sleep.

Of course, once the body is refreshed the soul is only going to foster psychic complaints again, and the old erotic cravings are likely to return with a vengeance. Thus Ayckbourn's Norman, as much as Updike's Harry, demonstrates that, no matter how much the human animal twists and turns, runs away or stays home, the unresolved tension created by the body-soul mix persists. This is what it means, after all, to be more than an animal running around with clothes on, to be in fact a loving, existing, soulful human being.

Affirming Life

John Updike once told an interviewer that "a person who has what he wants, a satisfied person, a content person, ceases to be a person. Unfallen man is an ape."[5] The fact that human beings are perpetually dissatisfied does not mean that it would be better to have been born an ape and not have to struggle with the irresolvable tensions of the body-soul mix. Human life, for all its challenges and difficulties, is still worth embracing.

We find Updike himself affirming life from his first novel on. *The Poorhouse Fair* (1959) closes with the voices of fairgoers and residents alike, the young and the old, the wise and the simple, chatting animatedly amongst

5. Plath, ed., *Conversations*, 34.

themselves, all enjoying the sheer bliss of human existence. And one of Updike's last novels, *Terrorist* (2006), concludes with the voice of a lone and fatigued but still life-affirming high-school guidance teacher pleading with a young Islamic zealot to let the sheer joy of life go on for the people around them. "Life," declares still another life-affirming Updikean protagonist, the Rev. Thomas Marshfield of *A Month of Sundays*, "that's what we seek in one another."[6]

Throughout the Rabbit novels Harry Angstrom maintains, often in the face of adversity, his own great love of life. There is a moment in middle age when Harry looks in a mirror and sees "a chaos of wattles and slack cords." Still, he thinks, "life is sweet. That's what old people used to say and when he was young he wondered how they could mean it" (626). Harry's "yea" to life entails affirming the whole of human existence:

> For a while Harry had kicked against death, then he gave in and went to work. Now the dead are so many he feels for the living around him the camaraderie of survivors. He loves these people with him. . . . Harry loves the treetops above their heads, and the August blue above these. . . . He loves Nature, though he can name almost nothing in it. . . . He loves money, though he doesn't understand how it flows to him, or how it leaks away. He loves men, uncomplaining with their potbellies and cross-hatched red necks (746).

An especially life-affirming moment occurs with the birth of Harry's first grandchild: "Oblong cocooned little visitor, the baby shows her profile blindly in the shuttering flashes of color jerking from the Sony, the tiny stitchless seam of the closed eyelid aslant, lips bubbled forth beneath the whorled nose as if in delicate disdain, she knows she's good" (1045). The baby is good because life, at bottom, is good—as the baby instinctively realizes.

Still, there is also a dark, tragic side to life that Harry can't help noticing: "When he contemplates it by himself, bringing a person into the world seems as terrible as pushing somebody into a furnace" (781). The affirmation of life, nevertheless, persists. The furnace may be there, but it is still good that we have been pushed, or "thrown" as Heidegger used to say, into life. When Harry's son, Nelson, shows signs of major fright on the eve of his wedding, when he appears, that is, to be on the verge of running from the life-affirming venture that marriage and family life entail—Harry reaches

6. Ayckbourn, *The Norman Conquests*, 144.

deep into his core convictions and says, "Look, Nelson. Maybe I haven't done everything right in my life. I know I haven't. But I haven't committed the greatest sin. I haven't laid down and died" (966). The greatest sin still consists in the refusal to embrace the greatest gift: life itself.

And behind that gift lies, however fitfully conceived, the thought of a giver. Thus Harry's musings at his son's wedding take, finally, a metaphysical turn. "Laugh at ministers all you want," he thinks sitting there in church, "they have the words we need to hear, the ones the dead have spoken" (841). The dead who yet speak (Heb 11:4) include the biblical writers pointing to God's telling "yea" as the ultimate ground and justification of life's goodness.

While Ayckbourn's British protagonist is certainly not as theologically expressive as his American soulmate, Norman, too, can be found saying yes to life in ways that suggest, however subliminally, metaphysical affirmation. "He's so bouncy this morning," Ruth observes of her husband on Monday morning following the hectic weekend with the family. "I could kick him" (216). Norman never loses that primal joy in life. Like Harry Angstrom, he never commits the great sin of lying down and saying "nay."

There is an especially illuminating moment when Norman is pressed to defend his life-affirming perspective over and against his harshest critic: Sarah. The two meet in the garden (shades of Eden?) where Norman has been taken after getting drunk on Saturday night. Sarah seizes the opportunity to have "a talk"—code language for putting Norman straight. But Norman has always known that Sarah's idea of the good life would essentially rob life of all pleasure and joy. He thus defends his affirmative perspective by recounting a proprietary-challenging parable: "When I was at my primary school—mixed infants—we had a little girl just like you. She was very pretty, very smart and clean—beautifully dressed—always nicely starched little frock on . . . . And she ran that school with more sheer ruthless efficiency than the head of the Mafia."

The little girl, it turns out, had usurped the prerogatives, not only of the teacher but of God: "She asked you to do something for her and you did it. You never argued. It was no good arguing with her. She was cleverer than you were. Precociously clever. She could reduce a nine-year-old thug to tears with her sarcasm."[7] The girl soon realized that Norman's opposition to her overweening pretensions was calling into question her whole control-freakish way of squeezing joy out of life. She therefore determined to make Norman's life murder.

7. Ayckbourn, *The Norman Conquests*, 184–185.

But then one day the tables were reversed. The little girl came round with her mother to Norman's house to have tea, and suddenly they were standing there, not in her territory, but in his: "And we stood there and we just looked at each other. And I thought what am I frightened of you for? A skinny little girl with knock knees and a front tooth missing—what on earth have I been frightened of you for, for heaven's sake?"[8] Norman finally picked the girl up, carried her to the bottom of the garden, pulled down her panties, and placed her on the biggest patch of stinging nettles that he could find.

For the longest time the two just sat there, not moving, just looking at each other, sizing each other up: "Then she got up, pulled up her knickers, very quietly took hold of my hand, gave me a big kiss and we went in and had our tea." After telling this story Norman comments, "I've never been in love like that again."[9] Clearly, this was a watershed moment for Norman Dewers. Even at this early stage of life, he was taking his stand on the side of life. And no domineering little girl, no one at all in fact would ever take that conviction from him. Not surprisingly, as soon as the story is over, Norman seduces Sarah, demonstrating in his own sweet way, his joyous, indefatigable yes to life.

Facing Death

Rabbit at Rest, the final novel in Updike's Rabbit tetralogy, opens, portentously, in the dying days of 1998. Harry is waiting in a Florida airport for a post-Christmas plane that abruptly becomes, in his mind, a symbol of his fast-approaching death. The plane imagery occurs again in the story as Harry relives the terror that the passengers on the Pan Am jet must have experienced when their plane exploded earlier that year over Lockerbie, Scotland. Then one day, while lying in a hospital bed in the wake of a near-fatal heart attack, Harry realizes that he is just like the people he felt so sorry for, falling from the burst-open airplane: he too is "falling, helplessly falling, toward death" (1209). The rest of the novel charts Harry's open-eyed plunge into the abyss.

Norman is also keenly aware that he is falling helplessly toward death and that there is nothing he can do about it. The painful realization comes, ironically, not at a low point in his life, but just when he learns that Sarah

8. Ibid., 185.
9. Ibid., 185, 186.

has become putty in his hands and that Annie is interested in a romantic rendezvous after all: "If you want to come to my room tonight, you'll be very welcome" (189). Alas, all this anticipated bliss simply drives home the realization that one day the bliss is going to run out, life itself is going to run out. The thought drives Norman into the black hole of despair. He decides to do exactly what Harry did when the American protagonist realized that *his* life had fallen into the psychic black hole: run. To Reg, Norman says, "Let's all of us—you, me, Tom—let's take a couple of weeks and just go. . . . And see things. And taste things. And smell things. And touch things— touch trees—and grass—and—and earth. . . . Let's see everywhere. Let's be able to say we have seen and experienced everything" (192).

But all Reg can think of is that his ankles are swelling again and he's going to get varicose veins if he's not careful. Norman's despair level, mean- while, grows ever wilder, and he ends up begging the heavens for more time to live and love: "Please don't let me die till I've seen it. Please don't let me die." Reg, by contrast, continues to cope through denial: "It's all right, Norman. You're not going to die, it's all right." Norman is thus reduced to mouthing simple pieties—"Let's stop hating and start to love, Reg"—and emitting elementary sobs. Sarah finally appears and dismisses Norman's anguished wails with the cold and uncomprehending if technically correct observation that the man is simply drunk. Norman continues to wail as he is pulled helplessly off stage (193).

Updike's Harry Angstrom similarly stares death in the face and re- fuses to minimize its horror. A vital conversation on this subject takes place between Harry and his former business associate Charlie Stavros during lunch one day just before Harry's date with the surgeon for open-heart sur- gery. Charlie attempts to comfort Harry with the story of his own successful heart operation. But the more Charlie talks about what the doctors did to him, the more disturbed Harry becomes. "They split your chest open and ran your blood through a machine?" Charlie insists it's no big deal: "Piece of cake. You're knocked out cold. What's wrong with running your blood through a machine? What else you think you are, champ?" (1265). But this is precisely the problem. Harry is horrified at the thought that he may be nothing more in the end than "a machine" that doctors break open and nature eventually tosses upon the scrap heap of an eternal junkyard. Surely to God (literally, *to God*), we are more than that.

What else you think you are, champ? This is what Harry Angstrom, ex-champion high-school basketball star and retired chief salesman for Toyota's Springer Motors, thinks he is:

> A God-made one of a kind with an immortal soul breathed in. A vehicle of grace. A battlefield of good and evil. An apprentice angel. All those things they tried to teach you in Sunday school or really didn't try very hard to teach you, just let them drift in out of the pamphlets back there in that church basement buried deeper in his mind than an air-raid shelter (1265).

Thanks to this gospel-imbued hope, Harry conquers despair and is able to face death unafraid. True, he remains sufficiently anxious (his name, after all, is *Angst*rom) that he opts for the less invasive, less threatening but also less effective angioplasty. Nevertheless, enough faith and trust fill Harry's heart that, from this moment on, he fairly runs to meet his death. Rabbit, to recall Harry's nickname once more, runs with courage and conviction and not least a powerful dose of insouciance. He throws incestuous inhibitions aside and makes love with his daughter-in-law. He fulfills a lifelong ambition and drives to Florida. He proves that he is still able to play basketball with the boys.

But naturally all this running around can't go on forever. One bright sunny morning Harry arrives at a Florida basketball court, spots a talented muscular black teenager shooting baskets by himself, and challenges the boy to a game of one-on-one. Harry knows, he must know, that he can't win, and that what he stands to lose this time may well be nothing less than life itself. Even so, he insists on playing the game. "'Come on,' he begs, growling the 'on.' "Gimme the ball" (1508).

The old marvel gets the ball from the boy and lets fly an old-fashioned two-handed set shot that drops smoothly into the net. Harry grabs the ball again and, full of the old magic, leaps ever so high only to feel his torso "ripped by a terrific pain, elbow to elbow. He bursts from within; he feels something immense persistently fumble at him, and falls unconscious to the dirt" (1510). Later in the hospital, his last breath imminent, Harry manages to hear his son Nelson shouting with grief and despair, "Don't *die*, Dad, *don't!*" (1516). Harry realizes that the boy needs help in facing the worst that any of us can face. Caringly, almost in a Christlike way, he utters his final, life-consoling, hope-engendering words: "Well Nelson, all I can tell you is, it isn't so bad" (1516).

Ayckbourn's Norman Dewers no doubt would never be caught dead uttering even such a modest expression of hope in the face of death. His literary creator, after all, is British, and the Brits are almost as stoic and secular as Harry's creator is American and religious. Still, there may be more faith and hope in Norman's outlook than first meets the eye.[10] Take, for example, what happens on Monday morning when all the characters in *The Norman Conquests*, exhausted from the weekend shenanigans and more than ready to go home, are foiled by Norman who alone is determined to keep the party going.[11]

Norman gets his opportunity when he and Ruth, whose misbehaving car has stalled again, are asked to sit in the car while Reg tows it to the top of the hill. "I'll tow you as far as the top of the hill, right?" Reg tells Ruth. "We'll disconnect the rope and then you're free to roll her down. But for heaven's sake wait till I'm out of the way" (220). Once Reg has disconnected the rope and driven off, Ruth can take her foot off the brake and activate the engine. Off they go, then. But when it comes time for action, Norman releases the brake prematurely, causing the car to smash into the rear end of Reg's car and forcing the couples to stay together, forcing in effect the party to go on longer.

We hear Reg shouting off stage, "You bloody fool." *Reg stamps back on stage followed by Ruth and Sarah. Norman follows up the rear with Tom.*

REG: What the hell did you let him drive for?

RUTH: He insisted.

TOM: Everyone all right?

REG: Why him? Why him?

10. While Ayckbourn acknowledges that he has long since replaced an early adolescent commitment to God with art, he nevertheless maintains that "it is desirable to retain a faith in something which is 'bigger than yourself, preferably not another human being,' and values spirituality while confessing to embarrassment and self-parody when he tries to explain what this might be" (Allen, *Alan Ayckbourn,* 29). Updike, for his part, though a lifelong, Apostles Creed-confessing Christian, could hardly be characterized as a dogmatic religionist. He once told the editor of *Episcopal Life,* "I wouldn't say that I'm one of those who's certain that God is there at all. I find it hard to imagine anybody who is that certain, in fact. But it's always seemed to me that he should be there, and that our best self is called forth by acting as though he is" (Plath, ed., *Conversations,* 250).

11. A comment that Updike once made in an interview makes him sound very Normanesque: "Parties are somehow deadly serious. To say no to one is to say no to life" (Plath, ed., *Conversations,* 14).

SARAH: I feel terribly faint.

Reg and Tom storm off to phone home and announce the delay, leaving Norman alone with the three women.

NORMAN: Definitely my mistake . . .

[*A silence.*]

[NORMAN *stands regarding the three women who are now seated. They look at him.*] Well. Back again.

ANNIE: Oh, Norman. . . .

RUTH: If I didn't know you better, I'd say you did all that deliberately.

NORMAN: Me? Why should I want to do that?

SARAH: Huh.

NORMAN: Give me one good reason why I'd do a thing like that?

RUTH: Offhand, I can think of three.

[*Pause.*]

NORMAN: Ah. [*Brightening*] Well, since we're all here, we ought to make the most of it, eh? What do you say?

Norman smiles round at the three women, but one by one they stand up and, without a word, leave. The party, alas, is over. Norman is left standing alone, hurt, bewildered, shouting after them, "I only wanted to make you happy" (226). We can never have enough time, Ayckbourn seems to be saying here, enough time for life and love. Or in Updike's words, we can never eternalize "our most obvious possession, our most platitudinous blessing, the moment, the single ever-present moment that we perpetually bring to our lips brimful."[12]

12. The overwhelming significance of "the moment" is stressed by the theological student in Updike's oft-anthologized short story "Lifeguard." The story concludes with a mock meditation in which the student says, "I seem to be lying dreaming in the infinite rock of space before Creation, and the actual scene I see is a vision of impossibility: a paradise. For had we existed before the gesture that split the firmament, could we have conceived of our most obvious possession, our most platitudinous blessing, the moment, the single ever-present moment that we perpetually bring to our lips brimful?" Updike, *Pigeon Feathers*, 219.

Conclusion

All this would seem to leave us with a pretty feeble confession of faith in the face of death. Yet when has our confession of faith not been feeble, even in its strongest moments? Updike, too, despite his more explicit religiosity, never suggests that doubt and despair can simply be erased from human experience. One thinks of that disturbing scene in *Rabbit at Rest* in which Rabbit's daughter-in-law Pru voices her deepest fear to Rabbit:

> I've had my shot, Harry. I wasted it on Nelson. I had my little
> hand of cards and played them and now I'm folded, I'm through.
> My husband hates me and I hate him and we don't even have any
> money to split up! I'm scared—so scared. And my kids are scared,
> too. I'm trash and they're trash and they know it.

Harry replies, "Hey. Hey. Come on. Nobody's trash" (1362). But inside, we are told, Harry knows that "it's an old-fashioned idea he would have trouble defending. We're all trash, really, without God to lift us up and make us into angels we're all trash" (1362).

An old-fashioned idea he would have trouble defending. . . . Thus does the religious novelist from America confess the built-in limitations of the hopeful outlook that he shares with the more secular playwright from Britain. The faith and love are still there, but so are the limitations. Or in the language of the Bible, we see through a glass darkly, and even very darkly. Nevertheless, we do see. And what Harry Angstrom and Norman Dewers manage to perceive, however fitfully and within the radical limitations of our common humanity, may yet be enough to give us encouragement and hope.

CHAPTER 8

A Potpourri of Reviews

WOLFGANG AMADEUS MOZART

By Karl Barth, Introduction by John Updike (Eerdmans, 1986)
Reviewed by John McTavish in *The United Church Observer*

"LIFE: THAT'S WHAT WE look for in each other," says a character in one of John Updike's novels. And life is what the theologian Karl Barth found preeminently in the music of Mozart.

In this slim volume, first published in 1956 in celebration of the 200th anniversary of Mozart's birth and now reissued in an English translation on the 100th anniversary of Barth's birth, the theologian tells how, by listening to Mozart's vital music, "one can be young and become old, can work and rest, be content and sad: in short, one can live."

Mozart helps us live without especially trying to help. Unlike Bach, for example, "Mozart does not wish to say anything; he just sings and sounds." And in contrast to Beethoven, he does not pour forth his subjective feelings. Burdened neither with formal "messages" nor personal "confessions" Mozart simply—plays.

But, oh, how he plays. "Beautiful playing," declares Barth, "presupposes an intuitive, child-like awareness of the essence or the center—as also the beginning and the end—of all things. It is from this center, from this beginning and end, that I hear Mozart create his music."

How strange that the dignified court composers of the day did not know this center the way the billiard-playing, woman-chasing, punch-drinking Amadeus knew it. Whether Mozart had a unique, direct access to God, Barth hesitates to say. But "we must certainly assume that the dear Lord had a special, direct contact with *him*."

As a result of this contact, Mozart was able to translate into music "real life in all its discord" yet always with that triumphant turning in which "the light rises and the shadows fall, though without disappearing, in which joy overtakes sorrow without extinguishing it, in which the Yea rings louder than the ever-present Nay."

John Updike, who supplies the foreword, notes that "Mozart's music, for Barth, has the exact texture of God's world, of divine comedy." It certainly has something other than the thump and grind of today's top forty, or the slushy Muzak that adults often confuse with music.

John Updike's foreword to Karl Barth's little book on Mozart is reprinted in Odd Jobs *(228–30).*

RABBIT AT REST

By John Updike (Alfred A. Knopf, 1990)
Reviewed by John McTavish in the *Huntsville Forester*

John Updike's quartet of Rabbit novels constitutes, below the surface, an epic retelling of the tale of Peter Rabbit. The mischievous Peter, you recall, hopped into Mr. McGregor's garden, gorged himself on the forbidden lettuces and beans and radishes, and then ran for his life when Mr. McGregor appeared, rake in hand.

Updike's own naughty but endearing rodent is first seen running in *Rabbit, Run* (1960), running from his dreary job and pregnant wife, hopping into the bed of a prostitute's warren, tasting the forbidden fruits, and then running for his life when Mr. McGregor appears in the form of a Protestant minister, Bible in hand. Harry "Rabbit" Angstrom (the nickname harks back to Harry's fleet-footed days on the high school basketball court) continues his adventures and misadventures in *Rabbit Redux* (1971) and *Rabbit Is Rich* (1981).

But all this running, we learn in *Rest*, has taken its toll. Just as Peter Rabbit sat down to rest after the chase only to discover "he was out of breath and trembling with fright," so Updike's Rabbit now finds "little squeezy pains tease his ribs, reaching into his upper left arm."

Early in the story, Rabbit suffers a heart attack during a near-drowning incident and the rest of the novel charts his slow but steady slide into nothingness. So much darkness and death. And yet the book, curiously, makes for an exhilarating read. Why?

There are the obvious reasons: the dazzling prose, the sexual fireworks (even with Rabbit virtually on his deathbed, Updike notices it's still a bed), the humor, the conflict, all the ingredients are there. Yet something else, something that can only be described as prophetic, even religious, makes this book, in the end, a strangely compelling read.

The prophetic word of judgment is easier to discern than the religious word of grace. Rabbit, after all, is clearly shown nibbling himself into the grave, sneaking peanuts and chocolate bars against his doctor's orders and granddaughter's preachments, snack-fooding himself to death. There is an obvious cautionary parable here for us in our overly consumptive, cholesterol-flirting, greenhouse-effect-causing private and social settings.

But there's also something else. At the outset of the tale, Rabbit observes a Jewish man shouting to his wife in a Florida airport, "Come *on*, Grace!" That shout can be heard reverberating through the Jewish writings of the Old Testament and answered in the New. It is echoed in Rabbit's final words to his son with their distant echo of Christ's final words of acceptance and trust spoken from the cross.

Another echo perhaps comes from Augustine (like Rabbit, another mischievous but lovable human animal) who said back in the fifth century, "Thou hast made us for thyself, Lord, and our hearts are restless until they find their rest in Thee." Certainly, this would seem to be the kind of rest that Rabbit finally enters upon. "Well, Nelson," he tells his son at the end, "all I can tell you is, it isn't so bad."

With a whisper of grace this book—and the remarkable Rabbit tetralogy as a whole, comes to a close. I am reminded of the closing words of the Bible spoken with reference to the One who embodies God's grace: "Come quickly, Lord Jesus."

Even so, "Come *on*, Grace!" and lighten our darkness.

NO OTHER LIFE
By Brian Moore (Knopf, Canada, 1992)

MEMORIES OF THE FORD ADMINISTRATION
By John Updike (Knopf, New York, 1992)
Reviewed by John McTavish in *The United Church Observer*

A Catholic slow ball and a Protestant knuckleball: that's one way of describing these two novels.

In *No Other Life*, Brian Moore, the Catholic novelist, plunks his hero down in a dismal no-win situation. Ganae is a fictional cross between Haiti and Nicaragua, and Father Jeannot, the country's newly elected democratic leader, must turn decades of poverty and corruption around with the moral earnestness and wily compromises of liberation theology as his only weapon. Fat chance. Father Jeannot can talk about justice all he likes. But once the elitists start fighting back there isn't much he can do but fight fire with fire, thereby escalating the violence and handing the army (not to mention the tut-tutting Vatican) a handy rationalization for reinventing the dictatorial wheel.

The title of the novel relates not only to the political and economic life of the country but also to the dilemma of an older priest who narrates the story and finds himself in a personal no-win situation. Father Paul has heard the call and taken up the priesthood but, oh, those human longings and urgings, with even his dying mother telling him there is "no other life," not really, and so he might as well leave the priesthood and *get a life* before the lights go out permanently.

The depressing message is pitched, as I say, as a slowball right down the middle of the plate. An easy book to read—and knock. On the other hand, Updike's book is easier to miss but more satisfying once we connect. The story here concerns James Buchanan, the US President before Lincoln, a man normally damned by historians for fussing and fretting and saying his prayers while rage between northern abolitionists and southern slaveholders escalates to civil war. As Updike's narrator recounts the story, however, Buchanan is the consummate mediator, an accommodator in an age not given to accommodation, a statesperson unfairly maligned for making the best of a no-win situation.

Still another no-win situation is experienced by the narrator, a romantically wired history teacher from an all-female junior college in New

Hampshire. Should Professor Clayton leave his spouse ("The Queen of Disorder") and marry his mistress ("The Perfect Wife"), or think twice before wading through all that blood and guilt?

The characters in both novels demonstrate that there really isn't much, domestically or politically, that one can do. Updike, however, seems more reconciled with the prospect, the Protestant novelist recognizing that our lives, after all, are justified not by works but by faith. Which may explain why *Memories of the Ford Administration* says virtually nothing about the do-nothing President featured in the novel's title. Nothing and yet everything if the invisible motions of grace, rather than external deeds, determine finally the meaning and shape of history.

When Memories of the Ford Administration *was published in 1992, Canada was in danger at the time of breaking apart as a nation. Many people in the largely French Canadian province of Quebec wished to secede, and the rest of the country wasn't sure we wanted them to stay. The Prime Minister, Brian Mulroney, was desperately trying to hold the country together in the wake of a looming referendum. Despite his best conciliatory efforts, Mulroney drew blame from all sides. While I wasn't a member of his Conservative Party, I nevertheless found myself empathizing with the man. Then I read* Memories of the Ford Administration *and discovered an analogy between Updike's hero James Buchannan and our Canadian leader. Both statesmen were widely reviled for simply trying to hold their country together during a period of great civil unrest. I decided to send Mr. Mulroney a gift copy of Updike's novel. The book was delivered by hand by my local Member of Parliament who then sent me a picture of himself presenting the book to the PM. I in turn sent the picture to John Updike along with a copy of my review of* Memories. *In reply, Updike wrote:*

> "Dear Reverend McTavish: Good to hear from you again, my faithful [sic] Canadian fan. As to Mr. Mulroney, the thought that is clearly running through his head, his bemused expression tells us, is, 'God, the things politicians get asked to do! This is worse than kissing a fucking baby!!' I'll put it right in my album, which is years behind anyway."

I never heard back from Mr. Mulroney, but I continue to treasure Updike's letter in which he went on to say: "You write a great swinging review, in the style of a man born to it. Poor old solemn Brian Moore! Poor old convoluted Updike, summed up—rather accurately, I must say with 'Characters in both novels demonstrate there really isn't much, domestically or

politically, that one can do." Thanks for your intelligent and buoyant atten-
tions, and for the additional kind words in your letter. There's something
about me and Canadian clergymen, we really click."

CONVERSATIONS WITH JOHN UPDIKE

Edited by James Plath (University Press of Mississippi, 1994)
Reviewed by John McTavish in *Theology Today,* October 1995

Although he has published over forty books, the jury is still out on John
Updike. His fans, some of them literary critics of the highest order, claim
he is America's greatest living novelist and possibly the finest novelist of
the century. His detractors find such claims not only wildly overblown but
repellent. As a prose stylist, they say, Updike is all windup and no delivery;
as a moralist, he is so sexually obsessed as to border on the pornographic.

Updike himself does not appear to be overly concerned about the
verdict. He just wants to get the truth down on paper as accurately and
engagingly as possible, leaving others to test his report against their own
judgments. Updike is not looking for disciples but for critical, intelligent,
sensitive readers.

So why should this concern the readers of *Theology Today*? Because
John Updike is one of the very few contemporary literary figures with a
worldwide reputation who writes out of a distinctively Christian conviction. The man goes to church; he professes the Apostles' Creed; he prays to
God. If that is not noteworthy for a major literary figure in the '90s, then,
we're still living, Bonhoefferian catchphrases aside, in the religious '50s. But
in fact the world has moved on; and for many non-escapist readers living
in our secular world, John Updike is one of the few literary links with the
historic Christian faith.

His novels pry open the secret world of the minister (*A Month of Sundays*), explore the relation between theology and science (*Roger's Version*),
test the gospel against the pantheistic dreams of neo-Hinduism (*S.*), and
trace the outworkings of *das Nichtige* in the world (*The Witches of Eastwick*). His short stories offer parables of grace ("Pigeon Feathers"), calls
to faith ("The Lifeguard"), and celebrations of the church ("The Deacon").
His poems give us everything from testimonies to the resurrection ("Seven
Stanzas at Easter") to rhapsodies over God's lowliest creatures ("Mosquito").

And now, to satisfy our left-brain proclivities, James Plath has brought together thirty-two previously published interviews featuring Updike speaking about his craft and the religious sensibilities that inform it. These include Jane Howard's early *Life* magazine interview where Updike can be heard saying, vis-à-vis Barth's aphorism concerning the drowning man who cannot pull himself out by his own hair: "There is no help from within—without the supernatural the natural is a pit of horror. I believe that all problems are basically insoluble and that faith is a leap out of total despair." There's the BBC interview in which Updike states his literary creed: "I seem to see all my books in terms of children's drawing, they are all meant to be moral debates with the reader, and if they seem pointless—I'm speaking hopefully—it's because the reader has not been engaged in the debate." And in an interview conducted by *Episcopal Life*, Updike's rector is quoted as saying, "It's a joy to preach to him as a parishioner . . . John is a quiet and generous critic; he has a certain sparkle and twinkle in his eye so that you can tell when you're on. And when you're off, he masks it well."

Also included in this book are examples of the offbeat interview: the scoop given to the editor of the local high school paper; a piece involving a Japanese translator; and a conversation about the Rabbit novels with Phil Jackson, the coach at the time of the Chicago Bulls.

Interviews are hardly choice forums for Updike. His best work, his most real self, he staunchly maintains, is to be found in the writing and not the "milking" that goes on through interviews. Even so, here are thirty-two bucketsful all brimming with revelations. Harried Christians especially can take comfort from the sight of such an uncompromising literary artist buoyed by the reassurances of the gospel:

> I have never been an unbeliever, I guess you could say. Somehow it struck me quite early that the church, whatever its faults, was speaking to the real issues, and that without the church I didn't feel anybody would speak to the real issues—that is, the issues of being human, being alive. I've remained loyal to the church. Spires you see in a small town or a city do bring hope, and hope brings energy. It's certainly brought me energy.[1]

---

1. Plath, ed., *Conversations*, 259.

IN THE BEAUTY OF THE LILIES

By John Updike (Alfred A. Knopf, 1996)
Reviewed by John McTavish in *The United Church Observer*

In the spring of 1910, the Reverend Clarence Arthur Wilmot, a Presbyterian minister in Paterson, New Jersey, loses his faith while reading the works of a famous nineteenth-century atheist: "Ingersoll was quite right: the God of the Pentateuch was an absurd bully, barbarically thundering through a cosmos entirely misconceived. There is no god, nor should there be."

The consequences of Wilmot's spiritual collapse are traced through four generations of the minister's family in John Updike's seventeenth novel, *In the Beauty of the Lilies.*

The first consequence: Rev. Wilmot resigns from the ministry (after a tussle with his ecclesiastical superiors who can't see why Clarence should quit) and plunges his family into social grief.

Clarence's sensitive son Teddy "stops dead" going to church after his father dies, unable to forgive the God who would deny Teddy's father the sign that he so desperately needed.

Teddy's daughter, Essie, is given the gift of faith thanks to her church-going mother. But Essie ends up, not so much a believer as an object of religious devotion: a movie star. And Essie's son, Clark, raised in an almost totally secular environment, becomes ripe for a fanatical religious experience.

All four Wilmots are good people, not a mean streak in any of them. There's just that little mustard seed of faith missing, that tiny hole in the human heart.

Does it matter?

Updike is writing novels and not sermons, so *Lilies* doesn't provide a clear answer. Nevertheless, one wonders, at the end of this story, whether a great deal more than Clarence Wilmot's faith wasn't lost on that hot spring day in 1910.

In the process of dramatizing the soul-stunting consequences of unbelief, Updike shows the American Century unfolding from the days when people called each other "kid," "kiddo," "squirt," "honey-pie," frequented soda fountains, and cranked up the Victrola to listen to songs like "Peg O' My Heart" and "When the Red, Red Robin Comes Bob, Bob, Bobbin' Along."

The social and political upheavals of the century are seen impinging upon the relatively isolated American mind. ("That stupid Hitler," the teenage Essie thinks, watching a newsreel in a movie theatre in the '30s, "with his tiny mustache saying something angrily you couldn't understand.")

The gods and goddesses of the silver screen—Gloria Swanson, Deanna Durbin, Clark Gable, Marlon Brando—are seen shaping the American soul.

Lilies delights and entertains as well as challenges and probes.

And for once the squeamish reader doesn't need to worry about Updike's penchant for describing with brutal honesty the sexual heart of America. I mean, things were pretty tame in Clarence's day and even in Teddy's. And while they heat up a bit with Essie, harried movie stars aren't as sexy as you might think.

No, the real scandal in *Lilies* isn't the presence of sex but the absence of faith, rendering the sky overhead for all these nice folk in the Wilmot clan cloudy and gray.

COLUMNIST PREDICTS NOBEL WINNER

By John McTavish, *Muskoka Advance* Column, Sept. 27, 1998

Roger Skunk is a little animal in one of John Updike's short stories.[2] None of the other woodland creatures will play with Roger because he smells so bad. So the skunk goes to see the wise old owl who directs Roger to a wizard who, for a price, waves his magic wand and says the magic word.

Bingo! Roger is smelling like roses. All the other animals now gather round and invite him to join in their games of tag and baseball and hockey and pick-up sticks.

A happy little skunk runs home that night only to have his mommy wrinkle her nose and say, "What's that awful smell?"

And Roger says, "It's me Mommy. I smell like roses."

She says, "Who made you smell like that?"

And he says, "The wizard," and she says, "Well, of all the nerve. You come with me and we're going right back to that awful wizard."

The wizard's spell is soon reversed and Roger returns home with his mommy who hugs him and tells him that he smells like her little baby skunk again and she loves him very much.

2. The short story titled "Should Wizard Hit Mommy?" was originally published in *The New Yorker* on October 4, 1959, and later included in *Pigeon Feathers* (1962), *Olinger Stories* (1964), *The Early Stories* (2003), and the Library of America's *John Updike: The Collected Stories* (2013).

Updike's narrator is telling a bedtime tale to his three-year-old daughter who protests that Roger isn't allowed to smell like roses any more.

"But Daddy."

"What?"

"Then did the other little animals run away?"

"No, because eventually they got used to the way he was and did not mind it at all."

"What's evenshiladee?"

"In a little while."

John Updike's stories are often filled with symbolism and hidden messages. They entertain but also quietly invite us to *think* about our lives. The story about Roger Skunk is a case in point. Among other things, it reminds us that if we remain true to our deepest selves we may well give off a disagreeable skunk-like odor. On the other hand, if we conform, buckle under, go with the crowd, we may find approval and acceptance, but we'll disappoint Mommy. That is to say, we'll disappoint those who know us best and care the most about the expression of our deepest selves.

I once met John Updike's real-life mother. She told me that this story was her favorite among her son's works. Clearly, she saw herself as the *Mommy* who wanted her little boy to remain true to his own best self.

He has.

In almost 50 books since he first became famous in 1960 with the publication of *Rabbit, Run,* John Updike has been dramatizing the physical urgencies and spiritual anxieties of middle-class America. His books give off the skunk-like odor of realism with their lyrical but brutally honest portrayals of human behavior.

He has his critics but more and more people seem to be recognizing Updike's literary genius.

The highest expression of that recognition in international circles is the Nobel Prize. Though the selection is often skewed by shameless cultural biases, I don't think Updike, however white and male and religious and American he may be, can be ignored much longer.

In fact, I'll predict right now that next week John Updike will win the 1998 Nobel Prize in literature.

And if not, well . . . evenshiladee.

The above article which rashly predicted that John Updike would win the Noble Prize in Literature in 1998, appeared in our local Muskoka paper on

September 27, 1998. Alas, the Swedish jurors gave the nod that year to Jose Saramago. But read the last chapter of Bech at Bay *and one realizes that, prizes aside, Updike had the last laugh on this delicate subject.*

JOHN UPDIKE AND RELIGION: THE SENSE OF THE SACRED AND THE MOTIONS OF GRACE

Edited by James Yerkes (Eerdmans, 1999)
Reviewed by John McTavish in *Theology Today*

> *Interviewer: Let's talk about Barth a little more. Obviously, you do acknowledge your debt to Barth, saying that at one point in your life his theology seemed to be your whole support. Could you say something about what elements of the Barthian position particularly attracted you?*
>
> *Updike: I think it was the frank supernaturalism and the particularity of his position, so unlike that of Tillich and the entire group of liberal theologians—and you scratch most ministers, at least in the East, and you find a liberal.*[3]

English professors, you don't need to scratch. They wear their liberalism on their sleeves, eloquently smudging the question of whether, as Updike put it in his 1976 interview with Jeff Campbell, "it really *was* so, that there was something within us that would not die." These same scholars, however, can't help noticing—and often appreciating—Updike's literary pyrotechnics in the fifty-one substantial books that he has written. Still, what to do with all that "frank supernaturalism"?

Give James Yerkes credit for meeting the issue head on. Yerkes, a professor of religion and philosophy at Moravian College, has rounded up ten English professors along with three professors of religion, and pressed them to write about the role that religion plays in Updike's work. Yerkes himself contributes an essay in which he describes how the religious dimension manifests itself in the self-consciousness of Updike's characters, noting the various ways in which it becomes the locale, but not the source, of the breakthrough of faith, revelation, and God. Experiential fiction naturally mitigates against theological precision, but Updike's patented realism gives the Christian faith, when it does break through, all the more believability. "This," says Yerkes, echoing the Jack Nicholson film, "is as good as it gets."

3. Plath, ed., *Conversations*, 102.

Several contributors tackle the religious themes in Updike's seemingly most religiously offbeat novels. The Brazilean scholar Dilvo I. Ristoff, for example, shows Updike exploring the Christian paradox of life in death in *Brazil* through the romance that a young black man (turned white) strikes up with a young white woman (turned black). And David Malone (who alone among the contributors draws out the allegorical depths in Updike) argues that the latest low of moral decrepitude registered by Updike's hero in *Toward the End of Time* proves that Updike "is less interested in portraying the holiness of a saint or the depravity of a sinner than he is in depicting the more densely-popular territory occupied by people pierced by longings for both extremes but wholly committed to neither."

Stephen Webb's essay, "Writing as a Reader of Karl Barth," notes the formal similarities of the two titans, particularly how they both eschew apologetics in the hope that the truth will speak for itself:

> Just as Barth rejected modern trends in theology as faddish and thought that the most radical thing a theologian could do would be to ground theology in the church, Updike follows the apparently traditional but really radical path of a descriptive prose that exercises the human freedom of creativity without thereby negating the reality of worldly constraints on that freedom.[4]

James Plath, whose book *Conversations with John Updike* is frequently quoted by the contributors, himself contributes an essay showing Updike implicitly conversing with Nathanial Hawthorne's *The Scarlet Letter* in the demonic-riddled *The Witches of Eastwick*. Plath contends that evil here "is more than just a welcome diversion from the boredom and routine of everyday goodness. It's edifying." Yerkes makes the same slippery point: "One does not sin in order to produce goodness, which is what genuine antinomianism means, but one does indeed learn a lot about goodness in sinning that would not be understood without it."

The most lucid treatment of the religious dimension in Updike's fiction remains, in my judgment, Alice and Kenneth Hamilton's pioneering work *The Elements of John Updike*. Still, *John Updike and Religion* is an important and helpful book: important because it updates criticism on the work of an author who, as the smoke clears, stands virtually alone with his bracing interaction of realistic fiction and solid theology; and helpful because the contributors, while wise in the ways of the academic world, do not grind unpalatable ideological axes.

4. See Yerkes, ed., *John Updike and Religion*, 149.

A MONTH OF SUNDAYS

By John Updike (Knopf, 1975)
Reviewed by Kenneth Hamilton in The United Church Observer

John Updike's latest novel is a shocker. Updike's wife is reported to have said that reading her husband's novel *Couples* made her feel smothered in pubic hair. Those who found the explicit sex-scenes in *Couples* too much for them will find *A Month of Sundays* even more distasteful. Not only are the descriptions of sexual encounters just as frequent and detailed. The narrator of these exploits is a clergyman.

The Rev. Thomas Marshfield has been turned out of his (Lutheran?) church for repeated adultery with members of his congregation and with other women who came to him for counselling. He has been sent by his bishop to a motel in a western state for a "rest-cure". There, in the company of other disgraced clergymen, he is under the care of the formidable Ms. Prynne for 31 days. Ms. Prynne's rules are: writing ego-confessions in the morning; golf and sight-seeing in the afternoon; cards in the evening; and no Bible-reading or talk about religion anytime. Marshfield duly sets down the story of the events leading to his dismissal, so that it unfolds over the month of his enforced stay. His "cure" is problematic, since on the very last day he apparently seduces Ms. Prynne herself!

Material less likely to appeal to church-going Christians would be hard to imagine. Many outside the churches, too, will find the novel offensive.

Nevertheless, Updike is himself a Christian and a churchgoer. He calls his novel "a testament for our times". While he sees his first duty as a novelist to be that of reporting objectively on contemporary manners and morals, he has never been able to keep out of the picture his own Christian convictions. Increasingly, also, his novels have come to be parables in which a realistic story-line serves to conceal only barely a statement about modern man's relation to his eternal destiny. In *A Month of Sundays* he speaks more openly than before about Christian faith being the sole solution to North American desperation and collapse of morale.

There are four sermons in the novel. Marshfield is a disciple of Karl Barth (as is Updike), and he believes the proclamation of the Word of God to be the heart of the Church's task on earth. As each Sunday comes round, he drops his daily stint of confession and prepares a discourse on a biblical text: hence—a month of Sundays. He has not left the ministry, and he considers that he has still the cure of souls (his own included). His sermons are on the treatment of adultery in the Old and New Testament, the miracles of Christ, the importance of the desert in the Bible, and the Resurrection.

The sermons have no obvious connection with the unfolding of the story of the amorous adventures that brought about Marshfield's "fall" at the age of 41. Yet they actually dovetail into the episodes described in his ego-confessions and show his gradual self-awareness of the reasons for his fall. On the first day he had written lightly, "In *my* diagnosis, I suffer from nothing less virulent than the human condition." By the end of the month he has discovered that this statement was indeed, quite literally, a damning one; for it has failed to take faithfully the amazing miracle of the power of God's salvation through Christ. As St. Paul declares, the man who preaches to others may well become a castaway himself. This disgraced cleric has never doubted the truth of the Word, but he has had to discover it afresh through finding it true for his own life. This discovery made, he can then preach to his fellow-countrymen. His fourth sermon, he is surprised to find, carries on its final page the pencilled note in another hand, "Yes—at last, a sermon that could be preached."

As with all Updike's works, this novel contains an intricate pattern of symbolism. In his previous novel *Rabbit Redux*, Updike speaks of the expanding desert, both material and spiritual, that is threatening America. Marshland, the man who continues in the Nixon era to believe in the Word, is by his very name an individual who resists being assimilated to the spreading wasteland; though, equally, he is not "good ground" for receiving the seed of the Word. The motel to which he has been sent lies on the edge of a desert. It is shaped like an Omega. So it is The Last Resort for failed priests of the Christian mysteries, since from it they can contemplate the final state of a world deprived of the water of life, the nourishment supplied by the sacrament.

These are a few of the themes in Updike's novel, whose enigmatic ending is a symbol of Marshland's repentance that enables him to accept the world as God's gift. This complex parable teaches that faith is not the same as morality (though the two ought not to be parted) and that only the miracle of grace revealed in the unbelievable yet actual event of the Resurrection of Christ can bring 20th Century man to his senses. But will any one look away from all the pubic hair long enough to see what else Updike is showing us?

The above review stirred a small controversy in the United Church of Canada. The head office of the denomination had a bookstore in Toronto on the first floor of the building in which the denomination's national offices were located. William Bird, the Manager of the bookstore, was so impressed with Hamilton's Observer review that he ordered several copies of the novel and gave them prominent window display. Finally a best seller, it must have seemed, that sounded religious! Sales of A Month of Sundays *immediately took off only to be followed by a blizzard of complaints. So indignant in fact were the complainers that Mr. Bird finally had to remove the book from the store. The United Church is a very liberal-minded denomination. Even so, its members were not ready in 1975 for the sexual realism that interacts with the theological themes in* A Month of Sundays.

ROGER'S VERSION

By John Updike (Knopf, 1986)
Reviewed by John McTavish in *Theology Today*

A Month of Sundays found John Updike offering an updated version of Nathaniel Hawthorne's famous love triangle in *The Scarlet Letter* from the perspective of the adulterous minister. *Roger's Version* retells the nineteenth-century classic from the perspective of the cuckolded husband.

The new novel also offers John Updike's response to the modern-day love affair between science and theology. Recently, Canada's national newspaper *The Globe and Mail* threw light on this interdisciplinary romance, crediting some of the latest cosmological studies with giving modern-day skeptics a glimpse of "something inexplicable, unsystematised, irreducible to dates and history, but a kind of creator all the same: *God*, for lack of a better word."[5] This is basically the thesis that *Roger's Version* examines in the context of its modern-day dramatization of Hawthorian love politics.

Roger Lambert, the protagonist of *Version*, is a doctor of divinity who teaches courses in early Christian heresy in a New England seminary where students titter at the mention of "the revelationist severity of Karl Barth," Roger's own, he confesses, "rascally pet." Dale Kohler, a graduate student in computer science, approaches Professor Lambert with a request for grant money to help prove God's existence with computer-generated cosmological statistics. Roger agrees to help, not so much because he is intrigued by

5. *The Globe and Mail*, "Ending Up with God," June 21, 1997.

the student's quixotic venture into the unpromising waters of natural theology as that he is interested in Dale's friendship with Roger's sexually enticing niece. Roger, in other words, is thoroughly, even, if you like, lamentably human, even as his view of God is wholeheartedly divine. That is, he takes the Barthian position that God laughs at all our human towers of Babel and speaks to us in God's own self-revelatory Word, refusing to be treated as an object whose existence is dependent on the latest findings of computer science, or popularizations of the same in one of Canada's leading newspapers.

Dale Kohler ends up seducing Roger's wife just as Roger Chillingworth's wife is seduced by a theological animal in the original Hawthorian tale. But at a deeper level, Kohler seduces, or at least attempts to seduce, the gospel itself by forcing the revealed Word of God to conform to the theologically alien presuppositions of natural theology. Here, however, he is foiled by a real scientist whom he encounters at a cocktail party in Roger's home. Professor Kriegman wastes no time in crushing Dale's seductive thesis. Kriegman first cites a parody of the teleological argument that appeared in a recent magazine:

> A helluva funny piece . . . in which a bunch of rotifers are imagined in learned conversation concerning why their puddle had to be exactly the way it was—temperature, alkalinity, mud at the bottom sheltering methane-producing bacteria, all the rest of it —it was clever as hell like I said—and from the fact that if any of these things were even a little bit different—if the heat necessary to vaporize water was any lower, for example, or the freezing temperature of water any higher—this Little Puddlian Philosophical Society, I think it was called, but you can check that when you look it up, deduced that the whole operation was providential and obviously the universe existed to produce their little puddle and them! That's more or less what you're trying to tell me, young fella, except you ain't no rotifer![6]

Kriegman then goes on to demolish the cosmological argument that would have us believe that nothing can ever come from nothing and so there had to be something, some kind of supernatural presence or power behind the advent of all things. The scientist, however, points out that, no, even in a total vacuum there is still potential geometry. "A kind of dust," he says, "of structureless points" swirling around and eventually configuring and knotting and—bingo!—the seed of the universe pops into being: "Out of

---

6. Updike, *Roger's Version*, 299.

nothing. Out of nothing and brute geometry, laws that can't be otherwise, nobody handed them to Moses, nobody had to. Once you've got that seed, that little itty-bitty mustard seed—ka-*boom*! Big Bang is right around the corner."[7]

Dale protests, only to have Kriegman steamroll over him again, this time picturing the origin of things mathematically. The scientist reminds Dale that zero is composed of one and minus one with minus one being nothing but plus one moving backward in time until—bingo again!—the dust of Borel points gives birth to time and time in turn gives birth to the dust of points.

Frankly, I have no idea what the scientist is talking about here. Even Kriegman acknowledges that it may be nothing more than "glorified bullshit." Nevertheless, the professor says enough to indicate that the jury of cosmologists is still out on whether anything besides blind chance is needed to bring about something from nothing in the act of creation.[8] And that leaves Dale, indeed it leaves all of us, with nothing but speculation upon which to base our faith convictions. Unless, that is, God is willing and able to speak a self-convincing, self-disclosing Word.

The concluding lines of *Roger's Version* offer a tantalizing hint that the Word of God in the power of which God *does* speak, remains a living, dynamic force in our lives. Roger's wife, Esther (secular shades of Hester), has been an agnostic living almost entirely in the aesthetic realm. But suddenly Esther would seem to despair of that realm and take a Kierkegaardian leap into faith. She not only breaks off her affair with the computer scientist but announces that she is going back to church.

---

7. Ibid., 303.

8. Jim Holt once asked Updike to comment on the scenarios that physicists have recently come up with that would allow something to emerge spontaneously out of nothing in accordance with quantum laws. "But then, of course," Holt added, "you're faced with the mystery: Where are these laws written? And what gives them the power to command the void?" Updike replied: "Also, the laws amount to a funny way of saying, 'Nothing equals something. QED!' One opinion I've encountered is that, since getting from nothing to something involves time, and time didn't exist before there was something, the whole question is a meaningless one that we should stop asking ourselves. It's beyond our intellectual limits as a species . . . I have trouble even believing—and this will offend you—the standard scientific explanation of how the universe rapidly grew from *nearly* nothing. Just think of it. The notion that this planet and all the stars we see, and many thousands of times more than those we see—that all this was once bonded in a point with the size of, what, a period or a grape? How, I ask myself, could that possibly be? And that said, I sort of move on. . . . The whole idea of inflationary expansion seems sort of put forward on a smile and a shoeshine . . ." (cf. Holt, *Why Does the World Exist?*, 249).

Roger is amazed: "Why would you do a ridiculous thing like that?" Esther replies, "Oh—to annoy you."[9]

Kierkegaard often claimed that the gospel was an annoying scandal. How "ridiculous" to pin one's hopes in life to the ancient God-man and the unlikely community of faith that gathers in his name! Yet this would seem to be not only Esther's but Updike's own version of the way things are. What John Updike once called a "highly intellectually unhealthy leap into faith"[10] remains a scandal, not only to secularists, not only to spiritualists, but even to Word-proclaiming, natural theology-despising Barthians like Roger in *Roger's Version*. In the last analysis, what are all the scandals of life compared to the scandal of faith?

S.

By John Updike (Knopf, 1988)
Reviewed by John McTavish in *Theology Today*

S. is the third novel in John Updike's trilogy that reworks the theme of Nathaniel Hawthorne's nineteenth-century classic *The Scarlet Letter*. The S. in the title is the signature of Sarah Price Worth, a New England housewife who joins a friend's yoga group for exercise and ends up getting hooked on Eastern spirituality. Just as Hester Prynne left Dr. Chillingworth for a sexual-religious experience in the forests of Puritan America, so Sarah leaves her pricey, chillingly philandering doctor husband for a religious-sexual experience in Forrest, Arizona. Entering an ashram led by a charismatic Hindu known as the Arhat, Sarah "there mingles with the other *sannyasins* (pilgrims) in the difficult attempt to subdue ego and achieve *moksha* (salvation, release from illusion).[11] Sarah finds herself working like a dog in the commune and embroiled in dogfights of another kind at dinnertime. Factor in the hair-pulling and teeth-smashing that sometimes takes place during the dynamic-meditative sessions, and it becomes apparent that religious life in modern-day America is no less demanding in its own way than it was for the Puritans.

Nevertheless, the rewards are considerable. The Arhat himself glows with an aura to which, Sarah assures friends back home, the posters cannot

9. Ibid., 329.

10. Kakutani, "Turning Sex and Guilt into an American Epic," 21.

11. Updike, *S.*, dust jacket.

do justice. When he rides by in his limousine, "even at thirty miles an hour," the guru generates a peace that Sarah finds "unbelievable." And the Arhat's message is at once simple and profound. As Sarah describes it in one of her letters: *"As lonk as sere isse iggo, the happiness*—I really can't do his accent, he has the strangest, longest 's's, different from any sound we make—*sub happiness fliesss avay. Like sub pet birt and sub pet catt, zey cannot exists in ze same room. Ven sub Master doess nut preside, sub vun eatss se utter"* (41).

Sarah draws increasingly closer to the Master, eventually becoming his private secretary and finally his lover (or at least one of them). But then she discovers that the "Arhat is really Arthur Steinmetz from Watertown, Massachusetts." Watertown, of all places, thinks Sarah. The Arhat, or "A rat," as the locals insist on pronouncing it, is now forced by Sarah to bare his soul. Arthur Steinmetz, it turns out, is not so different from Arthur Dimmesdale, or for that matter, any of us. Certainly he's just as scared as the next person about death, and anxious to find in religion not only heavenly consolation but an earthly opportunity to squeeze whatever human comfort and joy he can get out of life before the lights go out forever.

Updike is clearly having fun telling this story but that doesn't mean he is mocking Arthur. On point of principle, John Updike refuses to mock any of his literary creations. Arthur, to be sure, is on the make. Nevertheless, there is a quest here for faith, for something, *anything* that can fill the hollow scared hole in the heart that has bedevilled Arthur since his secularized childhood. Those who laugh at the Arthur Steimetzes of this world may well be themselves subjects for tears.

Even so, at the end of the day, the reader can't help wondering whether all the strange gods and exotic religious techniques that Arthur discovers and appropriates for himself through his reading of Alan Watts and Krishnamurti and Salinger and Ginsberg and the Upanishads add up to anything more than Calvin's factory of idols churning in the human mind. In the language of "the revelationist severity" of Karl Barth, Roger Lambert's "rascally pet" in *Roger's Version,* one wonders whether the whole of Oriental mysticism, so popular today in the West, is anything more than the religious man's perennial attempt "to justify and sanctify himself before a capricious and arbitrary picture of God."[12]

On the other hand, if the road to enlightenment doesn't lead through mystical religion, where does it lead? Updike has already answered that

12. Cf. Karl Barth's chapter "The Revelation of God as the Abolition of Religion" in *Church Dogmatics,* Volume I, Part 2, 280.

question in *A Month of Sundays*. "Away with personhood!" cries the Reverend Thomas Marshfield. "Mop up spilt religion! Let us have it in its original stony jars or not at all!"[13] Spilt religion, watered-down religion (religion from *Watertown*), however beautiful or refined, cannot, in the end, help. What is needed is religion in its original stony jars, religion in the "clay jars" that hold "the treasure of the gospel," religion that bears witness to "the light of the knowledge of the glory of God in the face of Jesus Christ." (2 Cor 4:7)

This is not an argument, of course, but a confession of faith. Updike makes the confession not directly but indirectly, so that his fiction never tips over into religious propaganda. John Updike, after all, is primarily a novelist and not an evangelist. But as a novelist he still remains true to himself, and that self has been shaped in large measure by the Christian faith. Updike once observed:

> Blankness is not emptiness. We may skate upon an intense radiance we do not see because we see nothing else. And in fact there is a color, a quiet but tireless goodness that things at rest, like a brick wall or a small stone, seem to affirm.[14]

Perhaps the literary blankness in John Updike's fiction can speak to the theological emptiness that characterizes so much of our postmodern culture, whether in the religious East or the secular West. This, however, means appreciating not just the lines in Updike's stories but the images and myths that inform those lines and give them the weight and significance of—allegory.

AMERICANA AND OTHER POEMS

By John Updike (Alfred A. Knopf, 2001)
Reviewed by John McTavish in *The United Church Observer*

Care to read a scary poem? Try "Icarus" in this latest collection of John Updike's poetry. Published just before the terrorist events of 2001, "Icarus" virtually predicts the horror show:

> O.K., you are sitting in an airplane and
> the person in the seat next to you is a sweaty, swarthy

13. Updike, *A Month of Sundays*, 25.
14. Updike, *Assorted Prose*, 186.

gentleman of Middle Eastern origin
whose carry-on luggage consists of a bulky black briefcase.

The man says his briefcase contains his "life's work." He doesn't want to talk.
He keeps looking at his watch and closing his eyes in prayer . . .
However, the danger passes and nothing happens. This time.

But the possibility of impossibility will keep drawing us back
to . . .

Who says poets can't be prophets?

Twenty-seven of the sixty-two poems in *Americana* are not only
strong and lyrical but finely shaped sonnets. And almost all of these poems
are blessedly *lucid*.

There's also a wistful, valedictorian mood in many of these poems.
John Updike reached the biblically allotted three score and ten last month.
This collection shows him taking one last look around and telling us how
he feels about it all.

In "61 And Some" Updike asks:

How many more, I must ask myself
such perfect ends of Augusts will I witness?—
the schoolgirls giggling in their months-old tans . . .

"In the Cemetery High Above Shillington" finds the poet visiting the cemetery of his hometown and letting the tombstones speak to him of people
who filled his childhood with magic and love:

Never shall I lie here in trimmed green silence,
among the corners of the resting place . . .

He takes us into his psyche (exotic) and carcass (ailing):

Used bodies—who wants them
save Death, the great rag-and-bone man?

There is a lot of depression in life as we grow through and out of it. However, the poet also shares his consolations with us. In "A Sound Heard Early
on the Morning of Christ's Nativity" the thump of the newspaper on the
porch carries a gentle reminder that the world into which Christ was born,
for all the horror, is not always wrapped in a "Godforsaken gloom."

In "Jesus and Elvis" both the similarities and the differences are noted between the "lovely young man" who lives in his music, and the young man, "reckless and cool as a lily," who lives that we may all live.

Finally, "Religious Consolation" notes the bizarre, even laughable streak in religions. He finally asks who needs all these crazy manifestations of the spirit world, and answers:

> We do. We need more worlds. This one will fail.

Americana's attractive book cover displays a stamped yellow envelope from Updike's town, Beverley Farms, Massachusetts, dated November 1, 2000, and set on a powder soft blue background. The envelope in real life would seem to have carried Updike's invaluable manuscript to the publisher.

And now to you and me.

VILLAGES

By John Updike (Knopf, 2004)
Reviewed by John McTavish in the *Huntsville Forester*

Don't judge a book by its cover, people say. Yet why not? Covers often tell us a lot about books. Certainly the cover of *Villages* tells us a lot about John Updike's twenty-first novel. It's a remarkably beautiful cover, displaying a number of women, some young, most middle aged, but all of them real women and not stylized sex objects, relaxing in a Turkish spa. The sensuality is honest and yet alluring, a digitally refreshed version, it turns out, of Jean Auguste Dominique Ingres's 1862 classic, *The Turkish Bath*.[15]

Villages, to quote the summary of the plot on the fly leaf, "follows its hero, Owen Mackenzie, from his birth in the semi-rural Pennsylvania town of Willow to his retirement in the rather geriatric community of Haskells Cross, Massachusetts. In between these two settlements comes Middle Falls, Connecticut, where Owen, an early computer programmer, founds with a partner, Ed Mervine, the successful firm of E-O Data."

We learn a lot about the development of the computer in this novel. We also learn a lot about Owen's growing relations with the opposite sex, the modern versions of the lovely women pictured on the cover cavorting in a Turkish spa. Owen's sexual education in life, so vividly described in the

---

15. The original hangs today in the Louvre, where it was finally accepted after a gift of the painting had twice been turned down.

novel, is likely to trigger comparisons with the reader's own education in this vital if rarely discussed field.

Updike, for his part, doesn't hold anything back in any of the chapters of the book. His involvement with developments in computer hardware is described in the same exacting detail as is his development in those chapters dedicated to village sex.

And vice versa.

On the whole, Owen Mackenzie leads a charmed life. Yet when his luck runs out, as it does in "lucky number" chapter 13, it really runs out. Still, Owen manages somehow to wiggle out of the mess. As a child in Sunday school, he had been taught that suicide was the ultimate sin. This is certainly one sin that Owen never commits. He never kills himself with guilt or remorse let alone with a gun. Instead he takes the gift of life and, for better or for worse, in good times and bad, runs with it.

Which brings us back to the cover. One could look at this cover, I suppose, and see it as little more than a pornographic celebration of unbridled sexuality. In fact, when my wife and I were visiting Stratford, Ontario, shortly after *Villages* had been published earlier this fall, I noticed that it was discreetly tucked away on one of the shelves at the back of the store. There was no way the leading bookstore in a town hosting the internationally renowned Shakespeare Festival was going to include in its display window a book with such a smutty cover! Yet what is smutty about this cover or anything inside this book unless life itself must be deemed, in its most intimate moments, somehow smutty?

TERRORIST

By John Updike (Knopf, 2006)
Reviewed by John McTavish in *Theology Today*

John Updike's nervy new novel, *Terrorist*, tells the story of eighteen-year-old Ahmad Ashmawy Mulloy and how his devotion to God draws him into a terrorist plot in the United States. The novel hit the bookstores just as seventeen young Muslims (led apparently by another Ahmad—twenty-one-year-old Fahmi Ahmad from Toronto) were being charged with planning a massive, real-life terrorist attack in Canada.

Updike's fictional Ahmad is first glimpsed in the menacing corridors of his inner-city New Jersey high school. Ahmad is a bright, sensitive young man looking for meaning and purpose in life and disgusted by America's godless, sex-crazy, pleasure-loving ways. A thuggish teenager called Tylenol (some pain killer) is soon harassing the boy: "Hey, you. Arab." But Joryleen Grant ("Little Miss Popular") likes Ahmad and invites him to come and hear her sing at her black evangelical church. Ahmad warily accepts, and the service turns out to be a surprisingly positive experience. A healing sermon invites the spiritual children of Israel to face down the sons of Anak, those humanity-threatening giants that make us feel like grasshoppers, with faith in "the Lord of us all." But when Tylenol learns the next day that Ahmad followed Joryleen to her church, he throws a jealous boyfriend hissy fit, and the young Muslim comes close to being beaten to a pulp. "You all faggots, man," is Tylenol's parting shot as the bell summons the students to class.

Ahmad, we soon learn, has been studying the Qur'an at a local mosque with a dangerously fundamentalist imam. Yet where else can he go for spiritual nourishment, let alone acceptance and support? The novel helps us feel the remarkable moral strength and religious purity of the Muslim faith. But it also shows an intolerant streak and hatred for infidels that, in Updike's eyes, runs through the Qur'an. "Poor Jack," the wife of Ahmad's guidance teacher is heard saying at one point to her sister on the phone, "he's been knocking himself out to get this boy out of the grip of his mosque. They're like Baptist fundamentalists, only worse, because they don't care if they die."

The negative streak here eventually manifests itself in Ahmad's behavior, leading the high school teacher to ask, "Did the imam ever suggest that a bright boy like you, in a diverse and tolerant society like this one, needs to confront a variety of viewpoints?" But Ahmad has an answer: "Shaikh Rashid . . . feels that such a relativistic approach trivializes religion, implying that it doesn't much matter. You believe this, I believe that, we all get along—that's the American way." For Ahmad the American way is a slippery slope leading to debauchery and despair.

It's hard to argue the point while reading this novel. Lewdness and lasciviousness are everywhere, not to mention all the consumeristic, junk-food, gas-guzzling nonsense that cares not a blessed fig for what these excesses are doing to our bodies and souls and the planet itself. "America," Ahmad observes, "is paved solid with fat and tar." It's more than possible to see why such a morally earnest, religiously passionate young man might be drawn to the logic of terrorism. Get rid of the garbage once and for all in one huge, cleansing, explosive action. That's wrong, of course—tragically, monstrously wrong. But Updike's point seems to be that it is not enough for us merely to condemn the wrong. We need to understand where people like Ahmad are coming from—and how we may be part of the problem.

One of the epigraphs in this novel is a passage from the book of Jonah, the biblical myth in which Jonah is asked to bring the message of God's judgment and mercy to the people of Ninevah. He refuses, escaping on a ship only to be thrown overboard, swallowed by a whale, and spewed out again upon dry land. This time round Jonah obeys and delivers God's message. But the Ninevites repent of all things and end up enjoying God's mercy. This annoys Jonah so much that he voices the prayer that Updike uses as one of the epigraphs for his novel:

> "And now, O Lord, please take my life from me, for it is better for me to die than to live." And the LORD said, "Is it right for you to be angry?" (Jonah 4:3–4)

The terrorists would seem to be the Ninevites of our day. Clearly, they need to repent. But is it right for us to be angry? Updike isn't condoning their murderous behavior. But maybe there's a reason why the Third World is sore at us. Maybe we should try to understand that reason and do something about it, instead of simply filling the air with angry rhetoric.[16] This is the message that this elegant, hard-hitting page-turner would seem to be asking us to consider.

P. S. The Chip Kidd cover for *Terrorist* shows a man (a terrorist?) fleeing from the scene. Yet turn the cover upside down and the hunted suddenly becomes a shadow of the hunter. So many of Updike's covers are not only aesthetically pleasing but small interpretive masterpieces!

---

16. In an interview with *Time*, Updike spoke about "the decline of America," and "without being any less of an American myself, the piggishness of us all. Clearly there's going to be a global crisis in the amount of petroleum in the world. There's only so much, and there are more people wanting it. No wonder the Third World is sore at us. We're spending the limited resources about as fast as we can. Our solution is to waste it all and then punt and see what we might do next." See Grossman, "Old Master in a Brave New World," June 5, 2006, 42.

UPDIKE

By Adam Begley (Harper, 2014)
Reviewed by John McTavish in *The United Church Observer*

Half a century ago, a college friend handed me a copy of John Updike's racy novel *Rabbit, Run* with the hope that the book would disabuse me of any notions I had of becoming a minister. Alas, the novel succeeded only in bowling me over with its elegant prose and eye-popping realism.

Granted, the ministers in *Rabbit, Run* are terrible role models, one an exasperatingly wishy-washy liberal and the other a painfully unbending conservative. But I eventually realized that Updike was using them to illustrate how the motions of grace can reach us through the most unlikely channels.

A few years later *Couples* appeared, and *Time* magazine ran a cover story on the chronicler of the pill-inspired sexual revolution in Middle America. I now learned that while Updike had been composing *Rabbit, Run*, he was also experiencing an overwhelming fear of death that he managed to survive, he told *Time*, "only by clinging to the stern, neo-orthodox theology of Switzerland's Karl Barth."

I read these words and blinked, amazed that a writer of Updike's sophistication was confessing such indebtedness to the leading theologian of the day. Usually one's cultural heroes have no interest in faith, or at least no interest in sharing it.

John Updike died in 2009 at age seventy-six, leaving behind over sixty books: novels, short stories, poetry, literary criticism. He never won the Nobel Prize in literature, but readers who enjoy him often can't find high enough words of praise. The British novelist Ian McEwan recently extolled the intelligence of Updike's sentences, "with that odd little hard-to-define spring. Who else does that? Shakespeare, Milton and many, many other poets. Bellow does. Calvino. There's no end of them, really. But never so copiously as Updike. One can open him at random and find some felicity on the page."

And now the first major biography of the writer has appeared in Adam Begley's *Updike*. Riveting, elegant, lucid, Begley's book takes us through Updike's life in tandem with his writings, reminding us that the celebrated author was a churchgoing Christian whose faith is reflected in his work. "Surrounded by disbelief more or less politely concealed, he refused to play along," Begley writes.

Raised Lutheran in Pennsylvania, the grandson of a Presbyterian minister, Updike joined the Congregational church as a compromise with his first wife, who was Unitarian, and later worshipped as an Episcopalian with his second wife. The rituals of church gave him great comfort: "What could be more delightful, more unexpected than to enter a venerable and lavishly scaled building kept warm and clean for use one or two hours a week and to sit and stand in unison and sing and recite creeds and petitions that are like paths worn smooth in the raw terrain of our hearts?" Updike's narrator muses in the short story "Packed Dirt, Churchgoing, a Dying Cat, a Traded Car."

At the same time, faith was more than a pleasurable habit for Updike. It was an antidote to "existential terror," as Begley puts it. Updike himself admitted as much in his memoir *Self-Consciousness*: "Perhaps there are two kinds of people: those for whom nothingness is no problem, and those for whom it is an insuperable problem, an outrageous cancellation rendering every other concern, from mismatching socks to nuclear holocaust, negligible."

For Updike, this horror of nonexistence could only be subdued through belief. "The core of his religious conviction," Begley writes, was "his lifelong inability to make what he called 'the leap of unfaith.'" And when the abyss loomed, particularly during an anxious period in his late twenties, Karl Barth's Christ-centered theology was a lifeline. Neither a fundamentalist nor a doctrinaire liberal, Barth argued that God breaks upon us in Christ in all the fullness of divinity while yet completely sharing our humanity.

> "Barth was with resounding definiteness and learning saying what I needed to hear, which was that it really was so, that there was something within us that would not die, and that we live by faith alone," Updike told an interviewer in 1976. "What he [said] joined with my Lutheran heritage and enabled me to go on."

Religion is virtually omnipresent in Updike's work, shaping novels like *Roger's Version*, which explores the intersections of theology and science, and *In the Beauty of the Lilies*, a generational saga that suggests that, if too much faith is murderous, a little is needed or we die. He celebrates the church and the battle for faith that goes on within it in stories like "The Deacon" and "Lifeguard" while poems such as "Fine Point" ("The timbrel creed of praise / gives spirit to the daily; blood tinges lips") testify to his robust faith.

But this doesn't mean that Updike's fiction forces a Christian message on the reader. On the contrary, he always believed that his basic duty to God was to write the most truthful and fullest books he could. "I don't want to write tracts, to be more narrow in my fiction than the world itself is; I try not to subject the world to a kind of cartoon theology which gives predictable answers," he once reflected. Fallen clergy, self-centred philanderers: no one escaped Updike's penetrating eye.

Perhaps Updike's finest religious story is "Pigeon Feathers," about a teenage boy's quest for faith amid panic over mortality. Early in that story, young David can be found holding up his hands in the dark and begging Christ to touch them. He feels nothing and yet wonders if he may have been touched all the same: "For would not Christ's touch be infinitely gentle?" Later, as he buries dead pigeons in the yard, the infinitely gentle touch of the birds comes as a revelation. He marvels at the beauty of their feathers, marked with "idle designs of color, no two alike, designs executed, it seemed, in a controlled rapture, with a joy that hung level in the air above and behind him."

The awesome complexity of the humble pigeon's feathers not only attests Christ's word of life in the midst of death but distills John Updike's own philosophy of writing: "to give the mundane its beautiful due," as he phrased it; to celebrate reality, both human and divine.

Myth and Gospel in
John's Updike's Poetry and Short Stories

CHAPTER 9

Myth and Gospel in John Updike's Religious Poetry

THE BBC INTERVIEWER ERIC Rhodes once asked John Updike if he was religious. The writer replied, "I'd say, yes, I try to be. I think I do tend to see the world as layered, and as there being something up there."[1] That "something" for Updike wore the face of the God who assumes our humanity in Christ, shoulders the horrors of human suffering and death, absolves our guilt, and fashions a new creation in the midst of a fallen and imperilled world. Such a full-blown christological understanding of the gospel hinges on the resurrection of Jesus, and that is the theme of one of Updike's greatest poems.

Seven Stanzas at Easter

Make no mistake: if He rose at all
it was as His body;
if the cell's dissolution did not reverse, the molecules reknit
    the amino acids rekindle,
the Church will fall.[2]

The "if" in the first line of this stanza recalls St. Paul's pivotal preposition: "*If* Christ has not been raised, then our proclamation has been in vain. . . . *If* Christ has not been raised, your faith is futile and you are still in your sins. . . . *If* for this life only we have hoped in Christ, we are of all people most to be pitied" (1 Cor 15:14–19). Nowhere else does the Bible speak so drastically about any of its recorded miracles. It does not say that our faith

---

1. Plath, ed., *Conversations*, 50.
2. Updike, *Collected Poems 1953–1993*, 20. The next six cited stanzas are also from this poem.

will collapse *if* Jonah did not emerge from the whale, or *if* the water did not change into wine, or *if* the paralytic did not stand up and walk. It *does* say that the resurrection is critical. *If* Jesus did not emerge from the tomb in some real historic way, count on it, says the poet, "the Church will fall."

> It was not as the flowers,
> each soft spring recurrent;
> it was not as His Spirit in the mouths and fuddled eyes of the
>   eleven apostles;
> it was as His flesh: ours.

How did Jesus rise from the dead? Was the resurrection a physical event that objectively confronted the disciples? Or was it a spiritual experience that took place internally in their minds and hearts? If physical, one wonders how the mysterious resurrection can be distinguished from the crude resuscitation of a dead corpse walking around again. But if spiritual, one equally wonders how it can be distinguished from the countless spiritual experiences people have had of God's presence. The poet does not break off the poem in order to address such matters. He simply makes the point that whatever happened, in whatever mysterious way, Jesus convinced a number of his disciples and followers that he was alive again.

> The same hinged thumbs and toes,
> the same valved heart
> that—pierced—died, withered, paused, and then regathered
>   out of enduring Might
> new strength to enclose.

People have sometimes read into this poem (even as many have read into the New Testament) the notion of a crude resuscitation. But that is surely to overlook the nature of poetic language. The poet is not giving us a prosaic statement on the resurrection. However, in rich poetic language he *is* saying that the resurrection of Jesus, for all the mind-boggling mystery, was a real event in space and time.

The Gospel writers themselves attested the resurrection in language that is surely poetic at times. In John's gospel, for example, the risen Christ passes through closed doors: hardly a feat that a resuscitated corpse might carry out. Yet the same Gospel writer gives us the story of Thomas placing his hands in Jesus' side: hardly an act that can be reduced to the rise of faith in people's minds.

Let us not mock God with metaphor,

analogy, sidestepping, transcendence;

making of the event a parable, a sign painted in the faded

credulity of earlier ages;

let us walk through the door.

The reference to the door recalls the resurrection story from John's gospel (John 20:26–29), and is surely metaphorical in this context, representing the closed door of unbelief. The poet is saying that the risen Christ can walk right through this obstacle, whether the "door" is the unbeliever's dogmatic conviction that miracles do not happen, or the half-believer's wavering faith in a symbolic resurrection story.

The stone is rolled back, not papier-mache,

not a stone in a story,

but the vast rock of materiality that in the slow grinding of

time will eclipse for each of us

the wide light of day.

Jesus rose from the dead as one who truly died, even as we will all one day truly—and not simply metaphorically—die. As Jesus identified with us in our weakness and death, so we are given the promise of identifying with him in his life and resurrection: this, it would seem, is the holy logic of the gospel.

And if we will have an angel at the tomb,

make it a real angel,

weighty with Max Planck's quanta, vivid with hair, opaque in

the dawn light, robed in real linen

spun on a definite loom.

The "if" in this stanza is quite different from the "if" in the first stanza of the poem. The poet is not an undiscriminating literalist. John Updike knows how language works. He recognizes that the Bible often employs figurative language in the process of attesting God's real but mysterious self-disclosure in Christ. Yes, angels are mentioned in the Gospels. Yes, they may be real. But they may also be metaphorical constructs. We simply don't know. But *if* we are going to speak about angels in this context, let them be real angels just as the event they are attesting is real.

Note, incidentally, the stylistic patterns in "Seven Stanzas at Easter." The first and fourth lines of each stanza rhyme. The extra long expository third line is followed by a short, hushed, climactic fourth. This poem sings!

Updike tells us that the poem has figured in a number of neo-orthodox sermons on Easter morning—and no wonder. It is a stirring poem to recite.

> Let us not seek to make it less monstrous,
>> for our own convenience, our own sense of beauty,
>> lest, awakened in one unthinkable hour, we are embarrassed
>>> by the miracle,
>> and crushed by remonstrance.

I once heard John Updike himself recite this poem at Calvin College in Grand Rapids, Michigan.[3] When he came to that final word—"remonstrance"—he chuckled and repeated the word, clearly relishing it. It is indeed a delicious word for the occasion.[4] To "remonstrate" means to protest, demonstrate, counter with overpowering evidence. The resurrection is the protest of God's love, demonstrating once and for all God's definitive and universal victory in Christ over the powers of sin and death.

Religious Consolation

> One size fits all. The shape or coloration
> of the god or high heaven matters less
> than that there is one, somehow, somewhere, hearing
> the hasty prayer and chalking up the mite
> the widow brings to the temple. A child
> alone with horrid verities cries out
> for there to be a limit, a warm wall
> whose stones give back an answer, however faint.
>
> Strange, the extravagance of it—who needs
> those eighteen-armed black Kalis, those musty saints
> whose bones and bleeding wounds appall good taste.
> those joss sticks, houris, gilded Buddhas, books
> Moronoi etched in tedious detail?
> We do; we need more worlds. This one will fail.[5]

---

3. This address can be viewed on YouTube by Googling the John Updike Society and then selecting the "Updike Address at Calvin College."

4. In addition to its theological appositeness, Updike may have been chuckling before the latter-day Calvinists on account of a code word associated with the Dutch Arminian party in the seventeenth century which issued, at the Synod of Dort, a formal "remonstrance" against Calvin's "horrible" doctrine of double predestination.

5. Updike, "Religious Consolation," *Americana and Other Poems*, 93.

Updike published this beautiful sonnet in *Americana* shortly after reaching the threescore years and ten plateau that the Psalmist suggests is the normal span of our lifetime. "And if by reason of strength they be fourscore years, yet is their strength labor and sorrow; for it is soon cut off, and we fly away" (Ps 90:10 KJV). The poem registers a keen awareness of death's inevitability: "We need more worlds. This one will fail." The grim statistics of climate change alone give such an assertion pressing significance today. Is there, we might ask, any light in the darkness of our fading lives and imperilled world? Are there grounds for hope in the great cosmic and personal predicament in which we all find ourselves?

The poet looks to religion for consolation. Yet religion, as we all know, is often painfully ambiguous. There is great beauty and strength in religion, but also so much nonsense and even downright evil. Dietrich Bonhoeffer, sitting in a Nazi prison cell and reflecting on all the evil and nonsense, famously called for a "religionless Christianity," and praised Barth for calling "the God of Jesus Christ into the lists *against* religion, 'pneuma against sarx.'"[6] Though indebted to Barth's theology, Updike does not attempt in this poem to distinguish divine revelation from human religion.[7]

The poet, however, *does* speak about religion's "extravagances": Who needs "those eighteen-armed black Kalis" of Hinduism? Or "musty saints" of Catholicism? Or "joss sticks" of Confucianism, "houris" of Islam, "gilded Buddhas" of Buddhism, or "books Moroni etched in tedious detail" of Mormonism?

"We do," concludes the poet. However bizarre religious beliefs may be they attest the human longing for an eternal meaning and purpose in our lives. Thus people desperately clutch the crutches of faith! For without that meaning, we are condemned to live in a godless universe bereft of any lasting hope or redeeming purpose. Updike, like Wordsworth before him, therefore refuses to criticize religion's extravagances in and of themselves: "Great God! I'd rather be a Pagan suckled in a creed outworn; So might

---

6. Bonhoeffer, *Letters and Papers from Prison*, 148.

7. Which may not be a bad idea given that even Barth refused simply to demonize religion however much he may have distinguished it from divine revelation. The Swiss theologian always maintained that "a theological evaluation of religion and religions must be characterized primarily by the great cautiousness and charity of its assessment and judgments" (*Church Dogmatics*, Volume I, Part 2, 297). Barth recognized that the person for whom Jesus Christ was born, died, and rose again lives *within* his or her religion. To attack that person's religion is to attack that person. The task of the Christian is not to attack but to understand in the light of God's healing and reconciling presence in Christ.

I, standing on this pleasant lea, have glimpses that would make me less forlorn."[8]

> One size fits all. The shape or coloration
> of the god or high heaven matters less
> than that there is one, somehow, somewhere.

What matters in the end is not any particular religious truth or tradition so much as the fact that there *is* a God who relates to us in warm, loving, caring ways, who hears "the hasty prayer" and chalks up "the mite the widow brings to the temple."

> A child
> alone with horrid verities cries out
> for there to be a limit, a warm wall
> whose stones give back an answer, however faint.

I dimly remember a moment in my own childhood suddenly crying out for that all-important limit. My uncle had turned up at the house one day on crutches. I took one look at those crutches and fled to my bedroom, sobbing uncontrollably. Updike gives us an older and brighter child crying out for the limit in the classic story *Pigeon Feathers*. Fourteen-year-old David Kern, sitting in an outhouse, is suddenly

> visited by an exact vision of death: a long hole in the ground, no wider than your body, down which you are drawn while the white faces above recede. You try to reach them but your arms are pinned. Shovels pour dirt into your face. There you will be forever, in an upright position, blind and silent, and in time no one will remember you, and you will never be called by any angel. As strata of rock shift your fingers elongate, and your teeth are distended sideways in a great underground grimace indistinguishable from a strip of chalk. And the earth tumbles on, and the sun expires, and unaltering darkness reigns where once there were stars.[9]

The Bible, of course, also shows people constantly crying out for a limit, and never more so than in the book of Job. In that searing saga the children of Israel finally hear a voice that responds to their cry and encourages Job to

---

8. The lines are taken from Wordsworth's oft-anthologized poem, "The World Is Too Much With Us."

9. Updike, *Collected Early Stories*, 268.

find in the dry land of Israel's coastline a sign of the boundary or limit that God has drawn over and against chaos's threatening waters:

> Thus far you shall come, and no farther,
> and here shall your proud waves be stopped (Job 38:11).

The "warm wall whose stones give back an answer, however faint," may also allude to the wall of Jerusalem, that concrete (literally!) reminder that the rhetoric of God's love assumed our flesh and blood amongst the children of Israel and in Jesus Christ "the cornerstone" (Eph 2:20). It is he who finally assures us all that there is indeed a limit, an answer to our worst fears and greatest dangers: "In the world you face anxiety; but take heart, I have conquered the world" (John 16:33 NEB). Christ's conquering, hope-bestowing presence, however, is received through faith. And faith is not sight, faith is not proof. Hence the answer that the stones give back, however true, is also "however faint."

Jesus and Elvis

> Twenty years after the death, St. Paul
> was sending the first of his epistles,
> and bits of myth or faithful memory—
> multitudes fed on scraps, the dead small girl
> told "Talitha, cumi"—were self-assembling
> as proto-Gospels. Twenty years since pills
> and chiliburgers did another in,
> they gather at Graceland, the simple believers,
>
> the turnpike pilgrims from the sere Midwest,
> mother and daughter bleached to look alike,
> Marys and Lazaruses, you and me,
> brains riddled with song, with hand-tinted visions
> of a lovely young man reckless and cool
> as a lily. He lives. We live. He lives.[10]

At a critical stage in the Passion story the Roman governor, Pontius Pilate, asks Jesus if he is a king. Jesus acknowledges as much, though the acknowledgment costs him his life: "You say that I am a king. For this I was born,

---

10. Updike, *Americana and Other Poems*, 92.

and for this I came into the world, to testify to the truth. Everyone who belongs to the truth listens to my voice" (John 18:37). "What is truth?" Pilate huffs and moves on. Millions, however, have not moved on. Millions have stayed with this "lovely young man, reckless and cool as a lily," finding in him the gracious sign and telling manifestation of God's majestic presence.

Yet Jesus is by no means the only regal presence in people's lives. There are also political kings, financial kings, cultural kings. Among the latter, few loom larger than Elvis Presley, the king of rock and roll. Hence the comparison between Jesus and Elvis. The poet begins by noting the similarities between the two men. Both were too wonderful to die in the minds of their followers. Both have remained alive, their lives and ours feeding off each other. We live because these two kings live. And because we wish to go on living, we refuse to let either of them die.

In the ancient world, twenty years passed before the news about the "lovely young man" from Nazareth began spreading far and wide. Paul's letters to the emerging churches began to appear, and the "proto-Gospels"— those "bits of myth or faithful memory" that eventually formed the basis of the Gospel accounts—began materializing on papyrus rolls. Also, "twenty years since pills and chiliburgers did another in," tourists began flocking to Graceland and worshiping at Elvis's shrine.

The similarities between the two objects of worship are striking, but so are the differences. The poem quietly hints at these differences in the final line: "He lives. We Live. He lives." This would seem to mean: "Jesus lives. We live. Elvis lives." Jesus is the king of God's kingdom, the one who "came to Galilee, proclaiming the good news of God, and saying, 'The time is fulfilled, and the kingdom of God has come near; repent, and believe in the good news'" (Mark 1:14–15) The good news is that the healing, kingly presence of God breaks forth in Christ and enables us all to live and not die. And living, our culture lives with us, including our musical culture led by the king of rock and roll. And so the poem concludes: "He (Jesus) lives. We live. He (Elvis) lives."

Fine Point 12/22/08

Why go to Sunday school, though surlily,
and not believe a bit of what was taught?
The desert shepherds in their scratchy robes
undoubtedly existed, and Israel's defeats—
the Temple in its sacredness destroyed
by Babylon and Rome. Yet Jews kept faith
and passed the prayers, the crabbed rites,
from table to table as Christians mocked.

We mocked, but took. The timbrel creed of praise
gives spirit to the daily; blood tinges lips.
The tongue reposes in papyrus pleas,
saying, *Surely*—magnificent, that "surely"—
*goodness and mercy shall follow me all
the days of my life,* my life, forever.

As Mozart penned the last genius-inspired lines of the *Requiem* while lying
on his deathbed, so Updike penned this heartbreakingly beautiful sonnet
immediately upon receiving notice of his inoperable lung cancer. Martha
Updike once agreed with me that "'Fine Point' is a miracle," adding, "John
died only four weeks later, and he was as you can imagine very sick. But,
never did he waver in his faith. We prayed together, as usual, planned his
funeral, and because he was unable to get to church our rector came often
to him with communion."[11]

"Fine Point" begins with a reminder of the remarkable persistence of
the Jews in history and the promises of faith associated with their historic
name. How often has this people lost battles and been threatened with ex-
tinction! And not just at the hands of the ancient Babylonians and Romans.
We must never forget the horrors that the Jewish people experienced at the
hands of our own Christian forebears in Europe. For almost 1,600 years the
Jews were shut out from nearly all occupations in Europe (except money
lending and scavenging), and shut into ghettoes where they were packed
in like sardines and locked in at night. And when these restrictions were
finally lifted in the nineteenth century, they soon had Hitler's death camps
to face. It was not until 1948 that the Jews had a homeland again that they

---

11. Personal email to John McTavish, March 31, 2012.

could call their own, and yet somehow throughout their tortured history they managed to keep the faith, managed to pass the prayers, as the poem puts it, "the crabbed rites from table to table as Christians mocked."

We mocked, yes, but we also "took." We took the messianic hope of this people and made it our own, made it in fact everybody's hope. We also took their "timbrel creed of praise" and Passover feasts ("blood tinges lips") and "papyrus pleas" (scriptural writings), and made these things our own as well. "Fine Point" cites a line from one of the most beloved of these papyrus pleas: "Surely . . . goodness and mercy shall follow me all the days of my life." It then concludes with the words—"my life, forever"—only these last words, note carefully, are set in normal and not italicized print.

What do you think the change in font at the end suggests? Is the poet breaking away from the consoling biblical passage at this point and uttering a cry of despair as if to say, "Not to put too fine a point on it, but we are talking about . . . MY LIFE, FOREVER!" It would be understandable if John Updike had felt that way in his last painful days. But in fact it would seem that the man of faith is still speaking in this poem, and speaking in a re-markably strong confessional way. Here is the ending of the biblical Psalm with Updike's final words from the poem italicized: "Surely goodness and mercy shall follow me all the days of *my life*, and I will dwell in the house of the Lord *forever*."

CHAPTER 10

Myth and Gospel in John Updike's Short Stories

DAVID UPDIKE PLAYED A lot of golf with his father over the years. I once asked him what his dad's language was like when the ball disappeared into the woods or an easy putt was missed. Did John Updike respond stoically or release a stream of colorful expletives—or what? David smiled at the memory and said, "My dad's language was always very tame and respectful. When he got really frustrated on the golf course he might say something like 'Sugar!' But that was about it."

Sugar?

Language was obviously a sacred tool for John Updike. But sacred also was his determination to let his characters speak as freely and authentically in *their* voices as he spoke in *his*. Accordingly, Updike never pulled his punches on the page. That said, the punches are delivered differently in the short stories than in the novels. There is something much more quiet and sedate, sugary if you like, about the linguistic texture of the short stories. This has nothing to do with timidity or dullness, and everything to do with tempo and mood. Updike's short stories are more like the adagio movements in a symphony: quieter and more meditative after the strong allegro movement of a novel like *The Witches of Eastwick*, or the raw, rousing rondo of a book like *Couples*.

Perhaps for this reason the myths are even denser in the short stories than they are in the novels. This chapter will direct the reader to a number of short stories where the mix of myth and gospel is particularly thick. The stories mentioned here can all be found, with one exception, in The Library of America's omnibus collection of John Updike's short stories.[1]

1. The exception is "Intercession," which appears in *The Same Door* (1959) and *Golf Dreams* (1996) but is not included in the Library of America anthology.

Collected Early Stories gives us the first 102 short stories that John Updike published in his career while *Collected Later Stories* gives us the writer's final eighty-four short stories.[2]

JOHN UPDIKE: COLLECTED EARLY STORIES

"Dentistry and Doubt"

A clergyman from Pennsylvania, who is studying theology at Oxford, has an appointment with a dentist called Dr. Merritt. During the session the clergyman learns that the world is structured not according to deed-achieving *merits* but according to divinely given grace. The discovery comes while the minister is repressing his usual urge to "do something" all the time, and notices that the (innocent) wrens and (greedy) starlings outside the window are "mixed indistinguishably, engaged in maneuvers that seemed essentially playful." Evil ceases to be a faith-destroying problem when the outside world is seen in the overall context of divine play or grace.

"Intercession"

Another grace story only this time a guilt-ridden man called Paul is playing a round of golf with a young boy who refuses to count his bad shots. Convinced that he can win if only the boy will play by the rules, Paul's final promising drive bounces once in the open and then vanishes—"as if a glass arm from Heaven had reached down and grabbed it." Like another Paul stopped in his tracks by a flashing light from heaven (cf. Acts 9: 1–9), the golfer needs to learn that the boy is right: we live by grace in a world where our strokes are beyond counting.

"The Kid's Whistling"

Sometimes grace camouflages itself in strange and even off-putting ways. This is the lesson that Roy learns one Christmas. Roy works in the display department of a department store and takes an artist's pride in painting the Christmas display signs only to have a teenage helper aggravate his nerves

2. This number does not include the vast majority of the Joan and Richard Maple or Henry Bech stories that have been reserved for collection in a future Library of America volume.

MYTH AND GOSPEL IN JOHN UPDIKE'S SHORT STORIES

one year with his constant whistling. Roy manages to battle through the irritation only to have things go wrong with his drawing just when he is applying the finishing touches. Roy immediately recognizes the source of the problem: "The kid had stopped whistling."

"Toward Evening"

This slight but tender story finds a man enjoying dinner with his wife and infant daughter in their Manhattan apartment. The meal becomes a near sacrament of grace recalling the story of the walk to Emmaus when the disciples constrained the risen Lord, saying, "Abide with us; for it is *toward evening*, and the day is far spent" (Luke 24:29). This was the first story, incidentally, that John Updike composed in Manhattan after returning from his year at the Ruskin School of Drawing and Fine Art in Oxford and joining the staff at *The New Yorker*.

"Snowing in Greenwich Village"

If "Toward Evening" was a near sacrament, "Snowing in Greenwich Village" dramatizes a near fall from grace. The narrator, a young husband, is the tempted one while the tempter is a young friend by the name of Rebecca Cune who is visiting the husband and his wife one night in their Manhattan apartment. The name Rebecca recalls the cunning prostitute of the book of Proverbs,[3] while her second name is a near miss for *cunt*. The opportunity for seduction appears later in the evening when the host walks his guest home to her apartment. Nothing happens on this occasion but the story ends with the comment: "Oh but they were close."

"The Persistence of Desire"

Again the snake of sexual temptation visits the narrator, only this time there is no question that seduction is more than close.

---

3. Cf. the Hamiltons' detailed discussion of Updike's symbolic identification of Rebecca with the prostitute of the book of Proverbs in *The Elements of John Updike* (56–61).

"Wife-wooing"

A surprising and delightful yet still realistic celebration of the joys of marital love and fidelity with no temptation, for once, in sight.

"Pigeon Feathers"

This is John Updike's finest religious short story and arguably one of the finest religious stories in world literature. David Kern's faith in God's love, made real for him in Jesus is shattered one day by H. G. Wells's "engines of knowledge." The destruction of the young boy's faith awakens a piercing dread of nothingness. In despair, David seeks help from his minister who demythologizes the problem away, saying, "David, you might think of Heaven this way: as the way the goodness Abraham Lincoln did lives after him." Even David's mother allows talk of God to collapse into anthropomorphic religiosity: "You think, then, that there is God?" "Of course I do." "He made everything?" "Yes." "Then who made Him?" "Why, Man, Man." David finally raises his hands in bed one night and begs Christ himself to touch them. He feels nothing but wonders if he had been touched all the same by one whose touch, after all, would surely be "infinitely gentle."

The infinitely gentle touch would seem to come to David at the end of the story after some pestering pigeons have been shot. While burying the birds, David notices that "across the surface of the infinitely adjusted yet somehow effortless mechanics of the feathers played idle designs of color, no two alike, designs executed, it seemed, in a controlled rapture, with a joy that hung level in the air above and behind him." He is suddenly robed in the certainty that "the God who had lavished such craft upon these worthless birds would not destroy his whole Creation by refusing to let David live forever." David has been touched, it would seem, by the quiet yet unmistakable word of the One whom he has been seeking all along, the Christ who says: "Are not sparrows two a penny? Yet without your Father's leave not one of them can fall to the ground. As for you, even the hairs of your head have all been counted. So have no fear; you are worth more than any number of sparrows" (Matt 10:29, 31). Updike does not spell out the moral lest he spoil the story, but the moral is certainly there.

"You'll Never Know Dear, How Much I Love You"

A child discovers that gain comes through loss, and that to lose one's life in a worthwhile cause, however small that cause may be, is to find it.[4]

"Lifeguard"

A sensuous, fun-filled Kierkegaardian parable reminding us that our spirits may drown if we persist in hugging the shore of religious nonchalance and never brave the open sea of faith.

"The Crow in the Woods"

A young husband and his wife dine with their landlord and his wife, return to their cottage-like home in the woods, dismiss the babysitter, retire to the bedroom, and make love. In the morning the husband uncharacteristically rises early, changes the baby's soaked diapers, dresses the child, and makes breakfast for her. His wife then rises and makes breakfast for him: "a boiled egg, smashed and running on a piece of toast." Meanwhile, a large black crow dives toward the house only to land unthreateningly on the branch of a snow-covered tree. The husband summons his wife to look but instead she says, "Eat your egg." And the story abruptly ends.

The black crow represents the defeated presence of evil in the world. Jack's relieved cry—"Claire!"—intends to draw his wife's attention to the glad sight that the crow has settled harmlessly on a high branch. But the woman already intuitively knows that redemption has drawn near. "Eat your egg," she tells her husband, recalling the one who throws metaphysics aside and simply says, "Take, eat; this is my body" (Matthew 26:26).

"The Christian Roommates"

The popular story of the prodigal son and his elder brother played out in a twentieth-century Harvard dormitory (cf. Luke 15:11–32).

---

4. Cf. Hamilton and Hamilton, *The Elements of John Updike* (14–25) for a detailed discussion of the extraordinary amount of symbolism packed into this seemingly slight story.

"God Speaks"

The New Yorker originally accepted this story in 1964, set it in type, and then killed it. The story was obviously confusing at the time. Today we are much more likely to understand. The story concerns an exchange student from Afghanistan who comes to Harvard and shocks a classmate with his religious skepticism. However, when the student, who is the son of the then ruler of Afghanistan, returns to Kabul upon the sudden death of his father, he immediately reverses all liberal trends and imposes a brutal cult of worship. The story in effect answers Updike's question, "After Christianity—what?" by pointing to the rise of Islam and its militant offshoots. Updike was to point again to Islam as the answer to what follows the collapse of Christianity in the secularized West by composing *The Coup* (1978) and *Terrorist* (2006).

"During the Jurassic"

A theologically liberal dinosaur attends a cocktail party a couple million years ago and charmingly but brainlessly speaks of Christ as a metaphor for the divine spark in us all.

"The Day of the Dying Rabbit"

God looms large in this story, the name being an abbreviated form for Godfrey, the baby in the narrator's family. The story itself is an abbreviated form of the story of Noah and his ark. It ends with the father and an older son bumping into a high bank in their kayak just as Noah and *his* sons came to rest on Mount Ararat in *their* kayak-like covered boat (cf. Genesis 8:1–4).

"The Deacon"

Another story that draws on the myth of Noah and his ark. Only this time a man wanders alone one night in a church sanctuary while the storm outside batters the building: "Miles feels the timbers of this ark, with its ballast of box pews, give and sway in the fierce weather, yet hold. . . . The storm seizes the church by its steeple and shakes, but the walls were built, sawed and nailed, with devotion, and withstand" (cf. Matthew 7:24; 16:18).

"The Carol Sing"

A fun and charming Christmas story that nevertheless reminds us of the darkness—"The holly bears a prickle, / As sharp as any thorn, / And Mary bore sweet Jesus Christ / On Christmas day in the morn"—that lurks in the background of even the merriest of Christmas's.

"Jesus on Honshu"

A pagan myth that illustrates how the story of Jesus loses touch with divine reality when understood along purely aesthetic lines.

"Transaction"

A married man enjoys an evening with a prostitute while on a business trip in an anonymous city. Intimate details of the sexual encounter are given along with imagery drawn from William Blake's poem *Auguries of Innocence*. The imagery links the story with the woman of the streets who broke open the bottle of costly perfume and poured oil over Jesus' head as a sign or augury of his approaching death. A surprising touch of innocence in both stories link them also with intimations of suffering and death.

JOHN UPDIKE: COLLECTED LATER STORIES

"Made in Heaven"

Faith is made in heaven and thus can't be manufactured on earth: so the title of this story would seem to suggest. The woman in this story is a woman of great faith who nevertheless loses that faith after a long and unsuccessful battle against cancer. Her husband's faith meanwhile has been awakened by her earlier example. But now he is forced to realize that in fact he has no faith: "he had believed in her all these years and could not stop now."

"Short Easter"

This story invites us to ponder the question of what goes missing when we sleep through Easter or rather when Easter sleeps through us.

"The Walk with Elizanne"

This story answers the question concerning what became of David Kern's faith in the wake of his epiphany in "Pigeon Feathers" (cf. The Afterword, pp. 173–76).

"Varieties of Religious Experience"

This story shows a variety of expressions of religion working themselves out in people who were all involved in the tragedy of 9/11. A transcendent word of judgment is spoken at the end, recalling the unwelcome and yet ever pertinent words of Jesus: "Why do you see the speck in your neighbor's eye, but do not notice the log in your own eye?" (Matt 7:3). Perhaps the unpopular moral of this moving story accounts for why *The New Yorker* declined to publish it!

"My Father's Tears"

A son remembers seeing tears in his father's eyes but once in his lifetime. Nevertheless, those lone tears were enough to communicate the certainty of a father's love. The reader may recall the one time in the Gospels when Jesus is said to have wept (John 11:35). A small moment that in this case communicates forever a divine parent's love.

"The Full Glass"

The full glass of water used to swallow down the pills for the day in the life of a man "approaching eighty" triggers memories of the social and sensual joys that the narrator enjoyed throughout his life. The story concludes with the narrator celebrating these joys in the quiet conviction that reality is ultimately on the side of life.

Meeting John Updike in Print and in Person

....

CHAPTER 11

Readers Share Discoveries and Recommendations

How did you discover John Updike? Which book or story or poem first communicated the magic of his writing and the depth of his vision? I once put this question to a number of Updike readers, and encouraged them as well to offer recommendations of a favorite Updike story or poem or novel for new readers. Here are their responses.

We begin with DON GREINER, the dean of Updike criticism, who discovered the writings of John Updike while he was a student at the University of Virginia: "Because those were the days after the deaths of Hemingway and Faulkner, Frost and Eliot, etc. we used to gather in a pub after leaving the library around 10 PM to drink a few beers and to argue about which current American writer would take the place of the recently deceased American modernists. Bellow was mentioned a great deal, but most of us put our money on Salinger. We did not know, of course, that Salinger had vowed not to publish again, a vow that he kept. But one of our group of beer-drinking 'intellectuals' insisted that I read his copy of *Pigeon Feathers* and then decide. I have been reading Updike ever since."

❋

It was one of those stories collected in *Pigeon Feathers* that first turned JAMES PLATH on to Updike: "Like so many, my first exposure to Updike came in high school, when I encountered a short story vaguely reminiscent of J. D. Salinger's that began, 'In walks these three girls in nothing but bathing suits.' With that first sentence, Updike grabbed the attention of every pubescent boy in every high school in America—even the back-row jocks who leaned in their chairs against the wall. 'A & P' appeared in the *Points of View* anthology, and it was easily one of the most accessible yet resonant stories we read in Honor's English. 'You know,' the 19-year-old narrator says, 'it's one thing to have a girl in a bathing suit down on the beach, where what with the glare nobody can look at each other much anyway, and another thing in the cool of the A & P, under the fluorescent lights, against all those stacked packages, with her feet paddling along naked over our checkerboard green-and-cream rubber-tile floor.'

"Apart from Salinger's *Catcher in the Rye*, I couldn't recall reading any literature with a capital 'L' where even a word like 'naked' or 'bra' appeared, much less a description of 'the two smoothest scoops of vanilla' inside it. Like the more graphic sexual descriptions which would follow in *Couples*, the *Rabbit* novels, and countless others, the metaphor seemed startlingly right. But I also thought Updike perfectly captured the disconnect, the unrequited love between high school boys and girls that, at this stage in their lives, might as well have been Greek goddesses, for all their inaccessibility. Other Updike passages from other novels and short stories resonate, but you never forget the very first time that a writer speaks, not just to you, but *for* you."

☀

BILJANA DOJCINOVIC was fifteen or sixteen years old when she went to the municipal library in Belgrade to borrow the recently translated novel everybody was talking about—*Couples*. But the librarian thought that she was too young for such a book, and refused to hand it to her, saying that *Couples* was a sociological study.

"Instead, she gave me *Rabbit, Run*. The closeness came in the scene when Rabbit comes back home and finds Janice pregnant and alcoholic in their messy apartment. Before he goes out again to fetch Nelson from his mother, Janice calls from the kitchen, 'And honey, pick up a pack of cigarettes, could you?' Her voice awakens in Harry a strange sensation: 'Rabbit freezes, standing looking at his faint yellow shadow on the white door that leads to the hall, and senses he is in a trap. It seems certain. He goes out.'

"It was this image of the character in the trap, between the door leading back to the hall/hell and the one which was seemingly the exit, that made the deepest impression on me. Anti-hero Angstrom, obviously marked by existential angst, facing the classic either/or of going with the family, problems and all, or moving outside and risking the loneliness and cold, spoke to my not-quite-conscious youthful dilemmas."

WILLIAM PRITCHARD recalls that "one of the first, perhaps *the* first time I became really aware of Updike's presence as a writer was at the end of 'The Happiest I've Been,' the final story in *The Same Door*. John Nordholm and his friend are driving to Chicago, and on the Pennsylvania Turnpike John's friend Neil lets him take the wheel while he sleeps. The following great sentence raised my consciousness:

> There was the quality of the 10 a.m. sunshine as it existed in the air ahead of the windshield, filtered by the thin overcast, blessing irresponsibility—you felt you could slice forever through such a cool pure element—and springing, by implying how high these hills had become, a widespreading pride: Pennsylvania, your state—as if you had made your life.

"I found attractive earlier parts of the story, a post-high school gathering of John and his friends, but it was the ending that took off, and I felt as exhilarated as our hero."

BERNARD RODGERS initially encountered Updike via "A & P" in a high school English class: "I was fifteen or so, and I already knew that I wanted to be a college professor of literature because of my discovery of writers like Updike whom I enjoyed so much. This seemed then, and still seems more than fifty years later, an amazing way to make a living: getting paid for doing what I love—reading good books—and then having the chance to share them with young people. . . . There was just something about Updike's tone of voice, and the beauty of his language, not to mention his subjects, that captured me from the beginning, even as an adolescent and has never let go. Yesterday, I went back to *Higher Gossip* to reread some of the pieces for a few hours in front of my fire in the midst of snowstorms here, and, as always, there was the charm, wit, and easy grace I find so congenial and welcoming. Such a pleasure to be in the company of his well-informed and inquisitive mind!"

KATHLEEN VERDUN read Updike in her junior year at Hope College: "A good friend who had (gloriously, I thought) gone on to graduate school dropped me a line. 'If you get a chance,' he wrote, 'take a look at Updike's collection *Pigeon Feathers*, especially the short story 'Lifeguard.' When I saw the Fawcett Crest paperback edition of *Pigeon Feathers* for sale on the bookrack of the local drug store, I bought it immediately—probably for something like fifty cents. I liked 'Lifeguard' very much, but I was most taken by the title story. Born on a farm, I could appreciate its rural setting; an avid reader since childhood, I sympathized with young David Kern's frantic running back and forth from book to book, from his mother's copy of H. G. Wells to his grandfather's worn Bible to the shallow platitudes of his catechism workbook; and of course I was moved by the circumstances of his sudden and personal confrontation with mortality.

"This was in the fall of 1963. Updike's name was still new, but his star was definitely rising, even—or maybe especially—at a small church-related college like Hope. The next Updike book I bought was *Rabbit, Run*, and there was enough campus interest for me to review it for the student newspaper. When I finally (rather to my surprise) found my way to a graduate program myself, I settled on Updike for the topic of my MA thesis. *Couples* had just come out to great acclaim (naturally I bought the issue of *Time* magazine featuring a portrait of Updike on the cover) and I felt that I somehow understood it. It was partly that Updike's protagonist, Piet Hanema, came from a Dutch Reformed background like mine; but more than that, I recognized a kind of longing in him, a stubborn drive for some kind of happiness, and the excitement I felt as I finished the thesis made even my cramped apartment endurable in the sweltering heat of a Washington DC summer.

"I still like these two books, *Pigeon Feathers* and *Couples*, very much, and they are probably the titles I would recommend to new readers of Updike. They present already the poles that famously define much of Updike's writing: the refreshing theological literacy that set him apart from the first but also the unflinchingly honest depictions of sexuality as it was playing out in what one of his characters calls 'the post-pill paradise.'"

※

GLEN SMITH also cites *Couples* as a favorite: "I remember it well, a paperback in a pinkish red color. The main character: Piet—roaming the streets of Tarbox (in his construction man's pickup on which someone has inscribed, in its dust, WASH ME), bedding all the nubile, young, willing wives of the town and finally settling on the newcomer; and Foxy—the earthy woman for whom Piet abandons his angelic wife Angela. *Couples* is a sexy book, of course, but the sex in *Couples* is real, its emotional context utterly convincing. This eloquent teller of home truths is the Jane Austen of the latter part of the twentieth century."

✳

BARBARA KAY is pretty sure the first book of Updike she read was *Pigeon Feathers*: "All the Maple Family stories captivated me. *Couples* certainly had me riveted. And the *Rabbit* series was tremendous. But I also loved his critical writing. I remember *Hugging the Shore*—the essays just kept astonishing me with his insights, his gorgeous writing and incredible referential range in literature."

✳

Shortly after JONATHON HOULON moved to Pennsylvania in 1992, he remembers asking a fellow graduate student in American literature who he would suggest was the most significant writer from the keystone state: "My friend growled, 'John Updike,' as if there could be any other answer. I picked up a copy of *Rabbit, Run* and it really knocked me out. It might have been my age (close to Harry's in that particular book) but I think it was mostly the lyrical writing. I am a musician. I hear books as much as I read them. There is not a false note in the Rabbit Tetralogy—an incredible accomplishment considering its length. I continue to learn from Updike and his painterly voice and apply the lessons to my song writing. I've read a fair amount of JU at this point. And there's certainly more to recommend than Rabbit. But, really, that's where I'd tell someone to start. If you want to learn what it means to be an American—'criminal yet never caught' is one way Updike describes his 'hero'—start with Harry Angstrom."

✳

PHILIP MARCHAND doesn't think he "discovered" Updike: "He was on my reading list for years before I ever got around to reading him in the early '90s, because of the publicity surrounding his work. Although he had his detractors, the general consensus of book critics was that he was among the major post-World War II novelists, along with Bellow, Malamud, Roth, etc. So on my reading list he went. When I did start to read him I was impressed by his sheer mastery of visual imagery and the psychological nuances of his characters. It was a rich, realistic tapestry he wove.

"I must confess some of the visual descriptiveness was almost excessive and the characterization overripe. I found *Couples*, for example, a hard go at times. But one novel I would without hesitation recommend is *In the Beauty of the Lilies*. That is one of the twenty great American novels of the twentieth century. The beginning, in which a Protestant minister suddenly loses his faith one fine day—just like that!—is unforgettable, along with some of the peripheral characters such as the dying man who realizes that he has never been saved and stoically accepts his eternal damnation.

"Among other things the novel is a history of American Protestantism, from the Calvinism of the New England Puritans to the cultism of rogue messiahs such as David Koresh. Along the way, Updike generates immense pathos, with never a note of excess or falsity."

⁂

John Updike first came into JIM PRIME's life when the latter happened upon an essay entitled *Hub Fans Bid Kid Adieu* in an anthology of classic baseball writing. "It was the best of introductions," Prime says. "Here was a man who captured the essence of my baseball hero, Ted Williams, not with cold statistics or rehashed accounts of Ted's on-field heroics, but with what amounted to poetry. Updike took one game, Ted's last, and used it to craft a small masterpiece. His writing gifted us with the drama, the pathos, the contradictions, the brooding darkness of an American icon. In short, he saw the complexity of the man and passed those insights on to us in the most palatable way imaginable.

"Later when I got to know Ted and co-authored a book with him (*Ted Williams' Hit List*), I appreciated the Updike introduction even more. Since Updike's piece debuted in *The New Yorker* on October 22, 1960, Ted Williams has been analyzed, psycho-analyzed and eulogized by an extraordinary number of writers—some wonderful, some pedestrian. Although these efforts have revealed new details, uncovered interesting new facts and facets, and reached varying conclusions, no one has been able to improve on the Updike classic. I suggest reading *Hub Fans Bid Kid Adieu* while looking at Norman Rockwell's *The Rookie* and sipping a single malt scotch.

✵

A school friend once handed JOHN McTAVISH a copy of *Rabbit, Run* in the hope of knocking religion out of McTavish. Instead, McTavish says, the book knocked Updike in: "I was simply overpowered by the stunning mix of emotional realism and poetic beauty. Still, I was slow on the uptake and didn't read anything by Updike again until *Couples* came out. But then I was definitely hooked and have never looked back."

Favorite Updike Books and Stories

Of the Farm is DON GREINER'S favorite Updike book: "The prose is exquisite, of course, but I like the contrast between the lovely prose and the intensity of the debates between Joey and his mother, debates that are certainly not 'lovely' particularly when Joey betrays Peggy to his mom. Although the novel is written in the first person, I find the novel to be Updike's 'James novel,' although I realize that James generally disparaged the use of first-person narration. Updike persuades me to have extreme reactions to Mrs. Robinson: sympathy for her loneliness, but distaste and even detestation for her selfish and dominating treatment of her son. I can only nod when Joey says, 'I think of myself as a weak man.' I don't know who wins at the end, but I know, with regret, that Peggy loses."

✵

BRUCE McLEOD notes that in the shrinkage of bookshelves occasioned by their move to a condo years ago, "I lost some old friends, but hung on to some special ones like *Pigeon Feathers* and *Roger's Version*. Picking up the latter today, I notice many margin marks and underlinings, especially in the early part of the book.

"I think I was attracted by the interrupting student way back in 1986. Only later did I begin to appreciate the deeper insights of Pascal and others, that the world provides 'enough light for those who desire to see and enough darkness for those of a contrary disposition.' And of course Updike's passing comments—like 'the pious often, I have noticed, have a definiteness that in others they would judge rude'—were always worth a margin stroke.

"Along the way, I loved his playing with words and images like Glenn Gould plays with notes and keys. I loved his 'noticing.' Or 'paying attention' where we look away quickly. I long ago marked a favorite paragraph in *Roger's Version*—his memorable description of the pipe-smoker (having once been one myself):

> The pleasures of a pipe. The tapping, the poking, the twisting, the cleaning, the stuffing, the lighting: those first cheek-hollowing puffs, and the dramatic way the match flame is sucked deep into the tobacco, leaps high in release, and is sucked deep again. And then the mouth-filling perfume, the commanding clouds of smoke. Oddly I find the facial expressions and mannerisms of other men who smoke pipes stagy, prissy, preening, and offensive. But ever since I, as an unheeded admonition to Esther some years ago gave up cigarettes, the pipe has been my comfort, my steeplejack's garb, my handhold on the precipitous cliff of life.

Who else would notice that, describe it so exactly, or deepen it to a comment on despair!"

⁂

ELIZABETH UPDIKE COBBLAH comments, "I read what crosses my path, largely on the recommendations of others, or what strikes my fancy at the moment, my father's work included. I suppose that makes me a grazer. I have to be careful reading my father's work as it is alluring and might also take me to a raw nerve of familiarity or feeling—potentially anything having to do with domestic life does so. It can also be comforting to read his work—a poem here, a snippet there. It brings him back, I hear his voice and the cadence of his sentences. Whatever feelings are evoked by the subject, I am always transported to a place of awe by the beauty of his words, his sensitivity and his ability to capture the essence of something."

⁂

MICHAEL UPDIKE recalls that at the time of his father's death he set out to read all of his father's fiction, poetry, and essay collections:

"I had read the Rabbits, *Marry Me, S., Brazil,* and *Gertrude and Claudius.* In addition to the novels completed there were some that I stopped reading before page fifty. I got stalled in *Roger's Version* reading the science-can-prove-God-exists theory. *Memories of the Ford Administration* was put down early when a scene involving cunnilingus presented itself.

Nor did I have better luck with *Seek My Face*. I had read about a third of the short stories. As each new book arrived by mail or in person after a round of golf, it felt like required reading. I had the best intention of getting to it before the reviews came out but I usually didn't and the reviews, good or bad, would convince me that there was no hurry. It always seemed that I was about to open the last book when a new one would arrive. The joke between my siblings was 'another book from father? I'm not finished not reading the last one.'

"In tackling the long list of unread Updike here is what I enjoyed. I have put the Rabbits aside. *The Centaur* was fabulous as a novel and I learned many things about my grandfather. *Of the Farm* is my favorite. It is such a spooky little gem that captures my Grandmother's 'ways' on the claustrophobic farm. *Roger's Version* was very enjoyable. I have aspirations to repeat the walk that the character takes down Mass. Ave. *Memories of the Ford Administration* wasn't so bad. I enjoyed *S*. It was very funny and doesn't deserve the anti-woman charge. *The Coup* needs to be made into a movie. It was hilarious. *Toward the End of Time* worked for me."

＊

PETER SELLICK has read all of Updike's fiction but comes back to *Couples* every few years: "I think it is his most theologically deft work. The novel is centred around four main characters: Piet Hanema the earth man, his wife Angela who is divine and abstracted, Foxy Whitman, earthy and real, and the dentist Freddy Thorne, demonic and nihilistic. The essence of the book is the outworking of the relationships between these four. After an agreement that Freddy would sleep with Angela in exchange for arranging an abortion for Foxy, Freddy proves impotent. The demonic may not penetrate the divine! The adulterous activities of the couples are judged by an act of God who strikes the Congregational Church with lightning releasing a shower of old sermons, one of which Piet reads. It shows how America has not lived up to its original hopes. In the end, Piet and Foxy, the incarnate couple, leave town, and the life of the couples reverts to the ordinary. *Couples* rewards rereading because of, among other choice felicities, its theological complexity and insight.

❋

GARY RIGG cites not a book or a passage but a favorite moment in one of Updike's interviews with Charlie Rose: "Pushed for a 'why' concerning his churchgoing, Updike, seeming a little uncomfortable about making any sort of avowal one way or another, replied, in his very droll fashion, 'It's the only place where they'll let me sing.'"

❋

BRIAN KENNEDY cites a short story from *Problems* as his favorite: "'Minutes of the Last Meeting' sticks in my mind. It has great insight into human nature and makes me chuckle every time I think of it. The story concerns the narrator's account of the minutes taken at a church committee meeting, but it's applicable to many of the meetings that many of us attend over a lifetime. I'm chuckling now just remembering it."

❋

JACK De BELLIS: "I would go with JU's own recommendation and say *Olinger Stories* (newly released, incidentally, in the Everyman's Pocket Classics). They are easier for a first reader and amply demonstrate Updike's genius with language, his three-dimensional characters, and his *knowingness*."

❋

JAN NUNLEY'S favorite Updike work is the poem "Seven Stanzas at Easter": "It's at the heart of what I preach every Sunday. It's my answer to any of my fellow progressives who scoff at the resurrection as 'fundamentalist nonsense.' Updike was no ignorant, credulous Bible-thumper, but a man of great intellectual gifts and sophistication, and I am proud to be in his company as one who has 'walked through the door' of faith. If I could get his poem into the next revision of the Book of Common Prayer, I would do it in a heartbeat."

❋

DON GREINER'S recommendation consists of six short stories: three stories with conventional form ("Pigeon Feathers," "The Bulgarian Poetess," and "A Sandstone Farmhouse"), and three with more experimental form— "Leaves," "Harv is Plowing Now," and "The Music School."

❋

ANDREW FAIZ: "The Rabbits."

❋

BRUCE McLEOD: "The poems always grab, and sometimes stick like burrs. They're not sweet; always (or often) a dark edge. I love 'Baseball' —"invented in America, where beneath / the good cheer and sly jazz the chance / of failure is everybody's right, / beginning with baseball." Also, 'The Rockettes' for sheer precision of word choice. And, of course, 'Religious Consolation': '. . . Strange, the extravagance of it, who needs / those eighteen-armed black Kalis, those musty saints / whose bones and bleeding wounds appall good taste, / those joss sticks, houris, gilded Buddhas, books / Moroni etched in tedious detail? / We do; we need more worlds. This one will fail.'"

❋

JOHN McTAVISH recommends *Marry Me* "with its portrayal of the beautiful but disturbing force of eros. Interestingly, Adam Begley in his biography of Updike suggests that *Marry Me* is John Updike's most *underrated* book. It is certainly a radical love story showing Jerry 'destroying his wife and wading through his children's blood' in order to gain—for the moment—his great love."

CONTRIBUTORS

–Elizabeth Updike Cobblah is an art teacher and John Updike's oldest child.

–Jack DeBellis is the author of *John Updike's Early Years* and other books on John Updike.

-Biljana Dojcinovic is Professor of Literature at the University of Belgrade in Serbia.

-Andrew Faiz is the editor of *The Presbyterian Record* in Canada.

-Donald Greiner has published several articles and books on John Updike including *John Updike's Novels.*

-Jonathon Houlon is a singer and songwriter based in Philadelphia.

-Barbara Kay is a columnist for the Canadian national broadsheet *The National Post.*

-Brian Kennedy is a former lawyer and now operates an antiquarian book business in Glen Williams, Ontario.

-Philip Marchand is a writer and former book columnist for the *Toronto Star.*

-Bruce McLeod is a minister and former Moderator of The United Church of Canada.

-John McTavish is a minister of the United Church of Canada and lives in Huntsville, Ontario.

-Jan Nunley is an Episcopal Priest serving the parish of St. Peter's in Peekskill, New York.

-James Plath teaches English at Illinois Wesleyan University and is the President of the John Updike Society.

-Jim Prime lives in New Minas, Nova Scotia and is the author of *Ted Williams' Hit List.*

-William Pritchard is the author of *Updike: Man of Letters* and a specialist in British poetry and contemporary fiction.

-Gary Rigg is a retired engineer and lives in America.

-Bernard Rodgers is an English professor and the editor of *Critical Insights*: *John Updike.*

-Peter Sellick is an Anglican Deacon and lives in Australia.

-Glen Smith practices law in Huntsville, Ontario.

-Michael Updike is a sculptor and John Updike's youngest son.

-Kathleen Verduin is an English professor at Hope College in Holland, Michigan.

CHAPTER 12

An Interview With John Updike

The Rev. Jan Nunley interviewed John Updike on February 3, 1993 for the now defunct magazine Episcopal Life. *Nunley then published this expanded interview in James Plath's* Conversations with John Updike *in 1994. The interview is reprinted in this book by kind permission of Jan Nunley and James Plath.*

As WITH SO MANY places in New England, you have to know where you're going to find this village. It's an appendage of the town of Beverly, a small, well-manicured seaside village a few stops out on the commuter rail from Boston. Its streets wind past Colonials and Capes with red doors; several private schools call it home; and in its midst is a ninety-year-old replica of an English country church, St. John's. Here, on a Sunday morning, you may find novelist John Updike sitting in a pew on the baptistery side; when the service ends he strides out and up the hill to his home.

The sixty-one-year-old Updike and his wife, Martha, who have seven children between them, moved here a decade ago. The writer joined St. John's about the same time. Raised a Lutheran, he was advised by a local Lutheran minister that in New England the Episcopal Church was closer to the "relaxed, establishment Lutheranism" of his Berks County, Pennsylvania home.

He'd detoured through the Congregational church while living in nearby Ipswich, but recalled the minister's advice upon settling in Beverly Farms.

"Episcopalianism is fairly close to Lutheranism," Updike observes, though with more emphasis on rite than creed: "a bit more of a 'works' kind

157

of place, I think. I notice that the theology is kind of 'do-it-yourself.' But I'm comfortable with that, and even happy with it. There is a kind of broadness to the Episcopalian outlook, a tolerance that you have to like, that makes it a very gracious church."

Updike is grateful for that. Churches, and the clergy in them, have not always been gracious places and people in the works of this writer, whose career spans nearly forty years and with just as many books. The struggle—and frequent failure—to be faithful, sexually and otherwise, while wearing the collar consumes characters like the Rev. Thomas Marshfield in *A Month of Sundays* (1975) and Prof. Roger Lambert in *Roger's Version* (1986). It's a theme that pops up often in his fiction: the links between religion and sex, both "modes of self-assertion, of saying, 'I am.'"

"What has interested me as a writer," explains Updike, "has been the betrayals: the clergyman who doesn't practice what he preaches. I think the most important ecclesiastical fiction I ever wrote was the story 'Pigeon Feathers,' which reflects my own shock when it seemed to me that the well-intentioned, sweet, bright, liberal Lutheran minister who was confirming me didn't really attach any factual reality to these concepts.

"I was distressed, because I saw that without these supernatural assurances we might as well all be dogs and cats and cockroaches. And so that boy's struggle as reflected in the fiction, I suppose, continues to tilt my portraits of the clergy. The Rabbit books have a couple of clergymen in them, and I guess I want the impossible for them. But then, I guess religion is the request for, if not the impossible, for the unlikely."

The series of novels recording the travails of Rabbit Angstrom included *Rabbit, Run* (1960), *Rabbit Redux* (1971), *Rabbit Is Rich* (1981), and *Rabbit at Rest* (1990).

But clergy aren't the only Updike characters who wrestle with religion.

"The books right up to and including *Couples* [1968] were rather specifically Christian," Updike points out. "I'm not trying to force a message upon the reader, but I am trying to give human behavior theological scrutiny."

Frequently those earlier works cite Karl Barth and Paul Tillich, the "crisis theologians" of the '50s and '60s, whom Updike says were "theologians I could trust. Not every theologian spoke to me—in fact some of them affected me sort of like the minister does the boy in 'Pigeon Feathers': the very hollowness of their voices frightened me."

He is still a Barth aficionado—"I haven't altered those views; I haven't really refreshed them either"—but his theology is less overt in more recent works.

"I don't want to write tracts, to be more narrow in my fiction than the world itself is; I try not to subject the world to a kind of cartoon theology which gives predictable answers."

His own faith, for all his Lutheran roots, has more than a little Anglican ambiguity in it.

"I wouldn't say that I'm one of those who's certain that God is there at all. I find it hard to imagine anybody who is that certain, in fact. But it's always seemed to me that he should be there, and that our best self is called forth by acting as though he is."

Updike sees faith as a response to anxiety about the possibility of death—"the natural product of having a mind that can foresee a future, which a dog, say, doesn't have. That is the human condition which leads us to theologians we can trust, leads us to a church on Sunday morning, leads us to pray in the space behind our eyelids."

Whatever leads him to St. John's, he's called a "faithful parishioner" by head usher Caleb Loring III. "He's very much part of the congregation," Loring says. "And he makes you feel that way as well." The rector, the Rev. James Purdy, says Updike seems to find "genuine joy in participating as a person in a pew, rather than as a person who is pressed forward. It's a joy to preach to him as a parishioner too. John is a quiet and generous critic; he has a certain sparkle and twinkle in his eye so that you can tell when you're on. And when you're off, he masks it well."

There isn't much trouble with "sightseers" coming to the parish to gawk at Updike: "We have other spectacles in this congregation," he teases. "And I don't think he's among them."

Indeed, the parish has a full list of activities for its 2,000 or so members, including English classes and resettlement for Cambodians in Beverly, a food pantry, clothes collection, and outreach to the homeless.

A frequent lector, the author sometimes writes the introductions to the lessons he reads as well. Each year he donates cartons of books to the parish fair, where autographed copies of his works are auctioned off.

He's also known for smaller generosities. Parishioner and friend Judy Cabot says that over the years, Updike has brought audio tapes he's made of his works to her mother-in-law, who's been blind from girlhood.

"'There's a real gentleness about John," she says, "a sweetness and a thoughtfulness. He seems to take pleasure in just coming into the village, to the post office, and then he comes into the kind of easy rhythm of the Sunday morning service."

It fits, somehow, with how Updike sees himself. "I'd say I was a hopeful person. Hope is only one of the three virtues that St. Paul enjoins upon us, and without lacking faith and charity I think I am truly hopeful. I think people are by and large well-intentioned and benign, if you let them be. They are beautiful, if you see them in the right light, and there is something inspiring about ordinary life as it is lived."

That's very Episcopalian, John.

"Oh, is it? Yes. Well, you see, maybe I am in the right church after all."

Q: What was your first encounter with the idea of the holy?

A: The memory that keeps coming to mind is attending my Aunt Hannah's funeral, when I was, I think, nine. It was an old-fashioned Lutheran burial in the country, and they propped her up in the casket and her profile showed against the hangings behind the altar. I don't know if that's holy, but it made a very vivid impression on me. Another early religious impression had to do with the ants that lived between the bricks of our little patio underneath the grape arbor. Their little teeming lives, running back and forth, seemed to transpose me into the position of the deity—these little scurrying ants, whom I occasionally stepped on, were, I supposed, a God's eye view of humanity.

Q: How did that make you feel about God as "the Other"?

A: God as the enormous Other, yes—and when many years later I came to read Karl Barth, the concept of the totally Other, the totally inscrutable Other, seemed congenial. But God had a friendlier face. [Shillington] was a small town, all white and mostly Protestant, divided very much between the Lutherans and the Reformed, and there was a geniality to the religion. My father was a Sunday school teacher, and a number of his colleagues were also Sunday school teachers, so the Sunday school and the church had a kind of familial, communal dimension that was not intimidating, but the opposite.

Q: How did those ideas change as you grew older and began to write?

A: Well, I'm not sure they did change. I think the function of a church . . . it's kind of a gratuitous thing, after all. People show up voluntarily. It's one of the few really voluntary things that people do—they could all still be at home in their bathrobes.

Q: Did that affect your ideas as a writer?

A: The sense of the sacred or the religious, let's call it, certainly does play into one's art. Art is also a gratuitous realm, where certain absolute standards seem to obtain. Just as the ideal Christian in his behavior does good acts that go unnoticed, so an artist tries to put a little something extra into the work of art for which he receives no money, and may not receive any credit. When you write, you do feel you're functioning by laws that aren't entirely human. They're somewhat absolute and otherworldly. The notion of the other world certainly figures in each time you write a novel, or even a briefer flight. You are trying to create another world. I don't feel my characters are ants and I'm looming above them. Rather, I'm among them as a kind of invisible brother. Not only am I [not] larger than they, but in a way I'm smaller, because I'm trying to get inside them and figure out what they're feeling and what they'll say next.

Q: That's very incarnational.

A: I suppose so. I wouldn't have used that adjective, but it's certainly empathetic. One tries to empathize. Christ advised us to empathize, and even a non-Christian writer is perforce obliged to try to empathize and try to feel what it's like to be in some shoes other than your own.

Q: In your memoirs, you talk about your struggle with stuttering and psoriasis. You frame those as part of what shaped you as a writer, gave you the ability to step outside the "universally human." Do you feel that outsider observational vantage point of being different, of being "other," is an essential element for a writer?

A: The artist and the writer is, to an extent an outsider and probably is attracted to it because he feels like an outsider already. Most writers begin with accounts of their first home, their family, and the town, often from quite a hostile point of view—love/hate, let's say. In a way, this stepping outside, in an attempt to judge enough to create a duplicate of it, makes you an outsider. That is, you are outside your material to the degree at least that you are writing about it, and indeed that is a big step, a big-feeling step when you begin to write fiction—the fact that you are on one side of the glass window and human events are on the other side. Yes, I think it's healthy for a writer to feel like an outsider. If you feel like an insider you get committed to a partisan view, you begin to defend interests, so you wind up not really empathizing with all mankind.

Q: How has that affected you spiritually—how you've grown in your relationship with God and human beings around you?

A: I don't know. I've been very grateful that I've been allowed to be a writer or something artistic. I wasn't too fussy as a child. I wanted to draw, basically, but I remain grateful that I've been lucky enough that in some ways my life has been charmed or my endeavor has been blessed, and to that extent I've tried to remain grateful and to give praise. Any act of description is, to some extent, an act of praise, so that even when the event is unpleasant or horrifying or spiritually stunning, the very attempt to describe it is, in some way, part of that Old Testament injunction to give praise. The Old Testament God repeatedly says he wants praise, and I translate that to mean that the world wants describing, the world wants to be observed and "hymned." So there's a kind of hymning undercurrent that I feel in my work.

Q: That reminds me of the idea that the act of observing, in a sense, creates reality.

A: So scientists tell us, and so indeed Berkeley and Locke and others have told us, and I suppose it's true: that reality is a mixture of stimuli from the outside and a recording, a sensitive ego that sees it. I've never, though, had the feeling that I am the only reality. I've always devoutly believed that the external is real, and what's frightening and dismaying about being alive is that the outside world would appear to be fairly indifferent to your presence. A thunderbolt in the wrong pace, a slippery road on the wrong night —all that can wipe you out in a twinkling.

Q: Particularly as a novelist, you've engaged in a form of expression that, at least in my mind, is closest to that of the biblical writers: the telling of stories rather than preaching sermons or creating an academic discourse. So your theology comes out in the story, rather than explicitly being stated, even when you're quoting. That tends to make for a wider range of interpretation from critics and the reading public. Do you find that they often miss what you intend?

A: A critic never quite describes the work that you thought you were putting forth. My most Kierkegaardian or Barthian, or whatever, fiction was, I think, that which was written in my twenties and thirties, and a book like *Rabbit, Run* is a fairly deliberate attempt to examine the human predicament from a theological standpoint. I'm not trying to force a message upon the reader, but I am trying to give human behavior theological scrutiny as it's seen from above, and the emotions the characters have. Rabbit is not a formal Christian, really. He's been exposed to it, but he proceeds by a few more basic notions: an instinctiveness that somehow his life must be important, even though there's no eternal confirmation of this—only the belief that the reality within must matter and must be served. A figure like Caldwell in *The Centaur* is a Christian, he keeps announcing, and is trying to lead a good life. So these books, right up to and including *Couples*, were rather specifically Christian. I think the later books were a little less so, although a book like *Roger's Version* certainly is, in a way, an essay about kinds of belief.

Q: Why do you think that movement happened, away from being specifically Christian, as your career has progressed?

A: Who knows? Maybe I'm becoming a less ardent Christian, or perhaps the struggle whereby I established my theological ideas climaxed in my early twenties in a set of conclusions along the lines of crisis theology, and I haven't altered those views; I haven't really refreshed them either. Also, I don't want to write tracts or to be more narrow in my fiction than the world is. God presumably sees Christian and non-Christian alike and is familiar with our modes of despair and absence, and so on. So I try to include those and not subject the world to a kind of cartoon theology which gives predictable answers.

Q: How does it feel to know that people will probably learn more about Barth, Tillich, and Kierkegaard from your writing than from reading them, or, frankly, from the pulpit?

A: I'm afraid if they depend entirely on my writing they won't learn enough, although I have actually reviewed Barth and, in a lesser way, Tillich. They were the poles, as I saw it, of possible theologies in the '50s and '60s, when I was concerned. I can't believe they will not remain important. I'm not a divinity student and never have been, so I have no idea what's in fashion now in the schools. I do notice that, when in a bookstore, you go to the theology section to see if they have any Barth in print, it's like Zen and various kinds of neo-Hindu tracts, and very little that I would call theology by anybody. . . . Earlier, for me to find, in this welter, books by Barth and Kierkegaard, it meant a lot to me. I can't believe, in short, what you say is true. It's always better to go to the source. I only really took out of Barth what I wanted and what I needed. There's a lot left over that I didn't use.

Q: In the end, you hope that you may lead people in that direction?

A: Yes, that would be nice—those who feel the need. There are various degrees of, various kinds of anxiety in the world, and many people don't seem to be anxious at all. I suspect that anxiety, fear, is the natural product of having a mind that can foresee a future, that can picture death, which a dog, say, doesn't have.

Q: Is being a Christian something that you do as an individual, or is it something you find as part of a congregation?

A: I think the sense of community is real enough, and a real enough comfort. The Christian religion is hardly something that you can do alone. It's quite a concoction, after all, and no single person could have invented it. I think it's helpful to be a member of a church. There is the danger, of course, that church observance becomes merely formal, and that the struggle part of it—the winning-through—you've left up to the rest of the group. As in any group endeavor, it's always a temptation to shift responsibility and ride along, so I suppose that could be said not only about the Episcopal Church, but any church. It can encourage a kind of spiritual laziness.

Q: Are you a fairly active churchman?

A: No, I've tried not to be. I've dodged—not that I've really been asked to do an awful lot, for which I'm grateful. I occasionally read the Bible verses of the day, and I'm active enough in the annual church fair, but I would say that that's about the extent of my activities. It was in the Congregational Church, oddly enough, that I got involved in the committees, and that was fun and useful and instructive, and it heightened, really, one's respect for your fellow parishioners, since you saw them trying to debate real issues—money issues, and so on. But I kind of had enough of that, and have been grateful not to have been asked to take it up again. It's hard, if you are a Christian, to say "no" to your pastor, but I have stayed out of the business end of St. John's.

Q: I found that what attracted me to the Episcopal Church was a "high tolerance for ambiguity," and I sense those themes in your writing.

A: I noticed that the theology is kind of do-it-yourself, as you said—a high tolerance for ambiguity. It comes out in the sermons, even in the kind of hymns we sing. But I'm comfortable with that and even happy with it. I think life and faith are both ambiguous. *Ambiguous* isn't quite the word—it's faintly unkind—but there is a kind of broadness to the Episcopalian outlook, a tolerance, that you have to like. The tolerance of each others' lives, spiritual lives, is what makes it a very gracious church to be a member of.

Q: You've dealt extensively with the intersections of sexuality and religion. So many of your fictional clergy are men—so far as I'm aware, no women yet—who struggle with their sexual lives in the context of wearing a collar. Why is that?

A: It's a problem I've noticed in clergymen, both the ones you read about and even the ones you know. You have a lot of time on your hands; a clergyman's weekdays are his own, more or less, to organize as he wishes. You have the freedom of peoples' homes; you go back and forth. It's an ideal set-up, if you're going to sexually wander. It's certainly an ideal profession as far as technically being able to do it, and it does happen. The first time that a young person sees it happening, you're thunderstruck by the incongruity of this sermonizer also being an adulterer. Later, it doesn't seem such a paradox, in a way. . . . In sexual encounter, you get the kind of confirmation of your own existence and tremendous intrinsic worth that you don't get elsewhere, except maybe in your mother's arms when you're an infant. So it's not surprising that churches are sexy places. The Puritan, the idealist in me or the shockable pre-adolescent is enough struck by it to have written a couple of novels about it: *A Month of Sundays* and *Roger's Version*. It's no paradox; religion and sex are traditionally linked in the United States, at least; the camp meetings our ancestors went to were also mating parties. It's kind of lovely, in a way.

Q: But the church struggles so much with coming to terms with that, at least in its public discourse: sexuality, women in ministry, *et cetera*.

A: You describe what seems to be the case, and it exists less out there in Protestantism, in Episcopalianism, than in many of our more Puritanical sister sects. Methodism and Presbyterianism had a long stew recently about appropriate sexual attitudes and the place of homosexuals in the church, and all that. It is a problem, but it's not my problem, and it's not a problem that interests me as a writer terribly much. . . . As to now, with the issue of consummating homosexual marriages or not, I have no idea what's right; it depends on how far you're going to ignore the Bible, which does have some things to say on these topics that aren't really in line with modern liberal thought. I recognize it as a problem for church administrators and for right-thinking churchgoers. The issue of the female clergy is, of course, behind us in the American Episcopal Church, and once you see them in action you realize how well suited the gender is for the pastoral function, and you wonder what the fuss has been about. And so it is with some contemporary problems. You may look back twenty years and wonder why you bothered. But the Bible does take some conservative positions on sexual behavior, and the church is caught between modern mores and biblical mores, and I don't think it's a false bind. It's an actual bind. Although, the Bible is a sexier document than our Victorian grandparents admitted, isn't it? There is sex in the Bible, not just the "Song of Solomon," but really constant acknowledgment of the power of sex—David's behavior, and so on.

Q: When you created Tom Marshfield and Roger Lambert, I sensed that despite your years of worldly wisdom and sophistication, there's still something in there that wants people to do what they say they're going to do.

A: Yeah . . . I do hold them to a higher standard, as I hold myself. I mean, I expect a lot of them, and this is unreal of me, but it does seem to be a part of me. My father's father was a clergyman, a Presbyterian—if you read *Self-Consciousness* I mentioned this—but a failed one. He didn't lose his faith, but he did lose his parishes and finally had to go into the real estate business. And my father was haunted, I think, by his own father's failure to uphold the faith somehow. It was a strange little shadow in the religiosity of our family.

Q: Failure to uphold the faith, or failure to uphold a congregation?

A: Well, they could have seemed the same thing—you know, if he had the faith, why didn't it work? Again, the expectation of a miracle, or maybe the expectation of earthly prosperity, to confirm our state of grace.

Q: There's John Calvin.

A: Yeah, the Calvinist notion that if you're good, where are the results? And my grandfather didn't come up with the right results, somehow.

Q: Is there still a strain of that in you, of that Calvinist uncertainty?

A: Probably, probably. It's not very fashionable, is it? But it's hard to get rid of it in myself. On the one hand, it's made America, it's what made the U.S.—that Calvinist drive. We became the wonder of the world through our Calvinism, and we mustn't be too hard on it now. It still is, I think, part of our approach and our high expectations. Clinton's inaugural address even reflected somewhat the sense that we can do anything if we work a little harder.

Q: According to the *Chronicle of Philanthropy*, Clinton was the only one of the candidates who tithed his income. Perhaps it's a measure of how far away we've gotten from our Calvinism, that sense of giving back to God in gratitude for what we've received. At some point we say, "Thanks for the keys to the car, Dad. I'm outta here!"

A: I don't want to sound pompous or pious, but I really have been strengthened and emboldened by the notion of gratitude and the idea that it is a service to both the universe and to one's fellow man to try to write entertainingly and accurately about the world. We've spoken about empathy and about giving praise, and there's something in what the fiction writer attempts, of searching out. . . . It's almost a scientific attempt to find those spots where a God shines through, as it were.

Q: Which is ideally what ministry is all about, as well.

A: I suppose so. But I must say that I never for one moment thought of becoming a minister. I admire people who are. To me it seems a very thankless recycling of the same human stuff that, like a heap of sludge, keeps coming back on you. Whatever I said about the ministers not having enough faith must be qualified with my admiration for their willingness to deal with human distress first-hand, not to sit in a room and write about it, but to actually go out and try to help it, to soothe it, to direct it, maybe.

Q: But in a sense, you're doing that as a novelist. It's a different kind of mediating function, but there's a sense in which it's a priesthood of its own.

A: There's a tendency of American writers to see themselves as priests, actually. Wallace Stevens said it, but I think many have felt it, that we are, in a way, trying to offer spiritual leadership, moral leadership. Even though my books strike many people as immoral or morally useless, to me they are really moral investigations of how we live, and harsh, perhaps, because the standards are otherworldly. I judge, in a way. I see my characters' confusion and rapacity and callousness against some kind of background of ideal behavior that I suppose is part of my Christian inheritance.

Q: That's what makes people squirm when they read them.

A: Somewhere Flaubert was described as reading the French people a series of lessons in human vanity, and in a way fiction could be said to be that. If nothing else, you're trying to read lessons in human vanity to your readers.

Q: Ecclesiastes?

A: Yeah. I have never been an unbeliever, I guess you could say. Somehow it struck me quite early that the church, whatever its faults, was speaking to the real issues, and that without the church I didn't feel anybody would speak to the real issues—that is, the issues of being human, being alive. I've remained loyal to the church. Spires you see in a small town or a city do bring hope, and hope brings energy. It's certainly brought me energy.

CHAPTER 13

John Updike, 1932–2009

J. D. McClatchy

When one of its 250 members dies, the American Academy of Arts and Letters, at a subsequent general meeting, asks another member to compose a tribute in honor of the deceased colleague. The Academy consulted with John Updike's widow, Martha, on the choice of a speaker, and she suggested the poet and critic J. D. McClatchy, who was then serving as the Academy's president. The following remarks were, thus, delivered at the meeting in November 2009. Among the Academy's guests for this occasion were Martha Updike and editor Judith Jones.

JOHN UPDIKE WAS A member of this Academy for forty-five years. He was not quite the youngest person ever elected, but nearly. Over those years he was awarded prizes (including the William Dean Howells Medal and the Gold Medal for Fiction), he served on every conceivable committee, he presided as both Secretary and Chancellor, he gave the Blashfield Address, and he edited *A Century of Arts and Letters*, the Academy's centennial history. I dare say he knew more about this institution than anyone among us today, and loved it enough to both cherish its traditions and gently mock them. On the one hand, he parodied us wittily in his Bech books; on the other, he once wrote a magazine squib about 155th Street as his favorite spot in New York City. "Manhattan's claustrophobic closeness lifts in this vicinity," he wrote, "the buildings throw short shadows, and the neighborhood's stately elements—the terrace, the walled cemetery, the Episcopal church across Broadway—stand as a kind of pledge the past once made to the future." And when he wrote about what happens inside this building . . . well, here is his sardonic little sonnet from 1992, called "Academy":

> The shuffle up the stairs betrays our age:
> sunk to polite senility our fire
> and tense perfectionism, our curious rage
> to excel, to exceed, to climb still higher.
> Our battles were fought elsewhere; here, this peace
> betrays and cheats us with a tame reward—
> a klieg-lit stage and numbered chairs, an ease
> of prize and praise that sets sheath to the sword.
>
> The naked models, the Village gin, the wife
> whose hot tears sped the novel to its end,
> the radio that leaked distracting life
> into the symphony's cerebral blend.
> A struggle it was, and a dream; we wake
> to bright bald honors. Tell us our mistake.

At my age, I am rarely surprised any longer by newspaper headlines. But I was genuinely shocked, last January, to read of John Updike's death. Why had I thought *he* would live forever, when all of us merely think *we* will? It was only later, reading the work of his last months, that one could see him wondering the same thing, watching with a wry detachment and a sudden fresh upwelling of old memories what had suddenly become his own last act unfold. Just a month before he died, he wrote a poem about two Shillington High School classmates of his who must that day unexpectedly have walked into the lamplight of idle consciousness, and whom he addresses—after a very specific account of their lives a half century earlier—this way:

> Dear friends of childhood, classmates, thank you,
> scant hundred of you, for providing a
> sufficiency of human types: beauty,
> bully, hanger-on, natural
> twin, and fatso—all a writer needs,
> all there in Shillington, its trolley cars

and little factories, cornfields and trees,
leaf fires, snowflakes, pumpkins, valentines.

To think of you brings tears less caustic
than those the thought of death brings. Perhaps
we meet our heaven at the start and not
the end of life. Even then were tears
and fear and struggle, but the town itself
draped in plain glory the passing days.

This is like a fable of his career: to have taken the types life offers, and rendered them with such detail as to make a moral allegory of the ordinary. And those final phrases—*plain glory* and *passing days*— were his abiding themes, despite the lavish ways he used to evoke them. No writer since his beloved Nabokov had manipulated, massaged, and mastered English prose as John Updike did. He laid down sentences like marble inlay in a grand corridor that led to the inner recesses of the heart. To linger again over those sentences is to admire a virtuosity so rare and exhilarating that we sometimes forget it was in service to something considerably beyond its own giddy pleasures.

But even before they got to the new sentences, writers picking up a just-published book by John Updike would invariably panic. The print size on the list of previous publications got smaller over the years to accommodate his titles. After five dozen of them, I think even the experts were confused about the exact number. Their range was prodigious—the novels and story collections, the poems and essays—as was his instinct to surprise us with a new narrative experiment or with an expertise in something obscure and compelling. But scanning those columns of books, what was most daunting at the heart of them was the Rabbit Angstrom books, long since properly gathered into a single massive volume that stands without question as the greatest novel of postwar America.

Early on, he told an interviewer, "My subject is the American Protestant small-town middle class. I like middles. It is in middles that extremes clash, where ambiguity restlessly rules." As a realist, he knew that the novelist's task is not merely the accumulation but the illumination of details. And that, in turn, is accomplished not merely by a keen observation of the murky secrets repressed behind the bright façade, but by revealing that tension between inner and outer in sentences of astonishing lyrical grace and rhetorical power. If sex and religion preoccupied many of his chronicles of American life, it is because he wanted to discover how we cling to the moment and to something beyond the moment, or what he once called "the tension and guilt of being human."

His least ambiguous faith, of course, was in language itself. But for a novelist who dealt so often with infidelity, he had a religious temperament. In a foreword to one of his favorite novels, Thornton Wilder's *The Eighth Day*, John said of Wilder that he "kept religion's bias—its basic gaiety," and in the novel itself, Wilder says that "faith is an ever-widening pool of clarity, fed from springs beyond the margin of consciousness." A bias that clarifies, a joy on the margins—these are about as good a definition of a contemporary American's religion as any. John wouldn't want to be in any world but a fallen one, and one that had fallen in a peculiarly American way, with our Puritan roots, with our evangelical fringes, with our restless, greedy, generous ambitions. Even in what we don't know, we know more than we suspect, *are* more than we hope. John Cheever once said that the characters in Updike's novels perform their lives in an environment suffused with a grandeur that escapes them.

In Harry Angstrom, he embodied all of these contradictions. Rabbit is one of literature's great characters—a rabbity and angst-ridden antihero who thought Ronald Reagan was like God in that "you never knew how much he knew, nothing or everything." In the Rabbit tetralogy, Updike used everything to explore the nothing. "Boys are playing basketball around a telephone pole with a backboard bolted to it. Legs, shouts. The scrape and snap of Keds on loose alley pebbles seems to catapult their voices high into the moist March air blue above the wires." So *Rabbit, Run* opens, with Harry watching them play. "He stands there thinking, the kids keep coming, they keep crowding you up." Hundreds of pages later—pages with the amplitude and address of the great nineteenth-century novels—*everything* has happened (happened in suburban beds and convenience stores and cars and sailboats, under copper beeches and on golf courses) until the nothing happens, and we look back on Rabbit's life as our own, our century's, our culture's. It is our great anatomy of desire. In the Rabbit books, Updike wrote of an American's empty dreams and passionate loneliness. The dreams are empty so that there is room to move around in them, to change them. The loneliness is passionate because each of us falls in love with being alone.

Few writers are given the privilege of writing down their time. And beyond his skills at the typewriter, Updike was a true bookman. His longtime editor at Knopf, Judith Jones, remembers him sending in a new manuscript every year, and considering it a point of honor that it make money. But there was never an agent, a contract, or an advance. He cared only about the book. He pestered the art department to design what was in his mind's eye. He had top stain and full-cloth bindings to the end. In the days of letterpress, he would pick up the first copy of a new novel, smell the pages, and run his hand over the type to feel the ink.

He was also a patient writer, a practical one. As *Rabbit Run*, which appeared in 1960, was being readied for publication, he became privately worried that its raw take on things like sex might get him hauled into local courts across the land. He had a family, after all, and tuitions to pay. So he suggested to Mr. Knopf that the firm's lawyers read the manuscript. They did, and came back with pages of anxious notes. Mr. Knopf telephoned John with the bad news, but was told that John was teaching Sunday school class and couldn't be disturbed. In the end, much of what readers of the day would have considered to be smut was deleted from the novel, and John waited patiently as, edition by edition, over fifteen years or so, bits of it were folded, like beaten egg white, back into the original batter. By the time the whole original text was finally between covers, the temper of the time had changed, and nobody ever noticed what had been done.

John Updike was, in every sense, our first man of letters, a man made of words which he chose—in ways always surprising and sublime—to give back to us, shaped like ourselves, like our lives, our sorry hearts. He let us see and understand them, love and wonder at their textures and terrors. His books, in the poet's phrase, beheld "Nothing that is not there and the nothing that is."

There is now an empty chair in this room, and always will be.

Afterword

THERE IS A SCENE in John Updike's novel *In the Beauty of the Lilies* where Uncle Danny is driving nephew Clark around the hilly outskirts of Los Angeles. Classical music is playing on the radio. Suddenly Danny exclaims, "Listen to that—pure milk and honey. And fire. That's Mozart. You should learn to listen to these guys" (392). A little later Uncle Danny says, "Now listen to that. That's *Sturm.* That's Beethoven. The Mozart gloves are off. Beethoven goes for broke every time" (395).

Like Beethoven, John Updike goes for broke every time. He does so, however, in a distinctly Mozartean fashion. That is, he keeps the gloves on. He doesn't indulge in brawling, over-the-top expressions of super-dramatic action. Machine guns going off! Bodies flying through the air! Muscle chiselled hunks! Drop dead gorgeous babes! No, what you get in Updike is the charm of the ordinary, the beauty, as he famously put it, of the mundane. Critics, Updike noted more than once, are constantly demanding madder music and stronger wine when what is needed is a greater respect for reality, its secrecy, its music.

This doesn't mean that John Updike's books are dull. It does, however, mean that they're not page turners in the conventional sense of the term. You don't race through an Updike novel while riding the subway any more than you soak up Mozart as background music at a dinner party. For a book to be good, Updike once said, it is not enough for it to be good: the reader has to be ready. And to be ready for John Updike means reading his work carefully, tasting the beauty of the prose, measuring human action qualitatively and not simply quantitatively, and not least following the tantalizing leads of the myths and images buried in the stories.

There is a moment in *Marry Me* when Jerry Conant comes across three small Vermeers in the National Art Gallery in Washington. "Oh, God," Jerry moans, "the drawing; people never realize how much *drawing* there is in a Vermeer. The wetness of this woman's lips. These marvellous hats. And this one, the light on her hands and the gold and the pearls . . . ."[1] Just so, the reader never realizes how much *drawing* there is in an Updike. His books are easy to read, but not easy to understand.[2]

This is why it helps to read Updike carefully, with an eye for the secrets in his stories. This truth was brought home to me afresh while composing this afterword. The valedictorian tone of it all stirred me to reread one of Updike's final, valedictorian-like stories: "The Walk with Elizanne."[3] I had read this story before, but now I really listened, really focused. The story finds David Kern attending a school reunion in the year 2000. Fifty years have slipped by since the class graduated from Olinger High School. This, of course, was the school where David had been a student during the momentous days of "Pigeon Feathers." In that earlier story David's faith had been shattered by the atheistic arguments of H. G. Wells. The resultant fear of death had driven the boy to despair. But then David had to shoot some pigeons, and while he was examining their feathers the worthless birds spoke to him, silently, the actual words of Jesus: "Fear not, therefore; you are of more value than many sparrows" (Matt 10:31).[4]

In "The Walk with Elizanne," David is more than half a century older than he was in "Pigeon Feathers," and thus closer to death than ever. Indeed, on the day of the reunion, David and his wife first visit a classmate in the hospital who is dying from cancer: a stark reminder of death's nearness. At the reunion itself, another classmate introduces David to Elizanne with the "aggressive" words, "Do you know who this is?" David has trouble at first remembering, but then it comes to him. Elizanne! "It was a name like none

---

1. Updike, *Marry Me*, 37.

2. "Your poems. Are they difficult?" Henry Bech asks Vera Glavanakova in "The Bulgarian Poetess." She replies, "They are difficult—to write." Charmed, Bech says, "But not to read?" She replies, "I think, not so very." The text makes it clear that Bech is speaking "brainlessly" (Updike, *Bech: A Book*, 49). He has forgotten the difference between words that are read and words that are understood. Similarly, Updike's words are easily read but not easily understood.

3. Updike, *My Father's Tears*, 38–54. Updike tips the reader off to the presence of myth in this story by having a terminally ill classmate of David's preface her remarks to him about the classmate's upcoming move to her final home on earth by saying that this will amuse David since he was "always into irony" (*Tears*, 41). There is an unusual amount of irony in this story, and with Updike irony is almost always the gateway to myth.

4. Cf. the Hamiltons' interpretation of "Pigeon Feathers" in *The Elements of John Updike*, 85–89.

other, pronounced, they learned as children, to begin with an 'ay' sound, like the mysterious 'et' in 'Chevrolet.'"[5]

Do *we* know who this is? The strange name, pronounced this way, reminds us of the song of the angels, the song that the church has been singing for over two thousand years. Kyrie eleison! Lord, have mercy. Christ have mercy. Elizanne, the embodied angel, steps forward to be kissed, her puckered mouth indicating the importance of the occasion. David responds, but his heart is not quite in it.

Then at the end of the evening, just before the classmates disperse, perhaps never to see each other again this side of eternity, Elizanne comes up to David and speaks to him once more. "David," she says, in a running murmur, "there's something I've been wanting for years to say to you. You were very important to me. You were the first boy who walked me home and—and kissed me."[6] David has trouble remembering the kiss let alone the walk. Would he also have trouble remembering, the long-time Updike reader can't help wondering, that all-important kiss of grace that came to him during his encounter with the dead birds in "Pigeon Feathers"?

Gradually, however, the forgotten walk is recalled along with the "dewiness" of the girl. By the time the two say good-bye, David is finally ready to make something of the occasion. Or so it would seem. But then all he can say is, "Thank you, Elizanne. What a sweet thing to remember. Hey, you look great. Unlike a lot of us."[7] Afterwards David wonders why he blew the moment. He now feels genuinely "inane," and "for days following, he tried to recapture that walk that had ended in a kiss."[8]

Kierkegaard's infinite passion of inwardness having finally seized David's heart, he now realizes that there could be "no better way to spend eternity than by taking that walk with Elizanne over and over."[9] "*Elizanne*" he wants to say, "*what does it mean, this enormity of our having been children and now being old, living next door to death?*"[10] The details of the all-important walk with Elizanne may be lost to *his* mind but not to that of his creator's: they arrive at her home just as the streetlights come on. "So soon!"

5. Updike, *My Father's Tears*, 44.
6. Ibid., 46.
7. Ibid., 48.
8. Ibid.
9. Ibid., 51
10. Ibid., 52. Italics in the text.

David exclaims. "You have a n-n-nifty-looking house."[11] Elizanne apologizes for chattering so much on the walk but David disagrees. "It was like you were singing to me," he says.[12] A car goes by "with a staring face in the passenger window, maybe someone they knew—a spy, a gossip."[13] Are the spies and gossips, one wonders, the people who complain that Updike, with all his singing prose, is all style and no content, worth little more than stares?

Certainly there are people who feel this way, and so be it. Reading is a deeply personal pleasure. We all get out of writers what we get or fail to get. Like love, it can't be forced. So there's no point really in complaining that some of the cars may hold staring passengers. Let them stare. But for those of us who find in John Updike nothing less than the singing prose of an Elizanne-like angel, we are happy to walk in his company forever. Here is how "The Walk with Elizanne" ends, and for once I will spare the reader of any attempt on my part to say what I think John Updike is saying. May he speak to you directly, now and always:

> "And there was even more," she said, giggling to show that she was poking fun at herself now, "that I wanted to say."
>
> "You will," he promised, breathlessly. His cheeks were hot, as if after gym class. He was worried about his father waiting for him; his stomach anxiously stirred. David felt as he had when, his one weekend at the Jersey Shore the past summer, a wave carrying his surfing body broke too early and was about to throw him forward down into the hard sand. "I want to hear it all," he told Elizanne. "We have t-tons of time."[14]

11. Ibid.

12. Ibid., 53.

13. Ibid., 53.

14. Ibid., 53–54.

Acknowledgments

CHAPTERS 2, 3, 4, 7, and 9 are enlarged and revised forms of articles which appeared originally in *Theology Today*, published by Princeton Theological Seminary in Princeton, New Jersey, and Westminster John Knox Press in Louisville, Kentucky. Chapter 2 appeared under the title "Myth, Gospel, and John Updike's *Centaur*," vol. 59, no. 4, January 2003 (596–606); chapter 3 under the title "John Updike and The Funny Theologian," vol. 58, no. 4, January, 1992 (413–425); chapter 4 under the title "Realism and Romance in John Updike's *Marry Me*," vol. 64, no. 2, July 2007 (221–232); chapter 7 under the title "Soul Mates: "Updike's Harry Angstrom and Ayckbourn's Norman Dewers," vol. 65, no. 4, January 2009 (475–488); and chapter 9 under the title "'Jesus and Elvis' and John Updike's Poetry," vol. 63, no. 4, January 2007 (433–441). I am indebted for permission to reproduce the material which appeared in those issues.

I am grateful to *The United Church Observer* for permission to reproduce revisions of reviews of Karl Barth's *Wolfgang Amadeus Mozart*; John Updike's *Rabbit at Rest*, *Memories of the Ford Administration*, *In the Beauty of the Lilies*, *A Month of Sundays*, *Americana*, and the review of Adam Begley's *Updike*.

And to the *Huntsville Forester* permission is gratefully acknowledged for reprinting reviews of *Villages* and *Rabbit at Rest*, and the article *Columnist Predicts Nobel Winner*.

Grateful acknowledgment is also hereby made for permission from Alfred A. Knopf, an imprint of the Knopf Doubleday Publishing Group, a division of Penguin Random House LLC, to quote from the following published works. All rights reserved:

"Peggy Lutz, Fred Muth 12/13/08" from *Endpoint and Other Poems* by John Updike, copyright 2009 by The Estate of John Updike;
"Academy" from *Collected Poems, 1953–1993* by John Updike, copyright 1993 by John Updike;

Grateful acknowledgement is made to reprint the following articles:

"John Updike's Prescription for Survival" by Alice Hamilton and Kenneth Hamilton, initially published in the July 5, 1972 issue of the *Christian Century*. Copyright 1972 by the *Christian Century.*

"Can A Novel Be Christian? John Updike and *A Month of Sundays*" by Alice Hamilton and Kenneth Hamilton, initially published in the May-June 1979 issue of *Radix* magazine, www.radixmagazine.com.

Grateful acknowledgment is also made to reprint excerpts from the following books or articles:

The Norman Conquests: A Trilogy of Plays by Alan Ayckbourn, first published by Chatto & Windus 1975. Published in Penguin Books, 1977, and used by permission of Haydonning Limited.

The Paris Review Interview by John Updike. Copyright *"The Art of Fiction XL111: John Updike"* by John Updike, originally published in *The Paris Review* issue 45 (Winter 1968), used by permission of The Wylie Agency LLC.

David Updike's "Tribute to Dad" is used by permission of the author and the editor, James Schiff, of *The John Updike Review*.

Jan Nunley's interview of John Updike in *Episcopal Life* is used by permission of Jan Nunley as well as James Plath who published an expanded version of the interview in *Conversations with John Updike*, University Press of Mississippi, 1994.

The memorial address, "John Updike, 1932–2009" by J. D. McClatchy is used by permission of the author as well as the editor, James Schiff, of *The John Updike Review* (cf. volume 3, number 2, Winter 2015).

Selected Bibliography

Cited Works by John Updike

Americana and Other Poems. New York: Knopf, 2001.

Assorted Prose. New York: Knopf, 1965.

Bech: A Book. New York: Knopf, 1970.

The Centaur. New York: Knopf, 1963.

Collected Poems 1953–1993. New York: Knopf, 1993.

The Coup. New York: Knopf, 1978.

Couples. New York: Knopf, 1968.

Collected Early Stories. New York: Library of America, 2013.

Endpoint and Other Poems. New York: Knopf, 2009.

Golf Dreams. New York: Knopf, 1996.

Higher Gossip: Essays and Criticism. New York: Knopf, 2011.

Hugging the Shore: Essays and Criticism. New York: Knopf, 1983.

In the Beauty of the Lilies. New York: Knopf, 1996.

Marry Me. New York: Knopf, 1976.

Memories of the Ford Administration. New York: Knopf, 1992.

A Month of Sundays. New York: Knopf, 1975.

More Matter: Essays and Criticism. New York: Knopf, 1999.

My Father's Tears. New York: Knopf, 2009.

Odd Jobs: Essays and Criticism. New York: Knopf, 1991.

Of the Farm. New York: Knopf, 1965.

Picked-Up Pieces: Essays and Criticism. New York: Knopf, 1975.

Pigeon Feathers. New York: Knopf, 1962.

The Poorhouse Fair. New York: Knopf, 1959.

Problems. New York: Knopf, 1979.

Rabbit Angstrom: A Tetralogy. New York: Everyman's Library, 1995.

Rabbit at Rest. New York: Knopf, 1990.

Rabbit Is Rich. New York: Knopf, 1981.

Rabbit Redux. New York: Knopf, 1971.

Rabbit, Run. New York: Knopf, 1960.

Roger's Version. New York: Knopf, 1986.

S. New York: Knopf, 1988.

The Same Door. New York: Knopf, 1959.

Seek My Face. New York: Knopf, 2002.

Self-Consciousness. New York: Knopf, 1989.

Terrorist. New York: Knopf, 2006.

Toward the End of Time. New York: Knopf, 1997.

Villages. New York: Knopf, 2004.

The Witches of Eastwick. New York: Knopf, 1984.

Cited Books on John Updike

Begley, Adam. *Updike*. New York: Harper, 2014.

Hamilton, Alice, and Kenneth Hamilton. *The Elements of John Updike*. Grand Rapids: Eerdmans, 1970.

Hunt, George W. *John Updike and the Three Great Secret Things: Sex, Religion, and Art*. Grand Rapids: Eerdmans, 1980.

Markle, Joyce B. *Fighters and Lovers: Theme in the Novels of John Updike*. New York: New York University Press, 1973.

Yerkes, James. *John Updike and Religion: The Sense of the Sacred and the Motions of Grace*. Grand Rapids: Eerdmans, 1999.

Cited Reviews, Interviews, and Articles on Updike

Baddiel, David. "Suburban Legend." *New Statesman*, May 2, 2014, 42–44.

Bloom, Harold, ed. *Modern Critical Views of John Updike*. New York: Chelsea House, 1987.

Gross, Terry. Audio interview, September 19, 2002. Download at the John Updike website at http://partners.nytimes.com/books/00/11/19specials/updike.htm1# audio2.

Grossman, Lev. "Old Master in a Brave New World." *Time*, 40–44.

Hamilton, Alice, and Kenneth Hamilton. "Can A Novel Be Christian? John Updike and *A Month of Sundays*." *Radix*, May–June 1979, 13–16.

———. "John Updike's Prescription for Survival." *The Christian Century*, July 5, 1972.

Holt, Jim. *Why Does the World Exist?* New York: Liveright, 2012.

Kakutani, Michiko. "Turning Sex and Guilt into an American Epic." *Saturday Review*, October, 1981, 14–22.

Marchand, Philip. "Seek My Face." *Toronto Star*, November 24, 2002.

Nunley, Jan. "Thoughts of Faith Infuse John Updike's Novels." *Episcopal Life*, May 1993, 248–59.

Plath, James, ed. *Conversations with John Updike*. Jackson, MS: University Press of Mississippi, 1994.

Pritchard, William H. *Updike: America's Man of Letters*. South Royalton, Vermont: Steerforth, 2000.

Time. "View from the Catacombs," April 26, 1968, 66–75.

Updike, David. "Tribute to Dad." *The John Updike Review*, vol. 1, no. 1, Fall 2011, 137–40.

Updike, John. "Updike Address at Calvin College," April 4, 1998. Google "The John Updike Society" and "Select Online Interviews."

Miscellaneous References

Ayckbourn, Alan. *The Norman Conquests: A Trilogy of Plays*. London: Penguin, 1977

Allen, Paul. *Alan Ayckbourn: Grinning at the Edge*. London: Methuen, 2001.

Augustine. *Confessions*. Translated by R. S. Pine-Coffin. Harmondsworth, UK: Penguin, 1961.

Barth, Karl. *Church Dogmatics,* Volume I, Part 2. Edinburgh: T & T Clark,1956.

———. *Church Dogmatics,* Volume III, Part 1. Edinburgh: T and T Clark, 1958.

———. *Church Dogmatics*, Volume III, Part 3. Edinburgh: T & T Clark, 1960.

———. *Church Dogmatics,* Volume III, Part 4. Edinburgh: T & T Clark, 1961.

———. *Dogmatics in Outline*. Translated by G. T. Thomson. London: SCM, 1966.

———. *The Word of God and the Word of Man*. New York: Harper and Row, 1957.

Bonhoeffer, Dietrich. *Letters and Papers from Prison*. Edited by Eberhard Bethge, translated by Reginald H. Fuller. London: SCM, 1953.

The Globe and Mail. "Ending Up with God." June 21, 1997.

Gollwitzer, Helmut, ed. *Karl Barth, Church Dogmatics: A Selection*. Edinburgh: T & T Clark, 1961.

Hamilton, Edith. *Greek Mythology*. New York: The New American Library, 1953.

Kimmel, William, and Geoffrey Clive. *Dimensions of Faith*. New York: Twain, 1960.

Pritchard, William H. "Review of *Museums and Women*." *The Hudson Review,* vol. XXVI, No. 1 (Spring 1973) 240.

Wood, James. *The Broken Estate: Essays on Literature and Belief*. New York: Random House, 1999.